"You know what I want. I'm willing to give you time to figure out if it's what you want, too."

She blinked. "How much time, exactly?"

The cagey little note in her voice had him smiling inside. He liked that in her, the determination to surrender only on her terms. Because he wanted her complete cooperation when they finally consummated this edgy chemistry they generated without even trying, he steeled himself to give her room to maneuver. But not too much room.

And not too much time. Twenty years was a long time to burn for a woman.

That decided, he allowed his private smile to show on his face. "I'm booked on the red-eye tomorrow night."

She took a deep, shaky breath. "In that case, you'd better stay for dinner."

Dear Reader,

The excitement continues in Intimate Moments. First of all, this month brings the emotional and exciting conclusion of A YEAR OF LOVING DANGEROUSLY. In *Familiar Stranger,* Sharon Sala presents the final confrontation with the archvillain known as Simon—and you'll finally find out who he really is. You'll also be there as Jonah revisits the woman he's never forgotten and decides it's finally time to make some important changes in his life.

Also this month, welcome back Candace Camp to the Intimate Moments lineup. Formerly known as Kristin James, this multitalented author offers a *Hard-Headed Texan* who lives in A LITTLE TOWN IN TEXAS, which will enthrall readers everywhere. Paula Detmer Riggs returns with *Daddy with a Badge,* another installment in her popular MATERNITY ROW miniseries—and next month she's back with *Born a Hero,* the lead book in our new Intimate Moments continuity, FIRSTBORN SONS. Complete the month with *Moonglow, Texas,* by Mary McBride, Linda Castillo's *Cops and...Lovers?* and new author Susan Vaughan's debut book, *Dangerous Attraction.*

By the way, don't forget to check out our Silhouette Makes You a Star contest on the back of every book.

We hope to see you next month, too, when not only will FIRSTBORN SONS be making its bow, but we'll also be bringing you a brand-new TALL, DARK AND DANGEROUS title from award-winning Suzanne Brockmann. For now...enjoy!

Leslie J. Wainger
Executive Senior Editor

Please address questions and book requests to:
Silhouette Reader Service
U.S.: 3010 Walden Ave., P.O. Box 1325, Buffalo, NY 14269
Canadian: P.O. Box 609, Fort Erie, Ont. L2A 5X3

Daddy with a Badge
PAULA DETMER RIGGS

INTIMATE MOMENTS™

Published by Silhouette Books

America's Publisher of Contemporary Romance

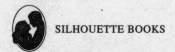 SILHOUETTE BOOKS

ISBN 0-373-27153-0

DADDY WITH A BADGE

Copyright © 2001 by Paula Detmer Riggs

This edition published by arrangement with Harlequin Books S.A.

® and TM are trademarks of Harlequin Books S.A., used under license. Trademarks indicated with ® are registered in the United States Patent and Trademark Office, the Canadian Trade Marks Office and in other countries.

Visit Silhouette at www.eHarlequin.com

Printed in U.S.A.

PAULA DETMER RIGGS

discovers material for her writing in her varied life experiences. During her first five years of marriage to a naval officer, she lived in nineteen different locations on the West Coast, gaining familiarity with places as diverse as San Diego and Seattle. While working at a historical site in San Diego she wrote, directed and narrated fashion shows and became fascinated with the early history of California.

She writes romances because "I think we all need an escape from the high-tech pressures that face us every day, and I believe in happy endings. Isn't that why we keep trying, in spite of all the roadblocks and disappointments along the way?"

SILHOUETTE MAKES YOU A STAR!
Feel like a star with Silhouette.
Look for the exciting details of our new contest
inside all of these fabulous Silhouette novels:

Prologue

He was alive. Barely. Now it was up to the cardiac team to keep him that way.

Sweat-stained and exhausted after the frantic struggle to keep the patient from bleeding to death, the surgeon in charge of the Level-1 trauma unit at George Washington University Hospital stripped off her bloody gown and gloves before heading down the sterile corridor in search of the patient's family.

While she and her team had been battling the almost impossible odds, a crowd had gathered—predominantly large, solemn-faced, broad-shouldered men with narrowed, watchful eyes.

Among the group were the two men who had ridden in the ambulance with the ashen-faced man now in surgery, their once pristine shirts bloodied while performing CPR until the medics had arrived.

All were members of the Special Investigations Branch of the Secret Service. The patient, Rafael Cardoza, was a senior agent in the same branch. His weapon as well as his badge and ID had been vouchered by the admitting clerk after they'd cut off his blood-soaked clothing.

Falling silent as she approached, they stood stiffly the way people do when they feel helpless, hands in the pockets of conservative suit coats, their carefully unobtrusive ties loosened, the requisite dark sunglasses tucked away in breast pockets.

"Excuse me, gentlemen, is Agent Cardoza's family here yet?" she asked, her voice reflecting her utter weariness.

In answer to her question, most looked toward a solid, massively muscled man in his mid-fifties who stood to one side of the crowded corridor, alone in a little island of deference. A pleasantly homely man, he had thick iron-gray hair, a granite jaw and steely blue eyes.

"Cardoza's parents are in Oregon. According to his wishes, they're to be notified only in the event of his death." He stopped, the unspoken question hanging in the air.

"He's alive," the surgeon hastened to assure him.

"Thank God." He took a deep breath and cleared his throat. "I'm his immediate superior and his friend. Name's Lincoln Slocum in case you need to know." That done, he sharpened his gaze. "Fill me in."

Though he spoke quietly, she had a ridiculous urge to snap to attention. She recognized the name as the newly appointed Director of the Secret Service, though in reality the photo in the *Washington Post* hadn't come close to portraying the powerful life force of the man.

"Agent Cardoza was hit twice in the chest," she related in a voice that was equally quiet. "One of the bullets punctured his left lung, the other may have nicked his aorta, which is why Dr. Forchet took him straight to the OR as soon as his blood pressure was stabilized."

He accepted that impassively, with only a slight movement of his stern mouth to betray his feelings. "Worst-case scenario?"

"He's lost a great deal of blood, which makes surgery extremely risky. His heart might also have been damaged. Dr. Forchet won't know until he cracks the chest."

No one spoke. The tension was palpable, a lethal black energy that seemed to suck all the air from the surrounding space. The silence was broken by a frustrated curse.

Finally Director Slocum released a long breath. "Rafe's as tough as they come. He'll make it."

She thought about the stripped-down body she'd seen only in clinical terms—lean and muscular and larger than average, bronzed where his skin had been exposed to the sun, paler where it had not. His shoulders were wide and packed with latent power, the torso long and corded with hard muscle, the waist narrow. Without an ounce of extra fat on the long frame, every superbly developed muscle, tendon and sinew had been outlined perfectly like an anatomy lesson come to life.

In spite of the Latin name, the man had a Viking's golden coloring and height. She'd had only a glimpse of his features before the second-year resident had inserted a breathing tube, but the rough-cut features had been overlaid with a rugged strength. Masculinity personified, she thought with a giddiness born of exhaustion. A beautiful tawny gold man with a heart that had faltered but fought on.

Did he have a mate? she wondered, thinking of her own adorably rumpled husband waiting for her at home. A woman with enough courage and strength to keep from being over-powered by his? A romantic at heart, she fervently hoped so.

"He's tough," she echoed, infusing her voice with a certainty she desperately wanted to feel. "He'll make it."

With a lot of luck, she thought as she turned away—and perhaps a little help from whatever benevolent deity looked after men like him.

Gut knotted even tighter now, Linc Slocum watched her until she disappeared behind the double doors to his left. Only then did he allow his stiff shoulders to relax.

He'd been at the White House, meeting with the President's Chief of Staff, when he'd been notified that one of his men was down, shot while guarding a witness at a government safe house in Maryland.

No, not just one of his men, damn it. His *best* man, his go-to guy. In spite of the fourteen years difference in their ages, they had a bond, he and Rafe—an immigrant steelworker's kid and the bastard son of a teenage runaway, brought up by a Mexican-American laborer and his wife after his birth mother had abandoned him in a horse barn.

"Any word, yet, sir?" Preoccupied with his own thoughts he hadn't seen Rafe's partner of three months approaching. Each year the new hires seemed to get younger, he thought with an inner sigh. Even Rafe, at a lean and muscular thirty-eight, had started complaining about feeling old. But then Linc doubted that Rafe had ever truly been young.

"He's holding his own," he said, smiling briefly to let the rookie know his concern had been noted and appreciated. "The doctor said it might take a while to patch things together."

Seth Gresham's lips tightened as he struggled to settle his emotions. "Twenty more minutes and I would have been there," he grated in an emotion rough voice.

"Any idea how the shooter found her?"

"Damned if I know, sir."

Rafe was too savvy to let himself be tailed. But this kid? It was possible, though unlikely. Among other things, Rafe had a way of getting the young ones up to speed fast.

Apparently Rafe had been in the kitchen making breakfast when the woman he'd been protecting had inexplicably—and against express orders—opened the front door to a man who'd claimed to be Rafe's relief.

It had been damn clever, the way the shooter had worked it. Arriving not too early to alert Rafe, but late enough to minimize the chance of being spotted.

"You think the shooter was Folsom himself?" Gresham asked tersely.

"Could be. Or he could have hired a pro."

"Damn frigging flu bug. Rafe never should have had to pull that kind of routine duty." Stan Vincent was head of the investigative branch—and Rafe's immediate superior—although both he and Stan knew that Rafe played by his own rules, which, given the unshakable integrity at the man's core, were far stricter than the ones in the book.

"We both know there was no 'should' to it, Stan. The woman only agreed to testify because Rafe convinced her she'd be protected. Nothing but an act of God was going to keep him from looking out for her.''

Slocum bit down hard on the rage that threatened to break free.

Jacob Peter Folsom was a cold, calculating predator, a swindler and a cheat who raped with words instead of his body. The specifics varied, but his M.O. was always the same. Contrive to meet a lonely—and well-off—woman on vacation, romance her with flowers and dancing and a healthy dollop of charm, winning her trust during moonlit strolls and candlelight dinners.

Alice MacGregor had been the principal of a prestigious boarding school located in Virginia's horse country. A dedicated scholar and empathetic teacher, she had entered her fortieth year a virgin with a spotless reputation and an empty womb.

While on a Mediterranean cruise she'd met a man who'd introduced himself as Jason Smythe-Jones. Cultured, sophisticated and well-read, he had claimed to be a history professor at Bennington in Vermont.

Still fit and athletic at forty-seven, he had beautiful silver hair and piercing blue eyes. In her statement Alice, as well as several of his other victims, had mentioned his remarkable resemblance to George Hamilton.

A highly intelligent, bluntly honest woman who knew all too well that her face would never be considered more than passably pleasant, she would have been immune to a traditional seduction. Instead, Smythe-Jones, aka Jacob Folsom, had praised her mind and her dedication to her students. To sweeten the pot, he'd asked her to be the mother of his children. For all her intelligence and sophistication Alice had been bedazzled.

They'd married in a flower-filled chapel in Venice before returning to Alice's small home on the school grounds. Two months later Alice had been bankrupt, her reputation in tatters, her job in jeopardy. After cleaning her out, her new husband had simply vanished. This time, however, he'd been caught when, in a wholly improbable coincidence he'd attempted to sell her highly recognizable vintage Mercedes convertible to the mother of one of Alice's former students.

Out on bail, he'd first tried to charm his bride into refusing to testify. When that hadn't worked, he'd threatened to kill her. Something in his eyes had made her believe him. Rafe had been the one to calm her fears. Now brave, heartbroken Alice MacGregor was downstairs on a slab in the hospital morgue, and the man who had tried to protect her was fighting for his life a few doors away in the OR.

"I don't get it, sir," Gresham said in a low, frustrated tone. "Ms. MacGregor was too trusting, yeah, but she wasn't a stupid woman. Just the opposite, in fact." He took a fast breath, his expression earnest. "In fact, none of the victims seem like the type to be conned. Near as we've been able to piece together, almost all are college graduates with responsible jobs. The one in Miami was a neurosurgeon and the one before Alice is an associate dean of women at San Diego State. As far as I can see, there's not a bimbo or airhead in the bunch."

Slocum was astounded by the man's naiveté. "Bimbos and airheads don't usually have fat bank accounts and platinum charge cards," he said tightly.

"He targets professionals in their thirties or forties because most of them have been too busy getting to the top to have time for romance," Stan amplified when Gresham's face reddened. "Most have biological clocks that are clicking down, which makes them especially susceptible to a man who professes to want children very badly."

Slocum felt a certain sympathy for the rookie, who still expected evil to make sense. "Folsom's smart and he's charming. He knows exactly what a woman wants—and he gives it to her." His jaw hardened. "If she's lucky, he'll only destroy her life before he walks away."

There was no need to say more. Every man and woman there knew that unless Folsom was stopped, there was every possibility that Alice MacGregor would not be the last woman to end up dead, simply because she fell in love with a monster.

Chapter 1

As soon as Dr. Daniela Fabrizio picked up her office phone and heard the tobacco-ruined voice of the repair shop mechanic on the other end, she'd expected bad news. In fact, it was worse than bad.

"Did you say eleven *hundred* dollars?" she forced out when breath returned to her body. "To fix that…that *lemon?*"

On the other end of the line Bruno of Bruno's Economy Automotive Repairs cleared his throat. "Uh, yes, ma'am. 'Leven hunnert it is. 'Course that could be a mite high on account of we might be able to get some of the parts used. I got my parts girl callin' around, but it bein' the start of the holiday weekend and all, it'll prob'ly be Tuesday or Wednesday before I know for sure."

"But you said it was *just* the transmission."

"Lady, there ain't no *just* to it when it comes to them foreign jobs. This here model of your'n is especially wonky."

"Wonky. I…see." Danni squeezed her eyes shut and tried

to find that safe place in her mind. Unfortunately, it seemed to have disappeared, along with darn near everything else she and her late husband Mark had accumulated during twelve years of marriage. Like the silver Lexus Mark had given her four years ago on their tenth anniversary and the healthy nest egg from his insurance settlement that she'd put aside for Lyssa's college education.

This morning on the way to the restored Victorian white elephant on the edge of Portland's historic district that she shared with two other psychotherapists, the nine-year-old hatchback that was now her only mode of transportation had started bucking like a deranged bronc.

By the time she'd made it to the nearest off-ramp, narrowly averting death by collision several times, her entire thirty-six years on earth had passed before her eyes. She'd barely made it to the ramp's shoulder when smoke had started pouring out from under the hood. The driver of the tow truck she'd called on her cell phone had recommended Bruno's.

"Couldn't you just fix *some* of the gears? I mean, I only need Drive and Reverse and Park. The others are just superfluous."

This time Bruno snorted something approximating a belly laugh. "That's a good one, Miz Fabrizio. Yes, ma'am, it surely is. But no can do."

"In other words, it's all or…nothing. Transmission-wise."

"That's about the size of it, yep."

She drew in a lungful of air. The pink hybrid tea roses she'd brought from home yesterday morning gave off a cloyingly sweet smell, and her stomach did a slow, clammy roll. The Cajun chicken salad she'd forced down at her desk five hours earlier had clearly been a mistake.

"So worst-case scenario, if I want it fixed, I have to come up with eleven hunnert—*hundred* dollars?"

"Yep. Like the man says, cash on the barrelhead."

No one said that these days. No one had said that for a hundred years at least. Nevertheless, the meaning was all too clear. No money, no car.

Like it or not, Lyssa would have to transfer to a middle

school closer to the house they were currently renting on Mill Works Ridge. It would break her daughter's heart to leave her friends in Lake Oswego, but even with a student pass, the bus fare was more than their already whisper-thin budget could handle.

She took another breath, fighting a sick feeling of helplessness. The phone rang twice in Paul Baxter's office next door before the service picked up. Outside, a MAX train swooshed past. A horn tooted cheerfully. It was the start of Memorial Day weekend, and downtown was emptying fast. Happy people rushing out to have fun despite the gray skies and icy wind.

The weather was due to break late tomorrow night, however, with the promise of sunshine for the rest of the long weekend. As a special surprise, she'd planned to take Lyssa down to the family vineyard near Ashland on Sunday. Fortunately Danni hadn't told her yet. Her little girl had already had too many broken promises in her twelve short years.

"Okay, say you *can* get those used parts," she said with determined cheerfulness. "What's the best I can hope for, cost-wise?"

"Hmm. Let me do some calculatin' here."

"With a sharp pencil, okay?"

"Ain't no need for a pencil. I got me a knack for figures, do it all in my head."

Which, as she recalled, was shaped exactly like a bullet. With a greasy "gimme" cap on top.

Torn between laughing hysterically or pleading piteously, Danni clamped her mouth shut and leaned back against the high back of her cushy executive chair. One by one she toed off her low-heeled pumps, then closed her eyes.

She'd been up since six, with scarcely a moment to herself since she'd dropped Lyssa off at school. Her calendar had been packed, with only a hurried twenty minutes for lunch. Her last session had been highly emotional, and she'd been drained by the time Cindy Habiz had left, calmer, finally, but still dangerously volatile.

Now it was nearly 5:00 p.m. and she still had patient notes to dictate so that their part-time medical assistant Ruthie could transcribe them over the weekend. Friday was also her night to stop at the market for groceries. Did taxis charge extra to carry groceries? she wondered, feeling a little giddy.

"Well, near's I can figure, the best we can do even with used parts would be a thou."

Sharpen the damn pencil again! she wanted to shout. Instead, she dropped her head and rubbed her forehead with her free hand. The spot above her right eyebrow was beginning to throb and her stomach was growing more iffy by the second.

"I can pay you a third now and the rest over the next three months." It would mean more belt-tightening, but—

"Sorry, little lady, I don't give credit. Got burned too many times by deadbeats, y'know?"

"Yes, I suppose you have." Danni felt truly queasy now. Humiliation had a taste, she'd learned. It was beyond bitter. She cleared her throat, but the bitterness remained. "Uh, let me see what I can do and I'll call you Tuesday morning."

There was a momentary silence before Bruno said in a softer tone, "Tell you the truth, I don't like takin' plastic on account of the service charge, but I s'pose I could make an exception, seein' as how you're expecting a little 'un and all."

A sudden wash of tears blurred the outlines of her mauve-and-blue office. The kindness of strangers, she thought. "I'm afraid that won't help, but thank you for the offer," she said in a wobbly voice.

Both of her platinum cards had been cancelled. In the bottom drawer of her filing cabinet was a thick file folder full of overdue statements and threatening letters. While she'd been basking in newlywed bliss—and her adoring husband's constant attention—Jonathan Sommerset, may he rot in the hottest bowels of hell, had managed to steal every cent of her liquid assets, sell her beautiful home on a bluff and all the furnishings before destroying her credit rating.

The damage he'd done to an innocent young girl desperate to feel a father's love again was his greatest crime, however. For that alone, the lying weasel deserved to spend the rest of his worthless life in a particularly nasty prison.

There was one bright spot however. Her own silver lining.

A tired smile curved her lips as she pressed her hand to her swelling tummy. Jonathan had given her a baby.

Her baby, and Lyssa's, not his. Never his.

As desperate as she was financially, she had still gotten the best of the bargain. Perhaps that was the best revenge, she thought with a small measure of satisfaction.

"Miz Fabrizio, you still with me?"

"Still here." Barely. "Uh, tell you what, Bruno, let me see what I can do about raising the money, and I'll call you on Tuesday."

"Yes ma'am. I'll be waiting." He cleared his throat. "Uh, Miz Fabrizio, say you wasn't able to come up with the money, I'd be willing to take that old hatchback off your hands for…say, four hunnert."

She sucked in a breath. "Cash on the barrelhead?" she couldn't resist asking as her headache suddenly increased exponentially.

"Why yes, ma'am." He chuckled. "You might do you some askin' around before you accept, but I promise you, it's a right fair offer. You're not gonna get a better one."

Her throat was suddenly clogged with tears. Somehow she managed to thank Bruno before putting down the phone. And then, alone in the office that was the only thing Jonathan hadn't been able to steal, she buried her face in her arms and cried.

Finally, after frustrating months of mistaken identities and dead ends, they'd scared up a lead. It was thin, little more than wishful thinking but even that was more than they'd had in weeks of chasing down dead-end leads.

Rafe had been running on the treadmill in the Treasury Building's basement gym when Gresham had come charging in, waving a fax from the Portland, Oregon office. The local authorities had put out a "wanted for questioning" alert for a man using the name Jonathan Sommerset who matched Folsom's description.

The charge was credit card fraud, swindling and forgery. The suspect's M.O. was strikingly similar. A "chance" meeting with a lonely widow on a luxury cruise to Acapulco, a whirlwind courtship ending in a romantic wedding in a chapel on the beach before sailing home.

The honeymoon had scarcely been over before he'd managed to have his name added to the deed to his bride's house and the title of a nearly new Lexus sedan. Naturally, he had insisted on adding her name to the deeds to his condo on Maui and the flat in San Francisco as well as his brokerage account and savings accounts, all of which existed only on official looking documents Folsom had created on his laptop computer. In turn, she'd given him total access to her bank and savings accounts, both of which were all too genuine.

Then, as was his pattern, he had convinced her to invest in a revolutionary new method of converting sawdust to decking material impervious to weather and pests. The process was real, as were the reams of supporting documentation. Only the stock certificates were phony.

Ten weeks after the wedding Sommerset arranged to take his wife and stepdaughter to England as a birthday surprise for the girl. Two days before departing, he'd pleaded a sudden business emergency, sending them on ahead. Excuse followed excuse until three weeks had passed. By the time the woman had gotten suspicious and flown home, Folsom had systematically emptied her bank accounts, sold her home and all the furnishings and maxed her credit cards before disappearing.

That had been almost three months ago, long enough for the trail to have gotten colder than a hooker's heart. Picking the victim's brain for some forgotten detail, some chance recollection that might put them on the scent again was their only hope.

They'd been on the red-eye that same night, landing at Portland just as the sun was rising this morning. The head of the Service's local office had lent them a vehicle, a no-frills sedan that smelled like a Texas honky-tonk, and drawn a map to the Portland PD precinct that had caught the case.

Even though it was raining steadily, Rafe had cracked the windows, front and back. The breeze that streamed through was flavored with pine and brought back memories of the crowded migrant camp by the river where he'd spent the first seventeen years of his life.

He shifted until his shoulders were wedged against the door. Even then and with the seat pushed back all the way, he couldn't stretch out his legs far enough to get comfortable.

Damn, he hated this, he thought sourly. Memories were a bitch, especially the mean, gut-twisting kind that snuck under a man's guard to deliver a sucker punch to the solar plexus. He'd known it was going to be rough being in Oregon again, but he'd figured to handle it fast and dirty, no more than forty-eight hours to find out all he needed to know, then he'd be outta here again. For good, this time.

It wasn't until he'd met with Detective Sergeant Case Randolph and heard the name of the victim that he'd known just how rough.

Twenty years ago he'd been wildly, blindly in love with Daniela Mancini.

In the case folder had been a photograph, taken of the happy couple right after their wedding. It was like a slice in his heart to see the photo of his adorable Princess looking stunningly happy in a flowing white Mexican wedding dress, her dark eyes glowing as she looked up into the face of Jacob Folsom.

He'd spent a lot of years telling himself she'd probably gotten fat and sour-tempered. Just his luck the young girl who had been a beauty at sixteen had matured into a sensuous, elegant lady with a body that could make a dead man weep.

"Nice neighborhood, this. Real homey like, you know. Almost makes a guy want to settle down and raise himself a couple of kids."

Jarred from his dark thoughts by the sound of Seth Gresham's perfect prep-school diction, Rafe opened his tired eyes long enough to shoot his talkative partner a sardonic look.

"Thought you were committed to playing the field." In contrast to Seth's cultured voice, his own was strictly blue-collar and inclined toward hoarseness when he was tired, a residual affect of the tube they'd stuck down his throat to keep him breathing. Women tended to consider the gruff texture a turn-on, something he wasn't above using to his advantage when it suited him.

"I said 'almost,' *compadre*," Gresham tossed back with a

grin. "As long as the ladies keep smiling back, I'm keeping my options open."

Seth nudged the seat back another notch and loosened his tie before pulling a folder from the hand-sewn briefcase at his feet. Inside were copies of Sergeant Randolph's notes.

The man had lousy handwriting, but he knew his stuff. It was a textbook report, concisely detailed, every question Rafe might have had answered. Just in case, he read it twice. By the time he'd finished the second read, his gut was twisted into an icy knot.

It was Folsom, all right. Rafe would bet his farm on it, the one he'd bought in the Maryland countryside about ten years back when he'd felt the need to have space and fresh air around him. He felt the same way now.

"Taxi just turned the corner."

Without moving, Rafe opened his eyes and glanced toward the end of the street. Mill Works Ridge was only two blocks long. On one side, far below the street was the mighty Columbia River. On the other was an alley leading back to Waverly Avenue, the main access road.

His gut tightened as the cab pulled to the curve in front of the house listed on the crime report as Danni's address.

"What the hell?" Gresham muttered under his breath as he shot to a sitting position.

"Could be a visitor."

"Definitely female," Gresham said as the passenger struggled to get out of the cab's back seat. Swathed in a bright red slicker, she made a vivid splash against the gray landscape.

As she emerged and straightened, Rafe felt his world tilt. It was Danni. And she was pregnant.

A driving rain stung Danni's face and obscured her vision as she struggled to balance two bulging grocery sacks, and the large shoulder bag that served as both a briefcase and purse. Ducking her head deeper into the slicker's hood, she edged crab-like toward the curb, only to have a sudden gust of wind bang the cab's door against her hip.

"Thanks for all the help," she muttered in the direction of

the grossly overweight cabby with really bad body odor who had refused to leave the protection of his equally smelly cab to help carry the groceries to her front door.

"Fact of life, lady," he said with a shrug. "I get paid to drive. Anything else costs extra."

Extra she didn't have. "I'd hate to have your karma," she muttered before ducking her head against the stinging drops.

Struggling against the wind, she finally made it to the safety of the curb, then turned awkwardly to slam the cab door. As she did, one of the sodden bags tore, spilling the contents into the muddy water surging along the gutter. Cold spray hit her shins as cans thudded onto the pavement. A large can of tomato juice smashed her toes, sending pain shooting through her foot.

She jerked back, only to lose her balance. With a cry, she dropped the other bag, and reached out desperately to keep herself from falling. He came from nowhere, a large man in a dark suit moving fast. An instant later, she was wedged against a chest as hard as granite, her head tucked against a bronzed throat. Steely arms held her steady while his wide back sheltered her from the rain and wind.

"Easy, I've got you." The voice came from far above her head, a deep baritone with a faintly hoarse quality. She smelled soap on damp skin and felt the edge of a starched collar against her cheek. Heart thudding, she clutched at the strong arms supporting her.

"Don't be frightened, Daniela, we're Federal agents."

Federal agents? Men in Black, or in this case a lovely charcoal gray? In safe and solid Mill Works Ridge, the same community known affectionately as Maternity Row? Hysterical laughter bubbled in her throat. She fought it down. Later, she would fall apart.

"If you're IRS, you're wasting your time. The old blood and turnip thing. I'm the turnip."

She thought he chuckled before she remembered that government types had no humor. "Good thing we're Treasury, not IRS, then."

He loosened his hold but kept his arms around her. After straightening carefully, she pushed back her hood so that she could see his face. At the same time he lowered his head so that his gaze met hers, and for a moment she felt as though she were poised at the top of a ski run, with a pristine slope of freshly-groomed powder falling away in a dizzying drop below.

She knew that face. Oh, how she knew it! Once she'd held it in her mind so that she would fall asleep thinking of him. After he'd left her, his image had tormented her in dreams for months.

The proud angles and strong planes were more sharply chiseled now, but still breathtaking. Beneath slashing brows the color of sun-washed sand, his eyes were an unusual sage green with sun crinkles at the corners and dense lashes. His chin was solid, with a hint of a cleft, his features boldly drawn, as though with swift, angry strokes on an imperfect canvas—all but his lips which had the smallest of curves at one corner. Like the beginning of the sweetest of smiles.

It wasn't really a smile, but a scar, one she'd put there herself when she'd been six and he'd been eight. He'd caught her crying because her brothers had gone fishing and left her behind, so he'd taken her to his own favorite spot along the Little Applegate.

Instead of a steelhead, she'd hooked him, then in her dismay jerked hard on the line, slicing his mouth as the hook pulled free. Blood had spurted like a fountain, and she'd gotten hysterical. He had ended up comforting her.

"My God, Rafe?"

His mouth slanted. That same cleanly defined mouth that had brushed hers in her first real kiss. "So you do remember. I'm flattered."

Remember? How could she forget? Suddenly cold to the marrow, she shivered violently.

His face changed, growing hard. "Give me your hand. You need to get inside."

Somehow she drew herself taller, pitting her five foot four inch admittedly out of shape form against six feet three inches of hard-bitten, decidedly intimidating muscle. "I'm not moving an inch until you tell me why you're suddenly on my doorstep after twenty years.''

''We'll talk inside.''

''Oh no we—''

His gaze narrowed, acting remarkably like a whiplash. She refused to be afraid. ''Inside, Daniela. Maybe you're immune to pneumonia, but I'm not.''

Without waiting for permission, he slipped the strap of her briefcase from her shoulder and slung it over his own, before tucking a big hand beneath her elbow. She started to turn, only to have his hand tighten.

''Gresham!''

Startled by the sudden bark of command, she glanced up to find him looking over his shoulder. As though conjured by Rafe's will alone, a tall, dark-haired man appeared, his suit blue instead of gray, his tie knotted in the same full Windsor Mark had preferred.

Ice blue eyes in a tanned, aristocratic face met hers with frank curiosity as he inclined his head a polite two inches then waited while Rafe performed a perfunctory introduction.

''Dr. Daniela Fabrizio, meet Special Agent Seth Gresham, of the Greenwich Greshams.''

The young agent's mouth curved into a boyish grin. ''A pleasure, ma'am.''

''Agent.'' Her voice came out too thin, and she took a fast breath. Heart thudding, she willed herself to calm down. Adrenaline wasn't good for the baby. It wasn't all that good for the baby's mom, either, she realized, as the dull headache that had gotten worse while she stood in the checkout lane took on a sharper edge.

''I need to get Dr. Fabrizio inside,'' Rafe informed his partner curtly. ''Make sure that rubbernecking cabby's not thinking about calling out 911 on us, then get the damn groceries.''

''Yes sir.'' Gresham shifted his gaze to her, then asked politely, ''Ma'am, are you square with the driver?'' His voice was Eastern, the diction perfect.

''Unfortunately, yes, the jerk.'' She drew back to glare at the cab driver who was leaning forward, staring white-faced through the passenger's window. "Took my tip, then refused to move his fat...self to help me."

Rafe's gaze flicked toward the cab. "Might be a good idea to rattle his chain a little, make him rethink the way he treats his paying passengers."

"Be a pleasure," Gresham said, his grin flashing white again before he turned away. The wind blew his coat back, revealing a gun in a holster hugging his side.

"Are you sure he's old enough to carry a gun?" she muttered, feeling more ancient by the moment.

"He's old enough." Rafe tightened his grip and helped her up the two short steps to the brick walk.

Grateful for his support, she concentrated on sidestepping the puddles formed by the walk's uneven surface. Water from the gutter squished in her sodden shoes, and her last pair of panty hose were now spattered with mud. To add insult to injury her mashed toes hurt like the very dickens, making her limp.

"What's wrong?" he demanded after only a few steps.

"I was attacked by a can of tomato juice," she shot back impatiently.

"Why the hell didn't you say so?"

"Because it's silly and—" Her voice ended in a gasp as she was suddenly swept off her feet and into his arms.

"Anyone ever tell you you're supposed to take care of yourself when you're pregnant?" he grated close to her ear.

Only everyone from her father and her doctor, Luke Jarrod, all the way down to Bruno of automotive repair fame, she thought peevishly. "I am doing my very best, I assure you," she said with as much dignity as she could muster under the circumstances.

Behind her, she heard the cab roar away, leaving more foul air behind. Though it wasn't quite six-thirty, the gloom had caused the streetlights to wink on. The rain was coming down harder, now, driven sideways by the wind.

"Is your daughter home?" he asked as they neared the small porch with its rose-covered trellis.

"No, Lys is..." She stopped abruptly and narrowed her gaze suspiciously. "How did you know I have a daughter?"

"It was in the file," he said as he climbed the three steps to the porch.

"What file?"

"Later." As he swung her around, her sleeve brushed one of the lavender roses climbing the terraces, and she caught a whiff of its perfume. Roses in the rain, her favorite scent.

"Where's your house key?"

"In my briefcase. If you'll just put me down, I'll—"

"Gresham, get your butt over here and unlock the damned door!"

She winced. What did he have to be so angry about? She was the one whose life was imploding. Reminding herself that she was a responsible, mature adult and not an hysterical six-year-old, she drew back her head and treated him to her coolest shrink look. "Wouldn't it be more sensible if you just put me down and let me unlock the damned door?"

"Probably." He flicked her an impatient glance. "In case you haven't noticed, you're still shivering."

She hadn't actually, but she noticed now. Noticed, too, that her head was splitting. Even more annoying for a woman who prided herself on her coping skills, it was becoming a struggle to keep her mind from wandering off on odd little side trips. Like remembering the last time she was smashed up against that muscular chest.

They'd both been naked and...

Oh God, don't think about that now, she thought, squeezing her eyes shut. It had taken years—*years*—before she stopped remembering every touch, every kiss, every fevered word they'd spoken to each other in the heat of passion.

"Sorry, had to get the rest of the oranges," Gresham said as he vaulted up the steps. "Sneaky little suckers rolled half-way down the block."

Remembering the sodden bags, she started to ask him how he'd managed when she saw the dark blue tote bag slung over a shoulder that wasn't nearly as broad as Rafe's. A stalk of celery protruded through the open zipper. Grateful for the distraction, Danni burst out laughing, then winced as pain crashed through her skull.

Rafe jerked his attention to her face. He'd spent time recently in the sun and the same rays that had burned his tan to a golden bronze had bleached his brows to a tawny hue. "What's wrong now?" he demanded impatiently.

"Trust me, you don't want to know." She sighed. "Even I don't want to know all the things that are wrong in my life at the moment."

His mouth softened, and time seemed to spin backward to the innocent days when she had run to him with all her problems, confident he would make everything better. "Put your head on my shoulder, Daniela," he commanded in that oddly hoarse voice.

"No, I'm fine." But suddenly her eyes were stinging.

"You always were part mule," he grated.

"Like you weren't," she muttered, but suddenly her cheek was resting against his shoulder and her eyes were drifting closed. Just for a minute, she told herself firmly. Until her head stopped clanging.

Vaguely, she was aware of Gresham unlocking the door. She heard the faint creak of the hinges as he entered. She frowned when Rafe didn't immediately follow. "If you're waiting for a polite invitation, consider it extended," she murmured in a voice that seemed oddly slurred.

"Shut up," he ordered brusquely.

Before she could answer, his companion returned. "It's clear."

She blinked. "What's clear?"

"Just checking your house for intruders, ma'am," Gresham said, smiling at her. "All part of the service."

Narrowing his gaze, Rafe shot his partner an impatient look. "You want to make sure you got all those canned goods?"

Gresham's boyish smile faded. "Yes sir."

As Rafe carried her inside with the same loose-jointed stride that could cover twice as much ground as her short legs, Danni roused herself to lift her head. "Okay, we're inside now. What's going on? Why are you here?"

He looked down at her. "To ask you a few questions."

"Questions about what?" She stared at that hard shuttered face and felt an inexpressible feeling of loss. Why hadn't he loved her? she wondered before ruthlessly pulling her mind back to things she could control.

"Not what. Who. Jonathan Sommerset."

She drew in a sharp breath. "Do you know Jonathan?"

"I know him."

Hope flared, and her heart gave a leap. "Do you know where he is?" she asked with a pathetic eagerness she hated, yet couldn't seem to disguise.

"No, that's why we're here."

"I don't understand."

"You will. First you need to get out of those wet things, and I need to make a phone call." He set her down gently, keeping one hand on the small of her back until she settled firmly on both feet in the center of the square foyer.

"But—"

He cast a lazy glance at her sodden suede pumps. "You're dripping on the rug. Pretty nice rug, too. Looks expensive. Be a shame to ruin it."

He was right, damn him. "Then get your big feet off of it!" she shot back before turning around to climb the stairs.

"Mind if I make some coffee?" he called after her.

"You lay one hand on anything in this house, and I'll sue!"

Chapter 2

After peeling off her sodden tunic and skirt, Danni couldn't seem to stop shivering. Even wrapped in her thick terry cloth robe, she felt frozen inside. Deciding a bath would help, she hurried into the bathroom and turned on the hot tap. As soon as the tub was full, she slipped out of the robe and into the steamy water. A blissful sigh escaped her lips as she sank to her chin and closed her eyes.

In her mind's eye she pictured a meadow with wildflowers. Nearby, a clear, sun-gilded stream rippled a soothing tune. The sun-warmed water was soothing and soft, bubbling around her bare ankles, and the rocks were smooth under her feet.

Secure in her safe place now, she took slow, even breaths, filling her lungs with steam-warmed oxygen until she felt her heart rate slowing to a normal rhythm. One by one she relaxed her muscles until the tension drained away. Relaxed and in control once more, she allowed herself to think of the man downstairs.

His father, Enrique, had been field foreman of Mancini vineyards since before she and Rafe had been born. His mother Rosaria had helped Danni's mother in the house until Mary

Elizabeth Mancini had died of complications a few weeks after Danni's birth.

Alone with four children under the age of eight Eduardo Mancini had brought Mary Elizabeth's spinster sister Gina to Oregon from her home in New Jersey to live in the big house and look after Danni and her three older brothers. With only Rafe to demand her attention then, Rosaria had become housekeeper, cook and, in many ways, Danni's second mother. It was only natural, she realized now, that she and Rafe—only two years apart—had become playmates.

Little by little they'd grown up tussling like bear cubs, fighting and making up like all siblings do, going to school together, running through the fields like gypsies during the summers and holidays. Year by year Rafe had gotten taller and stronger, until finally by the age of fifteen he'd towered over everyone but her two big brothers, Eddie and Vito. Little by little his bony shoulders filled out, then thickened with muscle. Naturally athletic, he made both the varsity soccer and football teams his freshman year.

Danni was changing, too. Finally, after being the ugliest of ugly ducklings, she became a swan—with breasts. Gloriously full, rosy-tipped breasts like all of the Mancini women. She'd also had curvy hips and a tiny waist that was the envy of all her girlfriends.

The boys in school started noticing. Her brothers began driving her crazy with warnings about the things boys would try to do to her if she wasn't careful. A perceptive woman, her aunt Gina had seen the way Danni looked at the tall, deeply bronzed boy with the look of a Nordic warrior about him and warned her brother-in-law of danger ahead.

Papa had just laughed. Both Rafe and Danni knew the way things worked on Mancini land. She lived in the big house, Rafe lived in the workers' camp near the river. They were friends, yes, but nothing more. It was good for her to test her woman's powers on someone who wouldn't take advantage of her.

Besides, Danni had been promised to Marco Fabrizio in her

cradle. Everyone in the valley knew they would marry on her eighteenth birthday, uniting two proud families.

Still, on her sixteenth birthday, Papa had sat her down and told her about her family bloodlines and her responsibility to keep herself unsullied for Mark.

Danni had listened, but she hadn't really heard. She only cared about Rafe, who, despite her developing body, treated her with the same brotherly affection as always. And then one hot August day it happened. She'd been washing Papa's new Mercedes, wearing only skimpy cut-offs and a halter top. Rafe had spent the day pruning vines and had stripped off his shirt in order to duck under the spray to cool off. They ended up fighting over the hose and her top had gotten soaked. The thin fabric had clung to her breasts, revealing nipples that stood out like hard pebbles.

Rafe's breath had hissed in, and he'd stood transfixed, the hose still in his hand. The laughter in his eyes had given way to a heated look that had made her mouth grow dry. It had taken her a moment to notice the distinctive bulge behind the fly of his worn work jeans.

As soon as he'd seen the direction of her gaze, he'd turned a fiery red, thrown down the hose and stalked off toward the river. After that everything was different. Instead of teasing her mercilessly the way he had for years, he'd taken to turning red every time she came close. When he'd tried to talk to her, he'd actually stammered.

That summer big, tough Rafe Cardoza started bringing her wildflowers. Lord, but she'd gloried in her new power.

All that changed when he kissed her for the first time. Then she'd been the one whose words hadn't come out right. The one who turned red with a melting heat that made her restless inside. She'd learned then that kisses were addictive. Like all addictions, however, she soon craved more. So, it seemed, did he.

They'd met in secret at first, usually in the grassy, sun-dappled spot beneath a corkscrew willow where Rafe had taught her to fish. No one in their families had known how things had changed between them. Not until Rafe had asked her to his senior prom. She'd been wild with excitement. Not even Mark Fabrizio's anger when he'd found out had dented her bliss.

The night before the prom had been unseasonably hot. The big old farmhouse hadn't been air-conditioned in those days, and the fan by her bed only served to move the steamy air around in a thick circle. When Rafe had thrown pebbles at her window to get her attention, then suggested a moonlight swim, she'd been more than ready.

Instead of taking her to their spot by the river Rafe had decided to go to the pond instead because the path to the river was treacherous at night, even when the moon was high. In the pond, hidden behind a thick tangle of blackberry canes, they'd played in the cool water like kids, splashing and ducking one another.

Realizing that sound carried, Rafe had stifled her giggles with his hand first and then his mouth. Those playful kisses soon grew more passionate, their mutual touching more intimate. Soon his hands were sliding into the cups of her bathing suit to massage her breasts, and hers were tugging at his trunks.

Bathed in silver, they explored one another awkwardly, driven by their wild need for one another. They'd made promises, spoken words of love that seemed shiny and new. She'd explored his body with a frank interest that seemed to arouse him even more, until finally something seemed to snap inside him.

It happened fast then, the two of them kissing frantically as they stripped off their suits. His eyes had grown hot when he'd looked at her naked body for the first time, and his hands had trembled as they'd explored her with a touching reverence.

With each virgin touch, new sensations had thrummed through her, until she'd been writhing beneath his hand, desperate for something she couldn't quite understand.

She'd been sobbing in pleasure and need when he'd parted her thighs. There would be pain, she knew, but it would pass, and then he would be inside her. Eagerly she reached for him, opening her legs wider. She remembered a feeling of moist warmth and then his body was covering hers. She braced for the invasion—and then he had rolled away from her, his breath coming in harsh gasps and those big fists clenched tightly.

He must have explained, but the words were lost to her now. Or perhaps she simply hadn't listened. The terrible feeling of humiliation and hurt, though, she remembered vividly to this day.

The next morning, with her eyes swollen from the copious tears she'd shed and her throat raw from the sobs she'd swallowed so that no one would hear, she'd found out that they'd been seen. By whom, she'd never known for certain. One of her brothers, probably. It hardly mattered. The damage had been done.

Her father's brown eyes had been filled with disappointment and sorrow when he'd told her that her brother had confronted Rafe with the truth and insisted that he marry her. Danni had felt a rush of joy, only to have her heart ripped in two when Papa had added in a tight, angry voice that Rafe had left the valley instead. If there was a baby, it was agreed between her father and Tonio Fabrizio that Mark would claim it as his own.

At first no one believed that she was still a virgin. But when her period arrived on schedule, they'd given her the benefit of the doubt. Or so she'd thought, until Mark had been visibly shocked on their wedding night to discover her untouched. Humiliated and angry all over again, she'd cried into her pillow after he'd gone to sleep.

She'd never seen Rafe again.

Both Rosaria and Enrique were careful never to mention him in her presence. On the rare occasions when she happened to run into one of his brothers or sisters, his name never came up. But he was always there, a silent, invisible presence.

Once the family star, he'd become a pariah overnight, his name erased from the tattered Bible that had been one of the few family possessions Enrique's father had brought with him from Mexico after his parents had been killed in a flash flood in their small village near Oaxaca.

Not only had Rafe shamed his family by violating the daughter of their *patron,* but he'd also added to his sins by refusing to restore her honor by marrying her. As far as Enrique was concerned, the son he'd once adored was dead. He was not to be welcomed into their home if he returned. No one was to speak his name or pray for him on Holy Days.

Rosaria was forbidden to cry for him. But she had, Danni knew. Sobbing into her apron in the pantry of the old farmhouse where no one could hear.

Danni had cried too. Buckets. She'd lost weight because she couldn't eat and cut her hair short because Rafe had loved it long. She burned her scrapbooks and photo albums and everything he'd ever given her. Nothing had helped.

It's just puppy love, cara mía, Papa had said, holding her while she sobbed.

It was better this way, she'd see. Rafe would never have felt comfortable in the big house on the hill and she hadn't been raised to live in a trailer in the migrants' camp. Rafe would never be able to provide for her the way she deserved. The best he could hope for was a job as foreman like his father, or maybe a job as a mechanic, if he really worked hard. No, it was better for everyone that he'd left.

Only now, it seemed, Rafe Cardoza had come back. Bigger, tougher, with eyes that looked as though they'd forgotten how to laugh and a dangerous edge to his personality.

A man of substance, Papa, she thought, breathing in steam. A man who wore beautifully tailored suits as though born to them and carried himself with a steely confidence. And unlike the last time she'd seen him, a man who was clearly accustomed to being in charge.

Of Agent Gresham, perhaps, she thought lifting her chin in a way her brothers would have recognized. But not of her, she vowed, reaching for the soap.

Once she would have willingly thrown away her heritage and her honor and her family's love for him. Now she simply wanted him to ask his questions and go away again. For good, this time.

Rafe opened cupboard doors until he found a serious looking coffeemaker. His spirits rose a notch as he pulled it out and plugged it in.

He'd given up his pack-a-day cigarette habit while he'd been in the hospital. Not that he'd had a choice, given the reality of life in Intensive Care. But once they'd weaned him off the ventilator and his lungs had learned to handle decent air again, he'd made it a permanent life change.

Caffeine was his only addiction now. He figured it would take another stint in ICU to wean him off the dozen or so cups of black coffee he drank every day.

"You want coffee?" he asked his partner who stood near the built-in pantry at the end of the work surface, dealing with Danni's groceries.

"Yeah, with a heavy shot of Kahlua."

"You wish, rookie."

Laughing, Seth dipped into his duffel and pulled out another can. Using the towel he'd found hanging on a peg by the sink, he wiped off the mud before putting it on the shelf.

"Did she tell you when the daughter was due home?" he asked as Rafe hung his suit coat on the back of a Shaker style kitchen chair.

"Started to, then got sidetracked."

One by one he unbuttoned his cuffs and rolled back his sleeves. He hated suits, but tolerated them the way he tolerated service politics and dumb-ass restrictions put on field personnel by ACLU types who hadn't a clue how rough it was out there on the streets.

"Have to say the lady's got great legs for a shrink. Nice ass, too."

Rafe felt his temper flash before he yanked it back. "We're here to pump her for information, not ogle her butt," he said in the steely tone he used when the rookie needed his attitude adjusted. One thing about Gresham, he was quick, Rafe thought as his partner's expression went blank.

"Think she still loves the bastard?" Gresham asked a few minutes later as Rafe filled the pot at the sink.

"Who can tell with women."

Rafe hadn't let himself think about more than the bare facts of the case. Seeing her softly rounded tummy had slammed him back hard, and he was still reeling. Thinking of Danni as a victim of fraud and forgery had been safe. Something that was familiar, part of his job. Imagining Danni in bed with that piece of slime, though, that would be a mistake.

Rafe didn't like mistakes.

Consequently he did the extra work required to make sure he didn't make many. In this case, that meant keeping the past blocked off and his mind focused on the job they'd come to do. Caffeine would help.

After conducting a methodical search, he found a bag of coffee grounds in an antique canister marked 'Lump Sugar' and measured out enough for a full pot.

Watching him, Gresham filched a chocolate chip cookie from a bag that had already been opened. Apparently Danni snacked as she shopped. ''Think she'll ask us to stay for dinner?'' he asked as he chewed.

''Jeez, Gresham, don't you ever think about anything but food?''

''Yeah, but you won't let me talk about my sex life.''

Rafe shot him a look as he switched on the coffeemaker. ''Talk about it all you want—as long as you don't blur the lines between private and personal when you're on the job. Mistake like that just might get you killed.''

It was advice he would do well to remember, he thought as he tugged his tie free of his collar and slipped open the button.

Daniela was just one more victim. He was a government cop determined to bring down one more bad guy, so he would ask his questions, make concise notes with cross-references and annotations, give her his card, and walk away—this time on his own terms.

This time without regret.

This time without tears in his eyes.

Chapter 3

Danni was halfway down the stairs before she smelled coffee brewing. Oh sure, just take over my house, she thought with a wild mix of emotions. On second thought, why not let someone else give it a shot? After all she wasn't doing such a hot job handling things herself.

Reaching the bottom of the stairs, she heard them in the kitchen, talking in low tones. Though she did her best to remain quiet as she walked through the living room into the dining room, the conversation ceased before she reached the kitchen door.

Rafe was standing in front of the fridge, transferring eggs from the carton in his hand to the door. He'd hung his suit coat over the back of a kitchen chair, loosened his conservative gray and red striped tie and rolled his blue striped shirtsleeves nearly to the elbows, revealing wide, corded wrists and thick forearms furred with curly hair bleached almost white by the sun.

Beneath the well-fitting shirt, his chest was a massive wedge of hard-packed muscle, his torso long and lean, his hips narrow. Tucked into a leather holster clipped to his belt was an ugly black gun that seemed far too enormous to be a simple hand-gun.

His partner still wore his suitcoat, a nifty double-breasted pinstripe. Standing with his back toward the door, he was stowing canned goods in the cupboard pantry, shoving them with a haphazard carelessness that had her teeth grinding.

"I hope you do windows," she said, glaring at them both in turn.

Rafe simply flicked her an impatient gaze. In contrast, Gresham turned to offer a friendly grin. "Only under extreme duress, ma'am."

He had dimples, too, she noticed, and beautiful manners. His hair, neatly styled and cut to mold a head that was definitely patrician, was the color of semi-sweet chocolate. He had a straight nose, an angular face and a perfect tan. He was—in a word—gorgeous.

"Feeling better?" Rafe asked, looking at her directly now.

"*Much* better, thank you," she said coolly.

"Coffee's ready." He closed the refrigerator door with a hard thump before tossing the empty egg carton into the trash can under the sink. "Made it strong. Figured it'd help drive away the chill."

His thoughtfulness made her feel petty. She bit off a sigh. What was wrong with her that he could cause her to regress to the level of an insecure teenager? "Unfortunately, I'm on restricted caffeine intake for the duration. Doctor's orders." She patted the bulge beneath Mark's old USC sweat shirt. "I'll just put on some water for tea."

He shrugged. "It's your kitchen."

"Exactly." For as long as she could swing the rent, anyway, she thought as she carried the kettle from the stove to the sink. As she turned on the water, she was aware that Rafe was looking at her belly.

"How far along are you?"

"Five months." She shut off the water, then carried the kettle to the stove and turned on the burner. She turned then, and deliberately met his speculative gaze. "I got pregnant shortly after Jonathan and I married. He said he didn't want to wait, and at the time…'' She took a shaky breath. "At the time neither did I.''

She caught the look Gresham sent Rafe and frowned. "Before I say another word, I want to know what right you have to ask me these questions.''

In response he retrieved a slim black leather wallet from the back pocket of his perfectly tailored trousers and flipped it open. Frowning, she stepped close enough to read the small print.

One side was a laminated card identifying the bearer, Rafael Martin Cardoza as a Special Agent of the Investigative Branch of the United States Secret Service. Attached to a removable black leather insert on the opposite side was a gold badge in the shape of a five-pointed star.

Surprised and a little awed, she lifted her gaze to his. "I thought Secret Service agents guarded VIPs.''

"Some do. In fact it's the first billet a new agent receives when he leaves the academy." He indicated his partner with a quick look. "Until a few months ago Gresham was assigned to the Vice President's wife.''

"What happened two months ago?''

"He got promoted.''

"To what?''

"Major cases like yours.''

She frowned. "Mine? I don't understand.''

"When the man you know as Jonathan Sommerset used your credit card, he committed fraud. Since the issuing institutions are in differing states, that makes it a federal crime.''

"The man I know? You mean that's not his real name?''

Instead of answering, he returned his ID to his pocket, then drew out what looked like a photograph. "Do you recognize this man?''

It was a mug shot, one of those frontal and profile views she was always seeing on crime-stopper shows on TV. The face above the numbers and the name Jacob Folsom was Jonathan's. Her stomach roiled. "This is Jonathan Sommerset, my husband.''

"His real name is Jacob Peter Folsom," he said without inflection.

She blew out air. "I need to call Case. He should know that."

"Case?"

"Detective Sergeant Case Randolph. He's the one trying to find Jonathan. He also happens to live next door, in the house with the fuchsia door. He's put out an APB or whatever you call an arrest warrant."

"I've read his notes. So far nothing of substance has turned up."

"Substance meaning what?"

Impatience tightened his mouth. She suspected he was far more accustomed to asking questions than answering them. "Meaning Folsom has gone to ground and no one has picked up his tracks."

Case had repeatedly warned her the more time that passed, the more likely they wouldn't be able to recover her assets, even if they found him. Even so, disappointment crashed through her. "Why is it with all the electronic gizmos and spy satellites and lightning-fast communications equipment you law enforcement people insist you need, no one has been able to find one middle-age swindler?"

Rafe turned his sleeves back another turn. "Miss him, do you?"

Her temper flared. "That's a stupid question, Rafe. The man cheated me! All I want from him now is a divorce—and my money."

Beneath the hood of dusty blond eyebrows his eyes crinkled with a sardonic amusement. "In that order?"

"In any order!"

After she rid herself of all ties to the man she now abhorred with every fiber of her being, she intended to devote herself to her children and her career, period. No more whirlwind romances for her. No more "Isn't it wonderful to be so gloriously in love?" fantasies.

As for her husband of less than six months, she only wanted him back in her life long enough to sign the divorce papers waiting for him on her attorney's desk and pay her back what he stole before they shipped him off to jail. Forever, if there was any justice left in this world.

"Where do you keep your mugs?" Rafe asked, lifting the coffeepot from the burner.

"Second cupboard. The ones with violets are for coffee, the daisies are for tea."

He shot her a measuring look before retrieving two violets and a daisy. "A little obsessive about your mugs, aren't you?"

"Needing to impose order on chaos is a perfectly healthy coping tool," she said with a shrug. "Besides, as you pointed out, it's my house. "

He poured coffee in the two mugs, left one on the counter for Gresham, then lifted his own to his mouth for a quick sip. "Your house until the Paxtons return from London, anyway," he said, watching her over the steam.

Surprise sifted through her. "Was that in the file, too?"

He lifted an eyebrow, his expression mocking. "No, I got that from one of those electronic gizmos."

She jerked the top off a cloisonné tin containing a selection of herbal teas. "My life is a train wreck and the man is playing 'Can you top this'?" she muttered, ripping the bag from its neat paper envelope.

"Oh no, ma'am, us G-men aren't authorized to indulge in games on duty." He slid the daisy cup down the counter toward her. As she caught it, she saw surprise cross Gresham's perfect features. Interesting, she thought, tucking it away for further study. Understanding and predicting human behavior was a passion as well as a profession. It made her feel secure to know within several plus or minus percentage points how someone would react to stimulus.

Rafe made her feel anything but secure.

"Nice house," Gresham said as he picked up his mug. "Reminds me of the place I lived as a kid."

His voice was part F.D.R., part J.F.K. Harvard, maybe? Definitely Ivy League at any rate. She suspected it hadn't been all that long ago since he'd graduated. Maybe four or five years.

"My daughter likes it." She would like Seth Gresham, too,

she thought, hiding a smile. Lyssa had recently discovered boys. Later than most in today's times, but that was partly due to lingering trauma. Knowing her daughter, she would rapidly make up for lost time. She wasn't looking forward to the mood swings and separation struggles that were part and parcel of navigating one's way through puberty, however.

Finished with the tea bag, she started to dump it into the trash, then thought better of it. Use it up, wear it out and never buy anything that's not been marked down at least twice—that was her motto now.

She could get one more cup from this sucker, even though it would be weaker than she liked. Conscious that both men were watching, she plunked the soggy dripping bag onto a saucer from the cupboard overhead. She'd become an expert at detecting pity. She saw only a flicker in Gresham's eyes, but not Rafe's. His were cool and watching, physically familiar, but otherwise the eyes of a stranger.

"Would you mind if we go into the living room?" she asked after fortifying her tea with two spoons of sugar. "If I'm going to be subjected to the third degree, I'd like to do it sitting down."

Without waiting for an answer, she led the way to the living room, more self-conscious about her altered body contours than reason dictated. It was instinctive, this awareness of the reaction she aroused in the male of the species, hard-wired into her psyche by eons of evolution like the fierce need to protect her offspring.

Not that she cared whether she ever attracted another man again in her entire life, she reminded herself firmly. Especially not one who looked at her with a stranger's coolness, even as her blood swam with the memory of his mouth hot on hers.

The Paxtons' living room was a mixture of tasteful antiques, comfortable modern pieces and accent pieces that ranged from priceless to endearingly homey, like the elaborate dollhouse Morgan had made for their daughter Morgana.

In the abstract, if not the literal, it had reminded her of the house she'd shared with Mark and Lyssa during what she'd come to consider the magic years. It had taken all of her control to keep from dissolving into a puddle of self-pity the first time she'd seen the exquisite little house.

"I sublet the place furnished," she said when she noticed Gresham looking at the array of ceremonial masks Morgan Paxton had brought back from South Africa after covering Nelson Mandela's release for his network.

"Interesting," was all that Gresham said. "Especially that guy with the yellow eyes."

Danni grimaced at the devil figure with its malicious grin. She preferred the benign face next to it, the one with the quizzical eyebrows and fuzzy yellow hair. The tribal equivalent of the archetypal jokester of Western mythology.

"The Paxtons' twin sons start kindergarten next year, and Morgan is taking a year's sabbatical in order to show his wife Raine and their kids Europe."

Gresham looked impressed. "Used to watch him reporting from Baghdad during Desert Storm. Man has more grit than sense."

"The Emmy he won is in the den."

Gresham lifted both brows. "What's he like in person?"

Her face softened as she recalled the generosity of both Paxtons. "Even more impressive than he appears on screen. And very kindhearted."

"How'd you end up renting his place?"

Danni recognized the attempt to establish rapport and wondered if Seth was the designated good cop. Rafe, on the other hand, had made little attempt to be more than marginally friendly. A professional decision or a personal one? she wondered as she forced a smile from her tired facial muscles for Gresham's benefit.

"You mean you don't already know every tiny detail of my life?" she teased, playing along.

His grin flashed again, revealing perfectly aligned, blazing white teeth. "That particular fact must have slipped by."

"My obstetrician, Luke Jarrod, lives on the corner across the street. He's also a colleague and a friend. When he found out I was essentially penniless and homeless, he talked the Paxtons into hiring a housesitter." She managed a smile. "Me, of course!'' Her smile faded. Her facial muscles felt stiff. Sometimes she felt as though she were strangling on her pride. ''The house wasn't available for a month so Luke and his wife Maddy let Lyssa and me stay with them until then.''

Though her budget was as thin as paper, she'd insisted on paying rent, both to Luke and now to the Paxtons—but at a far lower rate than a house like this would ordinarily command. Because she worked hard to keep the house and contents in perfect condition, she'd managed to convince herself that it wasn't really charity.

''Sounds like you have great friends.'' Gresham looked genuinely interested in her well-being.

''I do. And I'm very grateful.''

''Guess I envy you. This job being what it is I'm never home long enough in any one stretch to do more than nod at my neighbors in my place in Alexandria.'' Holding his mug in front of him, he wandered around the room, inspecting the eclectic memorabilia.

Holding his own mug, sipping occasionally, Rafe waited politely until she settled into the corner of the plush sofa with its heavenly eiderdown cushions before taking the chair opposite. Face impassive, he watched her steadily. The body language was classic, the dominant male of the pride sizing up his prey— or his next mate. Her skin warmed, then grew tight and itchy. She refused to squirm.

Cupping both hands around her mug, she lifted it to her lips. She inhaled the steam, then took a sip. It was an old habit of hers, stimulating both senses simultaneously.

''What are those, toys?'' Gresham asked, pausing in front of a curio case.

Some toys, Danni thought with a private moment of amusement. According to Raine, several of the small carved figures inside were worth more than the Lexus she still mourned.

''Those are Chinese chop marks. Mandarin warlords used them to make their marks on correspondence and military orders. Jade is relatively soft, so that it can be carved with the mandarin's name, like a stamp.''

''Clever.''

Rafe lifted one sun-bleached brow and tilted his head slightly. As a signal it was so subtle it would have eluded anyone but a trained observer. She herself wasn't completely certain until Gresham ambled over to another easy chair and settled comfortably.

Apparently Rafe had decided they'd succeeded in putting her at ease.

Looking deceptively relaxed, Seth took a couple of quick sips of coffee, then set the mug on a beaten silver coaster he took from the ornate holder on the table at his elbow. After producing a small notebook and pen from the inside pocket of his suit coat, he flipped to a clean page, then glanced up. Not at her, she noted, but at Rafe.

On the other hand Rafe was looking at her, a level, steady gaze that seemed to peel away the confident façade that had been her only protection in recent weeks. She felt a flare of resentment, and then humor surfaced. What difference did it make if he saw through her to the scared, humiliated woman beneath? she thought. Once a man had seen a woman naked, there wasn't much left to hide.

"I'll tell you all we know, and then I'd like to ask you some questions," Rafe said, his mouth curving slightly, but not far enough to engage the comma shaped creases that she knew bracketed his mouth when he truly grinned. "Fair enough?"

"Fair enough." Feeling a little chilled in spite of the warm tights and fleece sweatshirt that reached nearly to her knees, she curled herself a little deeper into the cushions, then rested her mug on her thigh.

Rafe took a sip, then leaned forward to rest both forearms on his splayed thighs, his coffee mug held between both large, callused palms. It was a masterful use of body language, an optical illusion of sorts that made him look smaller and less intimidating as well as encouraging her to think of him as a friend instead of an adversary. She had to admire his savvy, but then, he had undoubtedly undergone expert training in one of those ultrasecret facilities outside Washington.

In this case, his attempt to manipulate her only put her more on guard. She took a sip of her too-sweet tea and contrived not to grimace at the syrupy taste.

"Folsom was born in L.A. in 1952 and grew up in Las Vegas. The details of his early years are sketchy, but we know his mother was a part-time blackjack dealer and full-time prostitute. Folsom's first brush with law enforcement came at the age of eleven when he was picked up for trying to use a credit card he'd boosted from one of his mother's johns."

She realized he was waiting for her to comment and roused herself to admit, "He told me he grew up in a house on Philadelphia's Main Line and that his parents were killed when their yacht capsized in a storm off St. Thomas when he was a senior at Andover."

Gresham glanced her way. "That's one of his favorite scams."

"*One* of his favorite scams? That implies there are more."

Rafe flicked a look toward his partner. Gresham's face turned red. Clearly a blunder on the young agent's part. The mom in her wanted to pat his head and tell him this lion's roar was worse than his bite, but she wasn't all that certain she would be telling him the truth.

"Folsom's wanted for a long list of similar felonies," Rafe said without changing his tone.

"How long a list?"

The hesitation was little more than a flicker of the thick curly lashes framing those sage green eyes. "Fourteen that we've definitely traced back to him. Possibly more."

"He's swindled fourteen other women before me, and he's still running around free?" she asked, both incredulous and outraged.

Perhaps a less self-assured man would respond defensively. Rafe merely nodded. "He's been arrested five times. Only three of those arrests resulted in prosecution. Twice he was acquitted when the victim recanted her accusation under oath."

"And the third trial? Was he convicted?"

"He never went to trial." Something shifted deep in his eyes, and she felt her own narrow.

"Why not?"

His mouth flattened, and his eyes were suddenly haunted by some dark emotion. "The complainant was shot and killed before she could testify."

Danni's lungs seemed incapable of inflating, and then suddenly, they drew in air in a violent rush. "Are you saying Jonathan murdered her?" she cried after forcing the air out again.

"We don't know that for sure." It was the literal truth, no more, no less. The man who'd pumped nine bullets into Alice—and four into him—had matched Folsom's general height and weight, but so did half the adult males on the planet. The shooter's hair and face had been covered by a ski mask, his eyes hidden behind dark glasses. In Rafe's gut, however, he knew Folsom had either pulled the trigger or hired it out. Either way, the bastard was directly responsible for Alice's murder.

Danni's face was still too pale, and her eyes told him she was still grappling with another shock. "But…but you, personally, think he…Folsom did it." It wasn't a question. Even though he hadn't moved, he suddenly felt his back smash up against a solid wall.

The truth or a lie? Though it gave him no real pride to admit it, he had the knack of telling either with equal credibility. Because lying grated against every principle of decent behavior his parents had instilled in him, however, he preferred to stick as closely to the truth as the circumstances of the interview permitted. More importantly, the quick intuitive tug in his gut told him she would resent a lie if it was ever revealed. Which, in his experience, had a way of happening at the worst possible moment.

He sat back and kept his gaze steady on hers. "Yes, I think that one way or another he was responsible. The evidence was too sketchy to make a case, however, and the charges against him were dropped. We kept him under surveillance, of course, but he managed to slip out of town undetected during a bad snowstorm."

It jolted her, he saw, but she pulled herself together enough to ask calmly, "When…when did this happen?"

"December 2nd last year."

"I met Jonathan on December 27th."

"Where exactly was that, Doctor?" Seth asked.

"On board the *SS Holiday Pleasure*. My father and my brother had arranged for the cruise as a surprise."

"You went alone?"

"Yes." She took a breath, then looked down at her hands. Her nails were filed short with clear polish. She wore no rings. A platinum-and-emerald wedding set had been included on the list of stolen property. Hers from her marriage to Fabrizio, he assumed.

"My daughter Lyssa was severely injured in the accident that killed her father. She was in ICU for weeks with major internal injuries and then in and out of the hospital for months after that." She drew a breath. "The paramedics said that it had been a miracle Lyssa had survived. As it was her legs had been broken and one side of her face had been badly cut."

"No airbags?" Gresham asked quietly.

She shook her head. "My husband had just finished restoring an old Jag XK-150 and he'd driven it that weekend because he wanted to show his father. The state trooper who investigated said he probably would have survived if he'd been driving my Lexus or his Cherokee, both of which have airbags."

"You weren't with them, then?" Rafe asked, although he was pretty sure she hadn't been.

"No, Mark and Lys had gone down to the vineyard for the weekend, but I'd stayed home to catch up on case notes."

"Vineyard?" Gresham asked.

"Mark's family owns Fabrizio and Sons Wine. My father and brothers run Mancini Vineyard. The two properties adjoin one another in the foothills west of Ashland which is close to the California border."

Gresham's eyes lit up and he broke into a grin. "Great wines! I especially like Mancini's Pinot Noir."

Rafe shot him a look and he lost the grin.

"Thank you," she said with a brief smile.

"How is your daughter now?" Rafe asked before lifting the mug to his mouth for a sip.

"Bouncing back, finally, but it was a long haul."

"How about you? Are you bouncing back, too?"

Following his example she took a sip and tried to decide how much of herself to reveal. "It's funny," she said finally. "I ran a workshop in grief management when I first started practicing. I had all the tools, but somehow I was so busy taking care of Lys and trying to keep my practice going I guess I forgot to use them." She lifted an impatient hand and skimmed back the thick hair that still shimmered like a raven's wing in the sun when she turned her head. Her face had grown pale, highlighting the freckles splashed over the bridge of her nose. He'd counted them once between teasing kisses. Now he no longer remembered—or cared—how many there had been.

"I had sort of a meltdown on what would have been our twelfth anniversary. My family was already worried about me, and after that my father decided I needed to get away and relax. He arranged everything, even had my secretary reschedule my patients for the ten days I'd be away. I flew from Portland to L.A. the day after Christmas and boarded the boat the next day. I met Jonathan when he sat next to me at dinner the first night out." Her face tightened. "If he'd come on to me, I might have been suspicious, but he was a perfect gentleman."

She rubbed her palm up and down her arm as though trying to warm herself. "It seems even more horrible when I think about him touching me with the same hands he might have used to…to kill someone."

Suddenly, her cheeks turned the color of putty, and sweat broke out on her forehead. With a garbled moan, she set her mug on the glass-topped coffee table, then struggled to push herself out of the deep cushions.

Rafe put his own mug on the table with a sharp crack and got to his feet. Gresham did the same. Rafe reached her first.

"Danni—"

"Don't, please," she cried before clamping her hand over her mouth. Before he could stop her, she pushed him away and spun around to race toward the back of the house and the bathroom he remembered seeing there.

Chapter 4

"Danni, answer me, damn it! Are you all right?"

On her knees with her head over the toilet, Danni was too busy being miserably sick to reply. When the spasm passed, she grabbed a wad of toilet paper and wiped her mouth with a shaky hand. In recent weeks she had discovered a basic truth—morning sickness was definitely not for the fainthearted.

It was also, unfortunately, not confined to the morning.

"Danni!"

"I'm fine," she croaked.

"You don't sound fine," Rafe declared in a dangerous tone.

"You'll just have to take my word for it!" Too weak to move just yet, she sat down on the hard tile, and rested her head on her bent knees. The dizziness ebbed, only to be replaced by a growing clamminess that had her feeling hot on the inside and cold on the outside. She moaned, closed her eyes.

Obviously a man determined to have his own way, he rattled the knob. "Unlock the door, Daniela, or I swear I'll kick it in."

"Will you please go away?" she grated impatiently. "I'm being revoltingly sick in here, and I don't need an audience."

He greeted that with an ominous silence that lasted for several beats before he muttered a curse in Spanish that had her wincing. "Ten more minutes, and then I'm coming in to make sure you're all right."

Since she'd never known Rafe to make a threat he wasn't willing to carry out, she took a deep breath, then opened her eyes and pushed herself to her feet. Her head swam and bile surged to her throat. Her knees wanted to buckle.

I embrace perfect health and emotional serenity, she chanted silently. *I am strong and capable and confident.*

I am woman. Hear me roar.

She groaned silently. At the moment a newborn kitten had a louder roar.

Locking her knees, she forced her head up and opened her eyes. The wan face in the mirror staring back at her with hollow eyes was enough to make her queasy all over again.

After turning on the cold tap she grabbed a facecloth from the rod and bathed the hot skin until it started to tingle. She brushed her teeth until her gums felt raw, then ran her fingers through her lifeless hair and pinched color into her pale cheeks.

Oh God, could she really have married a killer?

Her lungs suddenly felt thick and sluggish, making it difficult to draw breath. How could she not have seen the violence in him? How could she not have felt it when he'd touched her? How could she know with any certainty that her judgment during therapy sessions was any sounder?

Dear heavens, what if her patients found out? How could they trust her? A humorless laugh ran through her mind. If her patients found out, she wouldn't *have* any patients.

Another thought rose, even more terrifying. Starved for a father's love, Lyssa had bonded with her new stepfather within only a few weeks. At the time she'd been touched by how sweet Jonathan had been with her. Now she knew it had all been part of his sick game.

She drew a shaky breath and tried not to think about the

images that Rafe's words had painted. What was it Harry Truman had said? Fatigue makes cowards of us all.

As soon as Rafe finished with his questions and left her in peace again, she would take a couple of Tylenol tablets and climb into bed. Lyssa wasn't due home until some time tomorrow afternoon, which meant she could sleep in for once.

After that...well, she would deal with the rest later. And deal she would, she vowed with more bluff than conviction. Daniela Mancini Fabrizio was no quitter. For good measure she patted the tiny cherub who was destined to come into the world without a father's love.

Don't worry, little dumpling. Mama intends to smother you with so much love you won't mind growing up without a daddy. One particular daddy, anyway.

Her jaw tightened as she thought about the legal steps she would need to take to ensure Jonathan Sommerset or Jacob Folsom or whatever he called himself would never ever have access to her child. No matter what, she intended to make sure that he never had a chance to hurt her babies again.

Determined to get past this without making it any worse than it already was, Rafe stationed himself at the end of the hall, far enough to give her privacy, but with a clear view of the door.

As he anchored himself against the wall and crossed his arms over his chest, he was so tense his muscles felt hot. As soon as he'd seen her, he'd been all stirred up inside. When he'd carried her up the walk it had brought it all back—the smell of her skin, the taste of her lips, the way she felt in his arms that night as he'd carried her from the pond to the soft grass beneath the long sheltering branches of a weeping willow.

Her skin had been translucent in the moonlight, her body as smooth as marble, her nipples dark and puckered, ripe little buds he'd been desperate to taste. He hadn't intended to do more than pet her into opening her mouth for him to explore, but when she turned wild in his arms, he'd forgotten everything but the hot pulsing need between his thighs.

Oh, he tried to play it cool. What self-respecting seventeen-year-old male would willingly admit he'd never been with a woman before? Especially one who'd been spoon-fed machismo along with his rice and beans. But inside, he'd been terrified. What if he hurt her? What if he was too clumsy to make it good for her?

As soon as he'd touched her, he'd been lost. Nothing had been more important than exploring every inch of that amazing body. His own had been so hard he'd been in real pain. When she'd touched him with those curious little hands, he'd nearly exploded.

He'd wanted to be inside her desperately, so desperately he'd ached. In the end it had been his respect for his parents and her father that had him jerking back an instant before he'd breached her maidenhead. He'd often wondered if Fabrizio had appreciated his sacrifice.

Danni sure as hell hadn't.

His heart raced as unwanted feelings crowded him hard. She'd been half-wild with hurt pride as she'd hastily pulled on her suit. No one had ever said no to Daniela Mancini on her father's land. Especially the bastard son of a Mexican field hand.

Nothing he said could soothe her. Still, in his halting way, he'd tried, pouring out his deepest feelings in a jumble of English and Spanish. All it had gotten him, however, was a slap in the face and a blast of that fine Italian temper.

After she'd stormed back inside the big house on the hill, he'd prowled the vineyards like one of the mountain cougars who inhabited the hills above the vines, walking for miles until his muscles burned and his mind blurred. Maybe that was why he'd simply stood there when Eddie and the others had come at him a little before dawn.

Mark had been leaving after visiting Danni's brother Vito and had seen them by the pond. Rafe had tried to tell them that he loved her. That he wanted to marry her. He hadn't gotten out more than a few words before Eddie had smashed his fist into his face, catching him by surprise and breaking his nose. He'd fought, but Ed's brothers, Vito and Benito, had held his arms while the two older guys had taken turns hitting him. Stronger than most, even as a kid, he could take a lot of punishment without going down. Consequently, he'd been in bad shape by the time he'd finally passed out. When he'd come to a few minutes later, his face sticky with blood and every breath an agony, Eddie had laid it out for him, all neat and tidy. He was to leave town that very morning, on the first bus out of Ashland and never come back. He wasn't to see or contact Danni ever again. If he didn't agree to those conditions, Ed would see that his father was fired from his job as vineyard foreman and kicked off Mancini land without a recommendation.

At twenty-four, Ed was already his father's right-hand man. Both of them knew he could do exactly as he promised. Both of them knew, too, that good jobs for a semi-illiterate Mexican-American day laborer with five young kids were hard to come by.

Spitting blood and with fury burning in his gut, Rafe had threatened to go to Ed's father. *El Jefe* was a fair man, a decent man. He'd even offered to send Rafe to trade school to learn auto mechanics so that he could go to work maintaining the vineyard vehicles.

He would never forget the satisfaction in Fabrizio's eyes. *Who do you think sent us out here?* he'd said with a smirk. *Even gave us money for your fare.*

Years later, Rafe had been able to see the logic in it. Eduardo Mancini wasn't a cruel man, simply a practical one. Danni was his only daughter. In the way of his father and his father's father, he had promised her to the eldest son of his best friend and rival vintner, Tonio Fabrizio. No mongrel with unknown parentage and few prospects would be allowed to threaten the dynasty he and Tonio Fabrizio had so carefully planned.

Rafe had known then what it was to hate.

Like everyone else in the valley *El Jefe* knew exactly how much Rafe owed to the Cardozas. His birth mother had been a fifteen-year-old druggie from California, who, with some guy she'd met in a truck stop, had stopped over to pick grapes for traveling money. One night during a spring storm the girl had given birth in one of the horse stalls, then split, leaving her hours' old son wrapped in a flea-infested scrap of blanket.

At the time Rosaria Cardoza had given birth to stillborn son only days earlier and still had milk. It was natural for her to take the baby. *El Jefe* had paid the attorney who'd arranged for Enrique and Rosaria to adopt him as their own.

Rafe had known from early on that he'd been adopted. How could he not know, a green-eyed blonde in a family of dark-eyed, dark-haired Latinos?

He'd been eleven when one of the other workers had gotten drunk and taunted him with the details of his birth. Rosaria had managed to soothe his hurt, but after that, pride had driven him to be the best at anything he tried.

As the eldest he'd always felt a responsibility to take care of the little ones. Maybe because he'd been adopted, he'd felt that responsibility more deeply than most.

After all that Enrique and Rosaria had done for him, he'd had no choice. So he'd swallowed the hate, along with his pride, taken the money and left. His face had been raw from the fresh bruises, and one eye had been swollen completely shut. Every time he'd moved, the splintered ends of his ribs ground together and breathing was agony. But he'd been determined to walk to the bus with his head high and his back straight.

With sweat pouring down his face and his stomach cramping with nausea, he'd finally made it on to the bus without passing out. He'd gotten as far as San Francisco before the pain of sitting for hours sent him in search of a bed. For a week he stayed holed up in a seedy hotel in the Tenderloin, living on junk food and aspirin while his body healed.

On the first day he was able to take a deep breath without passing out, he'd taken a cab to the nearest Army recruiter and enlisted. He'd been in boot camp when Danni graduated from high school, in Beirut when she'd graduated from Oregon State, slogging his way through the Treasury's own version of boot camp when she'd married Fabrizio. By the time her daughter had been born, he was no longer in love with the princess of Mancini Vineyards.

"Guess she's still puking her guts out, huh?" Gresham commented as he wandered into the hall from the living room, a fresh cup of coffee in his hand. Even though he'd removed his suit coat and loosened his tie, he still looked like a damn ad for twelve-year-old scotch.

Rafe shot him a sour look. "You learn how to talk that way at Dartmouth, did you?"

"Nah, that came straight from summer camp. Guys in my cabin took turns grossing each other out. I took grand champion three years running." Looking smugly pleased with himself, Gresham propped a shoulder against the opposite wall and sipped.

Still on the sunny side of thirty, with a trust fund in seven figures and serious political clout, Seth Aaron Gresham IV had the same lack of respect for rank that had caused Rafe no end of grief in his first few shaky years—until Linc Slocum had kicked his butt. For his sins—and according to Linc, they were legend—the suits in the big building had tasked him with whipping this particular high profile, gung-ho youngster into shape.

It was almost enough to drive a teetotaler like himself to drink, Rafe thought, corralling his chronic restlessness with more difficulty than usual.

"Question comes to mind why a guy famous for never losing his cool looks ready to explode because one pretty little woman has locked herself in the can."

Rafe shot him a sour look "You ever been around a pregnant woman?"

"Not my bag, actually. In fact, I tend to break out in a sweat the minute a woman gets that nesting gleam in her eyes."

Rafe checked his watch. Her ten minutes were nearly up. "I was six when my mom had my oldest brother. Mostly I remember feeling scared for nine months 'cause she was either hanging over the toilet or bursting into tears."

Seth took a sip, flexed his shoulders. "Guess I should be grateful I'm the last of three. Came along when my sister was almost nine."

Probably never slept three in a bed with at least one brother who peed the bed either. "Important thing to remember, a pregnant woman needs special handling. Last thing we need is a witness who falls apart on the stand. Tends to make juries do unpredictable things."

Provided they had a defendant and a solid enough case to take in front of a jury.

"Dr. Fabrizio seems pretty darn stable to me. Took the worst a lot calmer than most."

Rafe snorted. "Oh yeah, that sprint to the can looked real calm."

Gresham offered a reluctant grin. "She did look a little green at that." His grin changed to a frown. "Morning sickness, right?"

"Probably."

On the other hand he'd also seen burly, hard-eyed men toss their cookies after an emotional hit like the one he'd just given her. Laying it on her cold had been a tactical error, he realized now. Guilt bunched into a sick ball in his belly. Much as he hated to admit it, he had a strong feeling he'd rushed things because he wanted to spend as little time as possible in her presence.

"What now?" Gresham asked.

"We ask our questions, give her a list of contact numbers, and catch the red-eye back to D.C."

Gresham started to say more, but the sudden click of the bathroom lock had his gaze slicing toward the door. As she emerged and walked toward him, Danni gave them a quick smile designed to reassure. Instead, Rafe felt a jolt of alarm. Instead of queasy, she now looked truly ill. Her lips were pale, her hair damp around her face, and her eyes seemed glazed.

"Sorry about that." Despite her wan appearance, her tone was brisk, one professional to another. He recognized her need to retain her dignity at all costs.

"No problem." Rafe straightened and dropped his arms. Without the power suit and fancy high heels she seemed more like the mischievous hoyden with the metal grin and bubbling laugh who'd stolen his heart years before she'd blossomed into a beauty.

"Feel better now?" Gresham asked while watching her warily, as though expecting her to upchuck onto his shiny hand-sown Italian loafers.

Her too-pale lips curved. "Fine. I appreciate you being so patient."

Oh yeah, she was fine all right, Rafe thought, narrowing his gaze. If *fine* meant looking wrung-out and hollow-eyed. Despite her bedraggled appearance, however, she still managed to project enough sex appeal to have him shoring up walls he'd once considered impenetrable.

"Aren't you too far along to still be having morning sickness?" he asked more curtly than he'd intended.

"Actually morning is the only time I *don't* get queasy." She forced a laugh. "Luke says it's not all that unusual for a woman to have morning sickness through the second trimester."

In a deliberate effort to reassure her he broke his own rule and combined the personal with the professional "You probably don't remember, but Mom had to be hospitalized for dehydration while she was carrying Carlos."

Her mouth turned up at the corners. Damn, but she still had the most kissable lips he'd ever seen. "Actually I do remember, but only because while she was gone, I had to fix dinner three nights in a row before Papa got fed up with canned soup and grilled cheese sandwiches and took us all out to Napoli Gardens."

"Canned soup and grilled cheese would have been a treat compared to the stuff I managed to throw together for the kids and me while she was gone," he said with a smile of his own. "I still hate rice and beans."

Her eyes twinkled, and he grieved for that besotted boy who'd believed in fairy-tale endings. "Don't tell Aunt Gina, but I feel the same about red sauce."

"Since your aunt Gina would sooner refuse an audience with the Pope than spend even a moment in my presence, I think your secret is safe."

Her expression sobered. "She meant well, Rafe. From her point of view I had been promised to Mark in my cradle and my…infatuation with you frightened her."

Emotions he neither welcomed nor completely understood swam through him. It was tougher than he'd expected, hanging on to even the most justified resentments when the woman in front of him was looking more fragile with every breath she took.

"Come on, let's get some food in you before we get to those questions you promised to answer." He tucked his hand into the small of her back and started to guide her toward the living room. She took a few steps, and then faltered.

"Danni?"

She turned her head up to look at him, and her fingers closed over his arm, her nails digging in. She licked her lips, then took a shaky breath. As he looked down at her, her sloe-dark eyes glazed over, and her lashes fluttered like little dark brushes.

Alarm jolted through him as he curled one arm around her back. Bad guys he could handle. Even lousy memories that made him bleed inside were manageable, but a pregnant woman clutching him as though her very life depended on hanging on tight had him going ice-cold with panic. "Danni, talk to me," he demanded. Pleaded. "Is it the baby? Are you in pain?"

"No pain. It's just…I'm…sorry, Rafe, but I'm terribly afraid I'm going to…uh…I think…oh, hell." And then, just like that she crumpled against him like a limp, sad-faced rag doll.

His heart slamming with more than simple panic, Rafe scooped her into his arms and felt her settle bonelessly against him. Her cheek was pressed against his chest, her lashes resting on her cheeks and her mouth softly parted as though in a sigh, giving her a poignantly vulnerable look that pushed a lot of buttons he'd thought he'd disconnected long ago.

"Damn, this is turning into a disaster," he muttered, tightening his grip.

"Worse," Gresham replied, looking far from composed. "What do you think? 911?"

God! "Yeah."

"Phone's in my jacket," Seth said before hurrying into the living room. Rafe followed at a more careful pace.

"Hold off a minute," he ordered as Seth flipped open his cell phone. He figured five to ten minutes for 911 to respond versus a quick trip across the street to fetch her own doctor. He ran their recent conversation through his mind, sifting for the name. "She said her doctor lived across the street, right?"

Seth shot a fast look toward the window facing the side street. "Yeah, she did say that. Almost seems like Fate."

Rafe dismissed that with a scowl. "Jarrod, I think she said his name was. He'd be the best one to see to her if he's home. If not, then we'll go with 911."

Luke Jarrod had been a physician long enough to recognize panic when it flashed in a man's eyes—even a buttoned-up government type carrying a badge and an official looking ID.

He'd been settled deep in the ancient recliner Maddy considered mud ugly but grudgingly permitted house room, with his sleeping son curled like an exhausted angel in his lap, watching the Mariners play the Yankees when the guy had rung the bell.

While the agent paced the front walk, he'd tucked Ollie into his crib, kissed his sleeping wife on her cheek, and then because he never forgot to be grateful she was in his life again, kissed her one more time before collecting his bag from the closet shelf and hauled ass.

Knowing his Maddy girl the way he did, it was a pretty good bet she'd be spitting cat furious when she found out he hadn't roused her to help out a fellow member of the Mommy Brigade. He hated it when he had to play the tough guy, but he'd deal with it.

After nursing a cranky two-year-old through his first bout of the flu, she'd come down with it herself. The worst was over, but both needed their rest, and he was just the man to see they got it.

A sliver of lingering blue sky rode over the growing twilight to the west as he cut across Morgan's prized lawn, the preppy agent with the Yankee blue-blood name a half-stride behind. The guy's ID looked genuine, but what did he know about government agencies? Now, the nine-millimeter pistol he'd seen when the guy's coat flapped open, *that* was about as real as real got these days.

Not a suspicious man by nature, Luke had become intensely protective of Danni and her daughter. The other guys of the Row felt the same way. Though no one said the words out loud, each was privately hoping he'd be the first one to lay eyes on that bastard Sommerset if he dared show his face.

As soon as he got her checked out, he intended to give Case a quick call and ask him to use his cop's connections to find out what was going on. Right now, though, Danni needed his professional expertise more than she needed a surrogate big brother.

By the time Luke bounded up the front steps of the Paxton place, he'd run through everything he had retained from the notes he'd taken during Danni's last few visits.

Nineteen weeks gestation, no abnormalities, good fetal heart sounds, due for an ultrasound on her next visit. Other than frequent bouts of morning sickness, it had been a routine pregnancy.

"Door's unlocked, Doc," Gresham said quickly, but Luke had already shoved it open.

Inside, a tall, superbly built man in his late thirties, early forties stood guard over the sofa where Danni lay unmoving. As Luke had entered, one large hand had gone instinctively to the weapon riding on his hip before his piercing green eyes had spied the medical bag.

"Dr. Jarrod?"

Luke was neither surprised nor intimidated by the brusque tone. A man accustomed to command was a controlled man, and a controlled man was a useful ally if things turned sour.

"I'm Jarrod," he said, clipping his own words. "Who are you?"

"Rafael Cardoza."

Neither wasted time on a handshake.

"What have you done for her so far?"

Guarded green eyes cut back to the sofa. "Nothing other than the cold compress on her head."

"Did she complain of pain in her head?" Luke asked quickly.

"No, she just said she was feeling woozy, then went out fast." He flicked a glance toward his partner who confirmed his account.

"She did look a little green before the lights went out."

"Is it serious, do you think?" Agent Cardoza asked tersely.

"Too soon to tell." Luke set his bag on the coffee table, then went into the kitchen to wash his hands.

"She spent a lot of time in the can throwing up," Cardoza told him when he returned. "Wouldn't let me in to check on her."

"Any idea when she ate last?"

"No. She had some tea." His gaze touched the mug on the coffee table.

As Luke listened to Danni's heart, he felt those eyes boring into his back. "Has she showed signs of coming around?" he asked as he slipped the stethoscope beneath her shirt to listen to the baby's heart.

"Her lashes fluttered and she moved some when I put her down. Since then, nothing."

Danni's heart rate was steady and strong, but faster than he would have liked. The baby's rate, though, was smack in the safe range. He checked her pupils, then reached into his bag for the electronic thermometer that was God's gift to over-worked doctors and nurses.

He frowned at the read-out—101.6.

Mentally reviewing his findings, he returned the thermometer to his bag, then turned to face the silent agent. "Give me a rundown on what was going on before she passed out."

With an economy of words that Luke appreciated, the agent systematically chronicled the events leading to Danni's collapse. "Since she hadn't complained of pain and didn't seem to be having contractions or hemorrhaging, I figured she'd rather have you look her over."

The reasoning was flawless—and surprisingly intuitive. Either the man had medical training or he had more than a nodding familiarity with expectant moms. "Do you have children of your own, Agent?" he probed.

"No children, but I helped raise my five brothers and sisters."

"I figured you must have had some experience with pregnant ladies."

Cardoza smiled briefly. "Just my mother. Probably forgot more than I remember, though."

"Remembered enough to check for serious problems, which is the important thing." Luke knelt again and touched Danni's cheek.

"Danni, can you hear me? It's Luke."

She frowned, then licked her lips. "Mmm."

"Danni, open your eyes, okay?" He took her hand and rubbed her wrist.

"What's wrong with her?" Cardoza demanded, his voice gruff.

"Flu, combined with overwork, I suspect."

"Is it serious?"

"Can be, if it leads to complications. Danni's basically healthy, but stress can wear down even the healthiest person." Reluctantly, he dug into his bag for an ampoule of ammonium carbonate.

Instantly, Cardoza went on alert. "What's that?"

"Smelling salts," he said as he broke it open. As soon as he waved it under Danni's nose, she screwed her face into a knot and jerked her head to the side. Her lashes fluttered, then lifted.

"Luke?" she asked drowsily. "What…is it the baby? Oh my God—"

Luke rested a hand on her shoulder. "Easy, Danni," he said in a soothing tone. "The baby's fine. You just fainted, that's all."

Still disoriented, she lifted a curious hand to her forehead and frowned when her fingers encountered the folded dish-towel. "What's this for?"

"That stubborn head of yours," Luke said, his voice as stern as he could make it which, he had to admit, bordered on scary when he really concentrated.

Annoyed at the rebuke, Danni turned her head too fast and cried out at the sharp biting pain behind her eyes.

"Headache?" Luke asked gently.

She wanted to deny it, but the look in his eyes told her it would be a waste of time. "Like alligator teeth gnawing at my brain," she admitted wearily.

Luke studied her with sympathetic eyes. "How about chills? Muscle aches? Nausea?"

"All of the above." Damn, damn, damn. "It's the same thing Maddy had, isn't it?"

"Sounds like it, yeah."

Danni didn't even have the energy to produce a decent groan. She lifted the towel that was as hot as she was and handed it to Luke. As she did, her gaze fell on Rafe who was standing with his legs planted wide and his hands splayed on his lean hips, watching her impassively. It was a typical Rafe stance, she realized with a nearly unbearable feeling of nostalgia.

Exchange the glossy loafers for scuffed work boots and the tailored clothes for jeans and a faded cotton shirt with the sleeves rolled tight against his biceps and he could be the passionate young man she'd adored.

Basic truth number two, hormone overload had a way of turning a rational woman into a hopeless romantic.

"If I close my eyes again, will you all please just go away?" she said, her voice a little breathy.

Rafe's mouth slanted. "Not a real good idea at the moment, considering the way you tend to topple over on a regular basis."

"Once is *not* a regular basis."

"You forgot the swan dive at the curb when you got out of the taxi."

"The door smacked into my leg." She scowled. "I have half a mind to sue the taxi company for defective equipment."

"Probably win, too," Gresham said with a grin that looked a little stiff around the edges.

She sighed. "Can I get up?"

Luke stepped forward. "Let's see, shall we?"

Placing one big hand beneath her back, he eased her into a sitting position, then helped her turn until she was settled into the corner. "Feeling dizzy?"

She shook her head. "Just...sick. All I want now is sleep."

"Not until we figure out who's going to take care of you," Luke said firmly.

"I can take care of myself," she declared just as firmly. Or thought she did. Her words seemed to be coming from a very long distance, her body was suddenly freezing. She shivered, then hugged herself.

"Enough of this," Rafe declared, sounding angry. "She belongs in bed, and that's exactly where she's going."

Chapter 5

Twice in one day Danni found herself smashed up against Rafe's stone solid chest. "Stop squirming," he ordered, his breath warm against her temple.

"Recent events notwithstanding, I am a responsible, mature professional woman who does not need rescuing by a man," she muttered against his smooth bronzed throat.

She thought he chuckled, but perhaps he was just clearing his throat. "Even Wonder Woman couldn't save the world without help."

"Wonder Woman wasn't a shrink," she said peevishly.

"Makes a difference, does it?"

She intended to nod her head. Instead, she found herself nuzzling her cheek against his shoulder. "According to the shrink's code, we're required to be the sane and stable presence in the room."

"Sounds a lot like the T-man's code."

"Remember when we played cops and robbers, Rafe? You were always the good guy who saved me from the bad guys. Must be Fate."

"Guess that's one way of looking at it."

"Stop growling at me, it makes my head hurt worse." She opened her eyes, then closed them again when the photographs lining the staircase wall whizzed by in a dizzying swirl. Her head seemed oddly fuzzy all of a sudden, and her chest hurt.

"Which room is yours?" he asked when they reached the landing.

"Straight ahead."

A routine interview, that's what he'd told himself. Just another victim. A sad case, sure, but he'd handled plenty worst. All part of the job. No sweat, no pain. No emotional involvement. Not the kind that made it impossible to walk away clean, anyway.

The door at the end stood ajar. Larger than the two other bedrooms he'd passed, this one had pale peach walls, a plush rug the color of pecans and old-fashioned double hung windows framed by lace curtains. The furniture looked antique, probably genuine, given the Paxtons' wealth. The bed was shaped like a sleigh and covered with a thick satin comforter the color of the Concord grapes he'd once picked for days on end. A half dozen pillows edged with lace and fancy looking braid were piled against the curving headboard.

Oh yeah, there would be satin and lace for the princess. *El Jefe* would see to that. Why the old man hadn't covered her debts was just one of the questions he hadn't gotten around to asking.

He put her down gently on one of the pillows piled against the headboard, careful not to jar her head. Her face had lost what little color had returned after her stint in the bathroom, and tiny beads of sweat dotted her hairline. Wisps of corkscrew curls clung to her temples, giving her the look of a pagan goddess.

Did she ever think about that night? he wondered as she turned onto her side and breathed out a soft little sigh. Did she remember how she'd opened those silky thighs and begged for him to come inside her? Or how he hadn't been able to stop shuddering as he fought for control?

He dipped his hands into his pockets and looked down at her, reluctant to leave her alone. "Is there someone you can call? A neighbor maybe?"

"I just need to sleep, that's all." She blinked, reminding

him of an injured baby owl he'd tried to nurse back to health. No matter how hard he'd tried, he'd never been able to coax the terrified little thing to trust him enough to take food from his hand. He'd still been young enough to cry when it died.

"Give me a name, Daniela. Someone who can help you get undressed, help get you settled—unless you'd rather I did it."

It was an order, Danni realized. The big tough Fed had decided she belonged in bed, and that's where she was going to stay. Her temper gave a token flare, but the rest of her was unable to manage more than a scowl. "Do this, do that." She huffed out air. "You sound exactly like Eddie."

His face turned to stone. "You're wrong. I'm nothing like him." Anger had crept into his voice, making it hard and crisp.

"I was just teasing. You never used to be so sensitive."

"I never used to be a lot of things." He pulled his hands from his pockets and jerked the afghan over her. "A name, Daniela."

She forced herself to concentrate long enough to sift through a pathetically short list of friends to call in an emergency. "Try Liza Savage," she blurted when a name swam to the surface. "Luke has her number. But honestly, it's not necessary."

Rafe's gaze seemed to burn into her, reminding her of the boy whose hands had trembled when he'd touched her in the moonlight. Her breath suddenly jammed in her throat, and her skin was suddenly too tight for her body.

"Believe me, it's necessary," he muttered before turning on his heel and stalking out.

"Luke said two of these every four hours," Liza Savage said, dropping the tablets into Danni's cupped palm. "Safe for baby and good for mommy."

Danni managed a smile as she took the glass of water Liza handed her. It hurt to swallow, but she managed to down the tablets without choking. With Liza's help she'd changed into her nightshirt, then crawled gratefully into bed. Her muscles ached and her head was splitting.

"Thank goodness Lyssa's sleeping over at Jody's tonight," she muttered between sips.

"Finish the water," Liza ordered, looking like a dark-haired, dark-eyed Buddha in flowered tights and one of her husband Max's old police academy T-shirts.

Forced into retirement two years ago after a bullet in his spine had left him partially paralyzed, Max Savage had withdrawn completely for months before his love for Liza had given him the courage to fight back.

After nearly two years of grindingly hard therapy, he was able to walk again using only forearm crutches instead of the braces he'd worn for more than a year. Following the family tradition of medicine, he was now a full-time pre-med student at Oregon Health Sciences University.

Eight months pregnant with their second child, she and Max were transforming the third bedroom in their bungalow into a room for their son, Boomer, who would be two in a few weeks. Liza had been painting window trim when Luke had called, and she still had specks of steel blue paint in her dark hair.

"What're Max and Boomer doing while you're painting?" Danni asked between swallows.

"Boomer was sitting in his daddy's lap reading his storybook while Max read his hematology textbook. He has a final on Monday. Counts for half his grade so he's been hitting the books day and night. Even cut back on his therapy so that he could devote more time to cramming."

"How's he doing this semester?"

"Terrific!" Liza's eyes lighted. "Even carrying a heavier than usual load, he managed to bring his GPA up another couple of points to…*ta-da,* a sterling 3.4."

Danni managed a wan smile. "Good for him."

"I promised him a wild and wicked weekend at the coast as soon as he brings it up to a 3.5. I have my fingers crossed." She took the empty glass from Danni's limp fingers and put it on the nightstand. "Speaking of wild and wicked, who's the sexy guy with the big gun prowling like a caged lion downstairs? Luke just introduced him as Agent Cardoza. I assume he's FBI?"

"Secret Service." Danni slipped lower on the pillows. "He came to ask me some questions about The Weasel."

Liza smiled at the name Danni had coined during the manic

days after she'd discovered the depth of her new husband's betrayal. It fit so perfectly they'd all taken to using it when discussing Jonathan Sommerset.

"Have they found him, I hope?"

Danni heard echoes of her own eager question in Liza's voice. "Not yet." She squeezed her eyes shut. "It turns out he's a serial weasel. Has a long list of gullible victims like me."

"If they knew he was a crook, why didn't they arrest him?" Liza sounded outraged. Danni knew she would be too—as soon as she had the energy.

"Apparently they did. Turns out he just might have… murdered one of his victims before she could testify."

"Oh my God! Where? When? Do they think he's going to come back here? Is that why they're here, too?"

Danni managed to wedge open her eyes. "We were just getting to the details when I had to keep a fairly intimate date with the john. After that, things are a little fuzzy."

"That does it! I'm calling Max, and we'll stay here tonight. Boomer can sleep in one of the twins' beds. It'll be good practice for the little dickens."

Danni's lashes drooped again. "I appreciate the offer, but it's not necessary. Jonathan isn't dumb enough to come back here. Heck, why should he? All I have left for him to steal are my clothes. Even that old junker I bought to replace the Lexus is in the shop."

Liza sighed. "You're right, sweetie. Like Max says, I tend to leap before I think." She laughed. "Like swooshing blithely down this monster ski slope where I had no business being in the first place, with about a million tons of snow right behind me."

Danni recognized the effort to change the subject and felt a wave of affection for her new friend. The ladies of the Mommy Brigade had been a godsend. Another silver lining in her gray storm-filled life.

"Is that how you two really met?" she roused herself enough to ask. "In the middle of an avalanche?"

"Absolutely!" Smiling at the memory, Liza drew up the sheet, then tucked it in. She was, after all, the mother of a toddler. "Max just scooped me up like a sack of potatoes and shot across the slope like he was going for the gold. We both ended up in a snowbank and the rest, as they say, is history."

"You should write a book."

Liza laughed. "When? Between taking care of my two very high maintenance men and my day-care kids, it's all I can do to carve out time to shower every day and rub cream on my belly."

"Darn, I meant to get some of that cow balm stuff you told me about," Danni muttered, drifting now.

"I'll bring you some." She felt Liza's hand on her forehead, smoothing back her hair. "Anything else you need, sweetie, before I leave you in peace?"

"No, but thank you. 'Preciate it."

Danni had given up trying to pretend she was "just fine." After three and a half months of one crisis after another, one painful decision on top of the last, she needed some downtime. As R & R, a bout with the flu was way down on her list, but it would have to do.

"Damn, I forgot about Lyssa," Jarrod said, drawing his brows together. "Did Danni mention when she was due home?"

Rafe tossed down the last of his coffee, then grimaced at the acrid aftertaste. As a rule he liked his coffee strong enough to eat through steel, but this was even too bitter for his abused taste buds.

"According to the notation on the calendar by the phone in the kitchen, the daughter is spending the night with someone called Jody. There's a number next to the name, but I don't see any upside to calling the kid tonight."

Rafe paused to give the cowboy doctor an opportunity to offer an opinion. When he merely lifted his eyebrows, Rafe asked curtly, "Do you have a different take?"

"Nope. Best thing for Danni right now is sleep. Be good for her to shut down for a while and not have to worry about anything but building up her strength." Jarrod took a sip of coffee, then rested the mug on his thigh. "Ordinarily, I'd ask my wife to stay the night here, just in case, but Maddy's still recovering from this same bug. Prudy Randolph would be my second choice, but she's pulling night duty at the E.R. this week, and Stacy MacAuliffe is in Seattle this weekend.''

"What about Mrs. Savage?"

Luke looked thoughtful. "Liza would certainly volunteer, but she's only about a month from delivering herself. I hate to add to her stress level.''

Rafe's stress level was already well into the red zone and climbing. Good thing he'd thrown a pair of sweats into the carry-on bag he'd learned to take with him whenever he traveled, even when he had no plans to be gone overnight. Fifty percent of the time his plans took an unexpected turn. Like now. Along with clean shirts and underwear, he always packed jeans and his running shoes. He hated running, but it was the only form of exercise that kept his gut firm and his natural restlessness in check.

"My partner and I figured to catch the red-eye back to Washington once our business here was finished, but looks like we'll be staying over.'' In his mind's eyes he measured his six foot three frame against the sofa's length and decided it would be close. Still, he'd slept in a lot worse places. "Guess this is as good a place to bunk down as any,'' he decided aloud.

Jarrod narrowed his gaze. "No offense, Agent Cardoza, but I'm not real comfortable leaving my patient alone with a man neither of us knows—even if he is carrying a federal badge.''

Rafe leaned back and stretched out his legs. While the pretty lady with the flashing dark eyes had been up with Danni, he'd sent Seth out for Chinese. That had been nearly forty minutes ago, and he was so hungry the walls of his stomach were rubbing together.

"Daniela and I grew up together, Dr. Jarrod. My father is still Mancini Vineyard's field foreman.''

Surprise crossed the cowboy doc's tired face. "No lie?"

Rafe allowed himself a brief smile. "No lie.''

Jarrod studied him with a measuring gaze that seemed to peel away more layers than most. "You have any objection to my taking a look at your identification?''

"Not a one.'' Leaning forward, Rafe worked his ID out of his back pocket and tossed it over. Then while Jarrod studied his credentials, he studied the cowboy doc. A strong face, he decided after a moment's reflection. A solid jaw. Enough gray in his thick dark hair and character lines in his face to suggest a life that hadn't been particularly soft. Most important for Rafe's purposes, the man had honest eyes.

"Sorry, had to make sure," Jarrod said as he underhanded the wallet back to him.

"No problem. It's good to know Daniela has friends to look out for her."

"Not always, apparently," Jarrod said grimly.

Rafe returned his ID to his pocket, then leaned back against the soft cushions and flexed his shoulders. Danni's half-drunk tea was still sitting where she'd left it. About a million hours ago, he thought as he dug his fingers into the knotted muscles at the back of his neck.

Jarrod watched him with sympathetic eyes. Rafe had a hunch he'd had his share of rough days and nights.

"Did you ever meet Sommerset?" he asked, giving up on the knot that refused to yield.

"No. My wife and I sent a wedding present shortly after Danni called to tell me she'd gotten married. A few days later she stopped by my office on the way to the hospital to thank me. Said Sommerset was taking her and Lyssa to England in a few weeks, but when they got back she intended to have a party to introduce him to her friends."

"Seem happy, did she?"

"Very." Jarrod's mouth took on a sardonic slant. "Spent a good fifteen minutes raving about how wonderful he was with her daughter and how Lyssa finally seemed to be getting over Mark's death."

Rafe felt his jaw tighten. There'd been a time when he would have felt a vicious satisfaction at learning of Fabrizio's death. Not as much as if he'd taken the guy out himself, but enough to burn off some of his simmering hatred for the man and everything he stood for.

He wasn't proud of those feelings, but he understood them. He'd been raw for a long time after he'd left. There had been times, especially in the beginning when he'd missed his family so much he'd been sick with it. Rage had been all that had kept him going.

It had taken him a lot of years and a lot of growing up before he'd figured out that his anger was really directed at himself. Accepting that he'd allowed himself to become a victim had been a rough pill to swallow, but he'd forced it down—along with a vow never to let anyone push him around again.

The anger was still there, like fire in his belly, but he'd learned to redirect it toward lowlifes like Folsom.

"How'd the daughter take her stepfather's desertion?" he asked, studying the polished toes of his loafers.

"Badly. Danni has her in counseling with a colleague. Goes at least once a week, maybe twice." Jarrod looked troubled. "Couldn't have happened at a worst time for the kid, either. Puberty's bad enough for kids who aren't dealing with facial scars and a traumatic loss."

Rafe's attention sharpened. "The girl is scarred?"

Jarrod nodded. "Flying glass, mostly. Sliced her face pretty good, although that was the least of her problems for the first few months, considering she nearly lost one of her legs."

Rafe muttered a soft obscenity. "Must have been rough on Daniela, seeing her daughter go through hell."

"It was, but she amazed us all at how strong she kept herself for Lyssa. As far as I know, no one ever saw her so much as waver in all the months she spent at Lys's bedside and then later, during rehab. Impressed the hell out of me, I'll tell you."

Rafe tucked all that Jarrod had revealed into the mental file where he kept information that might prove useful down the road before asking, "Since I'm volunteering to play nurse, is there anything I need to know?"

Jarrod's gaze sharpened, and Rafe could almost see him slipping into a starched white coat. "Give her two more Tylenol tabs at 1:00 a.m. Try to get at least a full glass of water down her as well. I'll leave my thermometer and if her temp spikes above 102, give me a call. The number's on the pad by the phone in the kitchen."

At the sound of footsteps on the stairs, he flexed his shoulders, then got slowly to his feet. "I'll just run up and check on her one more time before I walk Liza home."

Chapter 6

Danni felt a hand on her cheek and wanted to whimper because it felt so cool against her burning skin. Pathetically grateful, she turned toward the comfort it offered, then groaned when pain sliced a jagged line through her forehead just above her eyebrows.

"C'mon Danni, open your eyes for me," a deep voice coaxed.

Frowning, she struggled to obey, but her lids felt leaden.

"That's it, honey. Open your eyes. You'll feel a lot better once you get these pills in you."

Pills? Drugs? There was something important she needed to remember. Something… "Not s'posed to take pills," she murmured. "Dangerous."

"These are only Tylenol tablets, Danni. Dr. Jarrod prescribed them, remember?"

She felt a strong arm beneath her shoulders, lifting her to a sitting position. Her head felt too heavy for her body and flopped forward. Her teeth were chattering now, and she started to shiver all over. Panic worked its way through the thick haze that seemed to fade in and out around her. Every part of her body ached, and something large and painful seemed wedged in her throat. She clutched the hand brushing her hair away from her burning cheeks.

"Am I dying?" Her voice was abysmally weak, scarcely more than a whimper.

"No honey, you have the flu."

"But I…don't have time to be sick."

Rafe might have laughed at the peevish tone if her cheeks weren't fever bright and her skin paper pale. "I'm not sure you have the choice," he said as he held the glass to her lips. "Drink a little water first. It'll make the tablets go down easier."

Her lashes fluttered, then lifted and she looked up at him. "Why…why are you still here?" she asked in a bewildered little voice that pushed a lot of dangerous buttons.

"Right now, I don't have a clue," he muttered through a tight jaw.

Those curly little lashes fluttered again, and he bit off a groan. He'd made some real dumb-ass decisions over the years, but volunteering to pull nursing duty for the only woman he'd ever loved was way past dumb. He thought about Gresham bedded down in the motel Jarrod had told them about near the hospital and clenched his jaw. Tomorrow night the rookie pulled nurse duty, no debate.

"Drink the water, Daniela," he commanded because issuing orders was something he knew how to do. Damned but if it didn't work too, he thought a little smugly when she meekly took a few swallows before looking up at him again.

He could smell her, sleep-warmed woman and flowers and some indefinable something that evoked images of that moonlight swim. Even as he reminded himself that she was extremely ill, and therefore off-limits, his body quickened. He blocked it out.

"Ready to take these pills now?" he asked a little brusquely.

She blinked, then licked her lips. "Why are you so mad at me?"

"I'm not mad."

"Then stop glaring at me."

"If I do, will you take these pills?"

A fierce little frown puckered her forehead. "Are you sure they won't…hurt my baby?"

"Scout's honor."

She sighed, then opened her mouth to let him put the tabs on her tongue.

"Drink it all," he ordered, holding the glass to those too-pale lips.

She obeyed, then let her eyelids drift closed. An instant later she was asleep.

Emotions churning, he rested his hand against her cheek, trying to draw some of the fever into his own body. Sweet Danni, his little scrapper. Even as a little squirt she'd given as good as she got.

Once he'd wanted nothing more in life than the right to fall asleep next to her every night.

Biting off a sigh, he withdrew his hand and snapped off the light. Then taking one of the pillows from the bed, he settled down in the overstuffed chair near the window, propped his stocking feet on a nearby trunk, set his mental alarm for twenty minutes, and closed his eyes. An instant later he was asleep.

Despite the tablets he'd bullied into her, Daniela's fever climbed steadily, terrifying him more every time he checked. Her skin was frighteningly pale, except for the feverish flush dotting her cheeks. Terrified that she would go into convulsions—or worse—he'd checked her temperature every few minutes, vowing each time that Jarrod was getting a call the instant it hit 102. Instead, in some kind of perverse cosmic joke designed to drive him into a cold sweat, it had stayed at 101.9.

Hell had to be like this, he decided as he bathed her hot face with a damp cloth. Her lips parted on a sigh, and he pressed the back of his hand against her cheek. "You'll feel better soon," he promised in a voice he tried to make gentle.

She opened her eyes, then licked her lips. "Rafe? You're not a dream, are you? You're really here?"

"Seem to be, yeah." He slipped an arm around her hot shoulders and lifted her so that she could drink from the glass he held to her lips. She took it all, but refused more. As he eased her back to the pillows, her fever-bright eyes searched his.

"Luke said the baby was fine, didn't he? I didn't just imagine that, did I?"

"He said the little one's doing great." He found a smile. "According to Jarrod, the little dickens has a strong heartbeat. Probably come out fighting, if he's anything like his mom."

"She," she murmured, her lashes drooping. "Lyssa wants a sister, so it has to be a girl."

The determination in her voice surprised him. "Do you always give her what she wants?"

"When I can, yes. I know it goes counter to every theory of child rearing but Lys is special." Her voice wobbled. "She's…she's been through so much. She deserves to be spoiled a little."

"What about Danni?" he asked quietly. "What does she deserve?"

She made a face. "A swift kick in my rapidly expanding posterior for being such a gullible ninny."

He kept his smile tucked safely inside. "Gullible, maybe, but not a ninny."

She puckered her forehead. "What would you call a reasonably intelligent, well-respected professional woman who falls for a con man?"

"Human."

"Oh I'm human, all right," she muttered. "Embarrassingly so."

"Don't be so hard on yourself, Daniela. You wanted someone to love. Folsom sensed that, and moved in. If there's any blame in this, it's his." Because he could no longer resist, he brushed those downy wisps away from her hot temples. Her lashes fluttered, and a sad smile curved her lips.

"I'm doing it again, aren't I? Running to you with my troubles."

"Is that so bad?"

"It was unfair. I didn't realize that until it was too late, and I'm sorry." She touched his hand, a tentative brush of her slender fingers against his. He told himself it was only common compassion that had him entwining his fingers with hers. "Big tough Rafe, you always made it better," she murmured, her lips curving.

He took a breath. "Some troubles are tougher to handle than others," he said carefully.

She understood, as he knew she would. "Who makes your troubles better?" she asked, her voice very soft.

"Us tough government types don't have troubles. Like they tell you when you sign up, if Uncle Sam wanted you to have a personal life, he would have issued you one along with the badge."

"And such a cute little badge it is, too."

He snorted. "Good Lord."

Her lips curved. "I really did love you, you know," she murmured as her lashes fluttered down.

His chest was suddenly filled with jagged rocks. Grieving a little for what might have been, he leaned forward to brush a kiss across her hot forehead. And then he settled down to watch over his star witness.

Luke was running late, although he consoled himself that it wasn't really his fault. Not completely, anyway. He'd been curled up next to his Maddy girl's soft warm body, waiting for the alarm to buzz, when she'd suddenly started rubbing her round little bottom against him. It had been an offer he couldn't refuse under the best of circumstances. After a really long week of enforced abstinence, he'd been more than eager to accept. Almost embarrassingly so, he recalled with something that felt a lot like a blush.

Consequently, he didn't make it to Danni's place until a few minutes before seven. As he waited for Cardoza to answer the bell, he unwrapped the granola bar he'd grabbed on his way out the door and thought longingly of the steak-and-egg breakfast he'd promised himself after rounds.

He was fixing to mash the bell again when the door suddenly swung inward. Looking right at home, Cardoza wore only sweatpants and a scowl. Shaving cream covered his jaw, with the exception of a wide swath next to his Adam's apple where his razor had scraped away the thick stubble.

Apparently fresh from the shower, he'd scooped his still damp hair away from his forehead and looped a towel around his neck. Beneath the towel his chest was heavily layered with muscle, his biceps bulging, even at rest. Knowing it was damned immature, Luke couldn't resist measuring him against his own six-one, two-ten frame. He sulked a little when he realized the guy had him by a couple of inches and forty or fifty pounds.

Exercising his two quarter horses a couple of times a week as well as bucking more hay bales than he wanted to count over the years kept him fit, but he wasn't all that sure he could take the guy down in a fair fight.

"Rough night?" Luke asked as Cardoza stepped back to let him enter.

"I've had worse."

But not many, Luke suspected, taking in the telltale signs of a sleepless night stamped on the man's face.

"How's our patient this morning?" he asked, automatically looking around, even though he didn't expect to see Danni on her feet for another eight hours minimum.

"Still sleeping when I checked on her about fifteen minutes ago. Fever broke around four."

Luke noted the dark smudges below sharply intelligent eyes that gave away damn little, even now. "How about you? Did you get any shut-eye?"

"Some." Soap dripped onto Cardoza's chest, drawing Luke's gaze to the surgical scar running from sternum to navel.

Cardoza's face tightened, and his eyes took on a hard sheen. "Took a couple of bullets a while back," he said by way of explanation.

Not more than six months, by the look of the degree of healing, Luke estimated silently before glancing toward the stairs. "Sounds pretty peaceful up there. I hate to wake her."

Cardoza followed his gaze, his mouth slanting. "Way she was sleeping when I used her shower, not much less than a full-on explosion could do that."

"Healing sleep," Luke said aloud. "It's a good sign."

Cardoza narrowed his gaze. "Wish I'd known that a few hours ago. Damn near gave myself a heart attack, worrying 'cause I couldn't wake her up to get more pills down her."

"Hell, man, you should have called me. I'm used to middle-of-the-night emergencies."

"Guess I should have figured that, but I have to admit I wasn't thinking all that clearly." He plowed his fingers through his hair, the first indication Luke had seen that he wasn't as detached as he'd first appeared. "Kept thinking maybe our showing up unexpectedly had been the last straw."

"Maybe, but Danni's been running on grit and vitamins for weeks now. Even though I've been keeping a close eye on her, I had a hunch some kind of crash was inevitable." Luke frowned. "That bastard she married should be hung up by his privates."

"Government frowns on vigilantism." His mouth turned hard. "Damn shame sometimes, though."

Luke chuckled. "I didn't hear that."

The sudden glint of humor in Cardoza's eyes went a long way toward humanizing him. "Coffee's only a few minutes stale, if you're so inclined. I'll be in the head if you need me," he said before turning away.

As he did Luke noticed the forty-five tucked into the small of his broad back just above the left kidney. Even though he told himself it was nothing more than habit, he couldn't shake the feeling that there was more to this routine interrogation than Cardoza was prepared to admit.

So far so good, Danni thought as she clutched the sink for support.

Between bouts of light-headedness, she'd managed to wash her face and brush her teeth. The next challenge was her hair which had dried in little tangled ropes all over her head, like Rastafarian dreadlocks.

Gritting her teeth, she took her brush from the drawer and set to work. Ten minutes later her brush was full of rats, her scalp hurt where the brush had torn the hair out by the roots, and she had worked her way through her admittedly sparse collection of expletives. Her hair still looked like a wind-tortured mess. Nothing short of a shampoo would help. Since her legs were beginning to go wobbly again, she decided to live with the windblown look a little longer.

Halfway to the bathroom door, a wave of weakness nearly sent her to the floor before a desperate grab for the towel bar saved her. Taking deep breaths she waited for it to pass, then using first the wall and then pieces of furniture for support, she managed to make it back to bed before her knees gave up completely. She was just pulling up the sheet when someone knocked on the door Luke had left ajar when he'd left.

"Come in," she called, her heart already speeding.

Rafe walked in carrying a tray. Dressed in faded jeans and a pale yellow polo shirt, with his hair haphazardly brushed he looked far too much like the Rafe she remembered.

Despite her weakened condition, her response was instantaneous—and annoyingly visceral, slowly unfurling ribbons of pure lust in her stomach and heat under the skin. It was still there, she discovered to her dismay. That powerful desire to be in his arms, skin against skin, with his mouth plundering hers.

Of course, she was experienced enough now to recognize the dynamic that had come into play. It was simply old tapes, set on auto play. It was a common enough occurrence, certainly. A simple matter to erase the tape.

"Good morning," she said brightly, determined to regain the upper hand in this unsettling reunion scenario.

"Morning." His mouth slanted briefly. He looked tired, she realized. And a little tense. "I brought you some tea and toast, doctor's orders."

She sighed. "What's that green stuff in the glass?"

"Sports drink with ginger ale," he said, holding the tray in one hand while making a place on the cluttered nightstand with the other. "Jarrod said it would balance your electrolytes."

"Not unless I can swallow it, which I doubt."

"I tried it. It's not bad."

Danni eyed the sickening liquid warily "It's the color of…well, something not discussed in polite company."

"Then by all means, let's not."

She laughed, then felt a rush of dizziness. "Oops, laughing is obviously not a good idea at the moment," she muttered, holding her head perfectly still.

His big hands splayed on his hips and eyes narrowed, he studied her thoughtfully. It was a stance she'd seen countless times before. "Still feeling rocky, are you?"

She pushed back a rebel lock of hair, only to have it flop forward again. "Remember that rag doll I used to haul around in that old red wagon? The one you rescued from Eddie's puppy?"

"As I recall, you got hysterical because the pup ate Raggedy's arm."

She'd forgotten that. Deliberately, she suspected. "You mopped up my tears and told me that if I wished on a star, then left her outside in the moonlight overnight, she would grow a new arm."

He handed her a napkin, careful, she noticed, to keep his hand from brushing hers. "Worked, didn't it?"

"With a little help from your mom." Her lips curved as she let herself remember it all. "It seems inconceivable now, but I honestly believed that tale you spun about why her new arm was a different color."

His sandy brows drew together. "What tale was that?"

"The one about how the fairies that made her new arm had baked it too long in their special oven."

His mouth slanted. "Good thing I didn't lay that one out for the priest in Confession. Probably would have gotten me a whole wagonload of Hail Mary's."

"As I recall you had the valley record at one time."

"And you had the record for the fewest. Saint Daniela in her prissy white gloves and little red purse." His gaze met hers. There was humor there and something else, something that made her insides soften and a lump come to her throat.

Sooty lashes dipped as she glanced down. "I didn't realize until you left that you'd been my best friend," she said softly. "I missed you for a long time."

The humor left his eyes, taking all the warmth in the room

with it. "You hung up on me when I called you on your birthday."

"I was still hurt." She smiled. "It was my fault, what happened that night at the pond. I never got a chance to tell you how sorry I was. I know now Papa and Eddie were wrong to try to force you, but at the time my pride was hurt."

"They forced me, all right. Forced me to leave."

Her head came up too fast and she fought dizziness. "What do you mean, forced you to leave?" she demanded when the room stopped spinning.

"I mean, Princess, that your brothers and your fiancé beat the crap out of me after you went back into the house, then offered me an ultimatum. Leave on the first bus out of Ashland the next morning or watch while Eddie tossed my parents and the little ones off Mancini land without a reference."

Shock stuttered through her. "Eddie said he broke his hand out riding early that morning," she said, remembering aloud.

He shrugged. "I can't be sure, but I have a strong hunch he busted his hand the same time he busted my nose."

She couldn't seem to wrap her mind around the enormity of what he'd just told her. It was simply too horrible to contemplate. Still, why would he lie now, after so many years? "But if Eddie forced you, why did you let Enrique think you ran away?"

His jaw flexed. "I tried to tell him the truth, but every time I called, he hung up on me. I sent letters and they came back." He shrugged. "I finally gave up."

And tried so hard not to care, she realized as tears filled her eyes. "Oh Rafe, I'm so sorry. I didn't know."

"You weren't supposed to."

"Is that why you've never gone home in all these years?"

He nodded, his expression carefully blank. "Never saw the point in pushing in where I wasn't welcome."

He'd buried it deep, she realized. The bitterness. But it was there. And pain. So much pain.

She felt her own pain returning. Such a tangled web, she thought. All because the pampered princess saw something she wanted and went after it. She had spent months nursing a broken heart before time had helped her heal. He'd spent years in exile because of her.

Her mouth took on a stubborn line. "As soon as I feel better I'm going to give my brother a piece of my mind, and then he's going to confess what he did to Enrique and Rosaria."

"No Danni. It's too late."

"Of course it isn't. They'll be so happy to find out the truth."

"Think, Danni. My dad is a proud man. He's never taken anything from anyone without giving something back. It would break him to find out I left to save him being humiliated."

"But it's not fair!"

His mouth took on a cynical hardness. "One thing you learn in law enforcement, Danni. Life is very rarely fair." He handed her a mug, the one with daisies. "Chamomile," he said with a brief smile. "According to the bag it's supposed to be relaxing."

She would let it go for now, but not forever, she decided, drawing in the pungent steam. Eddie had a lot to answer for, and she intended to see that he made things right. There had to be a way to reconcile Rafe with his parents without hurting Enrique's pride. She just had to figure out what it was.

Because he was watching she took a sip. The bitter taste stung her tongue, sending her into a flurry of coughing.

"Too strong?" he asked with a frown.

"It needs sugar."

"Sorry, I'll make a note." As though the words jogged his memory, he reached into his back pocket for a small notebook that looked well used and flipped several pages until he found the one he wanted. "There were a few messages on your machine this morning. I—"

He was interrupted by the buzzing of the beeper clipped to his belt. He glanced at the readout, his face giving away nothing. "My boss," he said when he caught her gaze. "Probably wants to hassle me about my overdue paperwork. If I don't call him back, he'll just keep bugging me." He tore the page from his notebook and handed it to her. "Want me to send Seth up with some sugar?"

She shook her head. "No, but thanks for the offer."

"No problem." He smiled, and for the first time his smile touched his eyes. "And Danni, drink your juice."

Rafe heard the underlying excitement in Linc's normally laconic voice and went on instant alert. "Finally got the results on that search you ordered on marriage license records. Turns out one Jacob Peter Folsom and Arlene Mary Clark applied for a license in Bellingham, Washington, on March 25, 1985. The social security number on his tax returns matches the one on the license."

Keeping a tight rein on his emotions, Rafe noted the information in his personal shorthand. "Did the search turn up an address for the wife?"

"Yeah. Got a pencil?"

Jake Folsom was a cautious man as well as a charming one. The charm had been innate, a gift from his whore mother, though he was honest enough to admit it had been rough and unpredictable in his early years. The caution had been burned into him in his late twenties after he'd nearly been busted for the murder of a hooker who'd been his partner in a crude stock option scam in Atlantic City. He'd played it too fast and too awkward and the mark had called the cops. Jake had stayed frosty, but the bitch had showed signs of turning. Killing her before she could squeal had been both a necessity and a pleasure. Killing mousy little Alice had been unavoidable. It hadn't brought him any pleasure, however. Just the opposite.

The Feds didn't take kindly to the attempted murder of one of their own. The fact that the bastard with the cold green eyes had survived was one of the reasons he'd gone looking for a place where he could hide out permanently, if it became necessary.

He was entirely certain that his success was due in part to careful planning and a ruthless attention to detail. Consequently, he made it a point to have several bolt-holes where he could lay low until the dust settled. One of his favorite spots was San Diego where he could slip into Mexico on a moment's notice. Since he was also a prudent man, he had money stashed in banks in both Tijuana and Juarez.

Even with NAFTA money fueling the economy, Mexico was still a primitive country. Recently, the government had made noises about confiscating the property of Anglos living in country.

Canada was much more civilized. He'd settled on Vancouver, British Columbia, because it offered escape by both air and sea. He'd driven north, using his own ID at the point of entry.

But once settled in the hotel, he'd taken yet another passport from the hidden compartment in his custom made suitcase. The photo was his, the name borrowed. The birth certificate he'd used to obtain both the passport, social security card and California driver's license was genuine. Michael James Carlyle had died shortly after it had been issued, undoubtedly causing his parents great grief. Jake considered it an act of divine providence.

"One more signature, Mr. Carlyle, and we're done." The glossy lady behind the new accounts desk at the downtown branch of Great Pacific Bank and Trust had promise, he thought, taking in the expensive suit as well as the glint of gold at her neck and earlobes. He'd been especially struck by the ring on her right hand, an exceptionally fine diamond solitaire nesting in a lovely circle of emeralds.

Jake had an eye for quality and expensive tastes, both of which cost money. He was sitting pretty now, of course, thanks to dear, trusting Daniela and all those lovely liquid assets. Still, a prudent man planned ahead to the time when he could no longer count on his charm and appearance to maintain him in the proper style.

It would mean moving up his plans by a few weeks, he thought as he obediently scrawled his signature to the card bearing Michael Carlyle's carefully constructed history.

"How long do you plan to stay in Vancouver, Mr. Carlyle?" Ms. J. Stephens asked as he slid the card across the pristine leather blotter. Her nails, he noted, were perfectly manicured—

and very red. A lady in the drawing room, a hooker in the bedroom, every man's dream. Daniela had been especially ripe, he recalled with a fleeting pang of regret. He'd planned to spend at least six months with her, but all that had changed when she began showing signs of a distressingly willful nature.

He liked his women meek and obedient, as well as financially comfortable. And then there was that brat of a daughter of hers. Always yapping at his heels for attention like an obnoxious puppy. It had taken all of his acting talent to keep from backhanding her into shutting up for more than five minutes at a time.

He would have to find out if J. Stephens had children before making his move. "My plans are somewhat fluid," he said with just enough of a smile to show that he was interested, but not desperate. "As I mentioned earlier, my partners and I have very specific requirements for the building site. Unless I get lucky, I suspect it will take me several weeks at least to come up with three or four possibilities to take back to Santa Barbara."

Ms. Stephens tucked the card into his file folder and closed it with a graceful twist of her wrist. "These checks will be good for a month from today," she said as she wrote his name on the cover. "The personalized ones should arrive at your Santa Barbara address within two weeks."

Jake pocketed the checks, then allowed a thoughtful expression to creep into his eyes. He'd worn his contacts to this appointment, turning Jake Folsom's dark blue eyes a rich deep brown. Following well-tested procedures, he'd changed his appearance as soon as he'd left Portland, adopting a longer hairstyle as well as touching up the gray. He'd also grown a mustache which he kept rakishly bushy. He was also toying with the idea of cosmetic surgery, although he hadn't yet made up his mind.

"Would it be too much trouble to hold off on sending those checks for a few days?" he asked with just enough warmth in his voice to sharpen the predatory interest he'd seen flashing into her carefully made-up eyes when he'd settled across from her forty minutes earlier. "I might just be staying longer than I had at first anticipated."

Rising to the bait with satisfying eagerness, she hastened to assure him that it was no trouble at all. Five minutes later Jake walked into the Canadian sunshine with an extra bounce in his step, and his mind already mulling over a tentative plan of seduction. He was still refining his plan when he arrived at his hotel in the heart of downtown.

Prudently, he stopped at the desk and requested a magnum of champagne be sent up to his room. "And two dozen red roses," he added as an afterthought, slipping the fresh-faced clerk a Canadian C-note.

"Mrs. Folsom is a lucky woman," she said with a bright smile. "Not every bridegroom is so thoughtful."

"Not every bridegroom has such a wonderful wife," he said, summoning the besotted expression the woman would expect—and appreciate.

A grim disgust ran through him as he thought of his impulsive marriage to mousy little Arlene Clark. Fifteen years ago he'd been broke and heading toward Canada to lay low for a while after a gold mining scam had blown up in his face when his rental car had been rear-ended by a bus. He'd ended up in traction in a hospital in Bellingham. Arlene had been his nurse.

When he'd gotten out, both legs had been encased in plaster. He'd needed a place to hole up for a couple of months until he healed and Arlene had seemed like the ideal cover. But she'd been a churchgoing lady with a lot of nosy friends so he'd married her.

He returned to her often enough to keep her—and her anonymous house in an anonymous neighborhood—available to him when he needed a place to lie low for a while. Pathetic loser that she was, she always acted so glad to see him.

Women were such stupid fools, he thought. They deserved to be fleeced. Sometimes they even deserved to be killed.

A cold smile stretched his lips as he waited for the elevator. One thing you could say about Jake Folsom, he always gave a woman exactly what she deserved.

Chapter 7

Arlene Mary Folsom lived in a surprisingly pretty enclave of midrange tract homes situated on a wide street lined by mature trees and neatly tended yards. It seemed a point of pride for the homeowners to keep their vehicles locked tidily in garages or carports, which meant that a strange car parked anywhere on the block for more than a few hours would certainly arouse Folsom's suspicion.

Bellingham PD had been cooperative, if not enthusiastic, about federal agents serving a warrant on their turf. Chief of Detectives Clarence O'Donnell had given Rafe enough flack to satisfy his hometown pride, then pulled strings to make things happen fast.

He'd personally driven them past the house in his SUV, even stowed his son's kayak on the roof for cover in case Folsom happened to spot the strange vehicle. As he drove nearby streets so that they could become familiar with the area, he'd filled them in on possible escape routes Folsom might have already mapped out.

Because there was little cover in the area and no overhead power or telephone poles to make posing as repairmen feasible, he'd suggested they pretend to be landscapers sprucing up the lawn in the house across the street. It just so happened his brother-in-law had his own landscaping business, and for a small fee, he'd be glad to rent the Feds enough equipment to make the pretense believable. Seth had been big time ticked at the man's nerve. Rafe had been more philosophical. He'd deal with the devil himself if that meant taking Folsom down.

Now three long days after they'd flown into Bellingham late Saturday night, Rafe's back ached from digging up the turf, and his knees were sore from kneeling in the dirt while he planted what seemed like dozens of annuals.

According to Mrs. Mavis Quinn, the sprightly sixty-something widow who had been delighted to let them dig up her front yard as a cover for a stakeout, "dear Arlene" and her husband Jacob had recently reconciled after a lengthy separation.

Able to charm the birds from the trees, he is, Mrs. Quinn had declared with a blissful little sigh. *And so distinguished looking. An international trade expert, you know, which is why he was always traveling.*

Rafe had been more interested in the description of the ring "dear Arlene's" recently returned husband had given her shortly after his unexpected arrival on Easter Sunday.

An absolutely magnificent emerald solitaire set in the prettiest platinum setting, Mrs. Q. had gushed with a romantic gleam in her faded blue eyes. Stripped down to basics, the ring sounded all but identical to the description Randolph had included in his report, the one Folsom had taken from the safe deposit box he'd insisted Danni rent for her valuables. The one to which he, too, had a key.

Mrs. Q. had gone on to explain that the happy couple had gone away for the long weekend. They were due back today or tomorrow; their unofficial informant hadn't been real clear on the exact day.

A barely leashed tension ran through him as Seth pulled the borrowed landscaper's truck into the driveway and hopped out. Like Rafe, himself, his partner wore a kelly green uniform shirt and a green and white ball cap.

Nights the PD handled the stakeout, using different vehicles parked at different spots along the street. So far, nothing.

"I got you a salad, too," Seth said as he tossed Rafe the sack containing his lunch order, a double cheeseburger with bacon, a double order of large fries. "Figured the lettuce would soak up some of the grease before it hit your arteries."

Rafe snorted. "I was raised on lard, amigo. It's the rabbit food my arteries don't like."

By tacit agreement they settled down in the shade of the towering pin oak that dominated the eastern half of Mrs. Q.'s yard. Situating himself so that he had a clear view of both ends of the street, Rafe settled back against the trunk and unwrapped his satisfyingly greasy cheeseburger.

"How much longer do you think we can pretend to be planting flowers?" Seth asked as he pulled out his own mess of sprouts and lettuce.

"As long as it takes, partner."

"Damn things make me sneeze." Seth eyed the neat row of petunias glumly. "Guess we could dig them up and move them someplace else."

Rafe took a bite before unscrewing his thermos. Brooding wasn't his style, but he couldn't seem to get Danni out of his mind. When he'd called Jarrod at his office this morning, the cowboy doc had assured him she was on the mend. The doc's wife and Mrs. Savage were taking turns watching out for her and her daughter. Probably better than he ever could.

"Do you think Folsom's wife knows what kind of a man he is?" Seth asked between bites.

"If she doesn't, she sure as hell will soon." He poured coffee into the cap, then took a sip. He grimaced at the stale taste. Just one more reason to hate stakeouts.

Seth shoved more greens into his mouth, then chewed earnestly. "You gonna tell me what kind of history's between you and Dr. Fabrizio, or should I use my imagination?"

Rafe figured he'd get hit with this sooner or later. The kid had hung on to his curiosity longer than most. "We were raised on the same land. My father worked for hers."

Seth frowned. "I thought you didn't have a family."

"Don't anymore." It still hurt, even after so many years. Talking about it with Danni had brought it all back again, stronger than ever. It was worse on holidays. Usually he volunteered to work, just so he didn't notice how empty his apartment was.

Down the street a garage door suddenly opened, and a baby pickup backed out. He watched as the driver, a young man with spiked hair floored it, spinning the wheels and sending out plumes of exhaust as he roared away toward the cross street to the west.

"Damn, where's a cop when you need one?" he said, shaking his head.

"Probably figuring out ways to gouge money out of brother officers," Seth muttered, digging in the bag for another packet of dressing. "When are you planning to tell Fabrizio about this new twist?" he asked as he squeezed the last drop from the packet.

"Which twist is that?"

"The fact that she married a man who is already legally married to someone else."

"Depends on how this shakes out."

"Guess that makes sense. No reason to upset her while—"

"Heads up," Rafe ordered, his gaze fixed on the dark blue late-model sedan just making the turn onto the street at the eastern end. According to their unofficial informant, Folsom's wife drove just such a car.

Since he was facing the house across the street, Seth kept his gaze straight ahead, but his body was suddenly coiled and ready. As the car approached, then slowed to make the turn into the driveway directly across from where they sat, Rafe's heart speeded. His mind, however, was already slowing, its focus narrowing. It was always that way when he braced for action, as though events were suddenly clicking through his brain in separate frames.

"Hot damn it's him, all right," Seth said, his blue eyes glittering as he pretended to drink his soda. "He's gotten rid of the gray hair and grown a mustache but it's Folsom, no doubt about it."

Rafe pulled up one knee and pretended to tie his sneaker while he watched the garage door slowly opening. A man who knew the value of planning, he'd already taken Seth through every possible scenario.

The one that seemed to have the best chance of success was this one, catching Folsom when he'd just returned, and before he had a chance to switch his mindset. To that end they had to make their move as soon as he got inside. Because the house was identical to Mrs. Quinn's, both he and Seth had memorized the layout.

There was small porch in the front, a deck in the back with a sliding glass door. The other entrance was in the garage. The small backyard was fenced, with a redwood gate leading to an alley. Under cover of darkness Rafe had checked out the gate's hinges and found them well oiled, swinging open and closed without making a sound.

Seth would cover the back, he would go in the front.

"Wife looks like a tiny thing," Seth offered as he tucked his half eaten salad back into the bag.

"Only takes a few ounces of pressure to pull a trigger on a real big gun." Still, the woman with the curly blond hair and mousy features was a well-respected nurse and an active member of her church. She had no skeletons in her closet, no arrest record, nothing to indicate she was anything but an innocent pawn. In her own way, Folsom's wife was just another victim.

Curbing his impatience, Rafe flexed his shoulders, working out the stiffness as he swept his gaze up and down the block. They'd caught a break this time, he thought. The street was empty. It was every cop's nightmare, some innocent law-abiding citizen getting in the way of a bullet meant for the bad guys. Before Alice, it had been his worst one. Now it was a pale second.

"We'll give him ten minutes to carry the bags inside," Rafe said as he dropped the rest of his burger into the sack and closed it with steady hands. "And then we move."

The area where the smaller commuter planes parked was at the far end of the oldest of the terminals at Portland International. Consequently it had smaller, shabbier waiting areas and fewer conveniences. It was also far less crowded than the areas where the major carriers were situated, a plus for the two Portland PD detectives waiting in front of the floor-to-ceiling windows overlooking the parking ramp.

Familiar with the special security screening they'd be forced to undergo before they'd be cleared to carry their weapons into the facility, they'd arrived in plenty of time to meet the 4:15 p.m. plane from Bellingham. Last time Case Randolph checked, it was due in on time.

Hurry up and wait, he thought as scanned the overcast sky for a glimpse of the small plane.

"Thought the doc ordered you to lose ten pounds," Case commented as his partner, Detective Sergeant Don Petrov pulled a chocolate bar from the sagging pocket of his ancient blue blazer.

"Missed lunch," Don said as he ripped it open with hands as big as oven mitts.

Never one to stifle a generous impulse, Case accepted a square and popped it into his mouth. "Guess that mess of greasy French fries I saw you stuffing in your mouth while you were typing your notes on the Sanders shooting was breakfast, huh?" he said as the chocolate melted on his tongue.

"Nah, just a midmorning snack."

Case checked his watch, then shifted his narrowed gaze to the tarmac directly below. He hated playing taxi service for the Feds, especially when it was his case they'd muscled in on without so much as a by-your-leave.

He'd pitched a fit to the captain, but they'd both known it was little more than a token bitch. Rules were rules, even if Case bent as many as he could manage without pulling down major flack. In this case, though, the federal warrant predated Portland PD's, and that was pretty much that. Which meant that despite all the work Case had put in, calling in markers and spending hours in front of a computer screen, looking for similar M.O.'s, Folsom was Cardoza's collar. The bastard would be tried in federal court, with the state charges second in line.

"Federal types give me heartburn," Petrov grumbled before tossing the candy wrapper into a nearby receptacle. After twenty years of working together they often read one another's mind. It came in handy when things got hairy.

"Cardoza's a decent enough sort," Case offered aloud. "Called me direct instead of reaching out to the brass like most of those buttoned-up types. Asked for local assistance real polite like, too."

Petrov looked unimpressed. But then, not much impressed the big guy. Not after thirty-five years in law enforcement. "How come you decided not to give Dr. Fabrizio a heads up on Folsom's arrest?"

Case watched a two-engine prop job swoop down from the cloud cover like a fighter jet streaking toward a carrier deck. "Prue says Danni's still not a hundred percent back from her bout with the bug. I figured I'd wait until the bad guy was in the pokey, just in case something went sideways." He sighed. "Besides, Prue would have my butt if I upset a mama-to-be who's already dealing with enough stress. Hell, she'd have the whole Brigade down on my head if I caused her any more problems. They've closed ranks around their new sister."

"I figure Cardoza will wait until the other passengers clear the area before bringing Folsom out," Case offered, watching the small commuter plane taxiing closer.

"Be the way I'd handle it." An appreciative gleam appeared in Petrov's hound dog eyes as a pretty, dark-eyed Asian-American airline employee slipped behind the counter. An instant later the P.A. system clicked on as she announced the plane's arrival. "You want to handle upstairs or down?"

Case shot a telling look at his partner's gut. "Guess I'd better handle the tarmac, just in case Folsom rabbits."

Petrov looked deeply offended. "I can still spot you two hoops one-on-one and clean your clock."

Case snorted. "Fifty bucks says you can't."

"Done."

The small, two engine commuter opened and the steps lowered. Petrov hitched his trousers a little higher over his gut, then ambled over to flash the pretty agent a smile first and then an instant later, his ID.

Case caught the startled look she sent his way. He tossed her his best "NYPD Blue" grin which he figured worked because she picked up the walkie-talkie and spoke a few words before accompanying Petrov to the door leading to the outside steps.

"I'd appreciate it if you didn't frighten the passengers, detectives," she said as she punched out the access code on the keypad by the door.

Case thought about the woman who'd died in a hail of bullets, bullets the prisoner on the plane might very well have fired, and turned cold as he pushed open the door.

With a huff of disgust Daniela tossed the classified ads into the wastebasket by Morgan Paxton's gorgeous rolltop desk and slumped back in the big leather chair. With the four hundred dollars Bruno was offering for the hatchback she had her choice of a twenty-five year old Pinto station wagon that "runs great," a Dodge Dart that "needs work" or a ten-year-old Kawasaki motorbike.

She'd taken the bus to and from her office today and would do the same tomorrow. Lys had complained bitterly about taking the bus to school, and Danni couldn't really blame her. A trip that was a zippy twenty minutes by car required twice that on public transit. Besides, according to Lys, the bus smelled "gross" and the other passengers stared at her.

Bottom-line, the Fabrizio family of two needed a car of their own. Ugly as it was, the hatchback was her best bet. Anything else was far above her means. Even cutting expenses to skeletal bones, she was barely keeping up with the basic monthly bills and the huge payments to the credit card companies. Now the hospital was dunning her for the balance due on Lyssa's last surgery. To their credit, they'd been more than patient, but it had been months since she'd sent them even a token amount.

Could they actually turn her away when it came time to deliver? she wondered, putting down her pencil before slumping back in her chair. Maybe she'd better research home delivery.

She could just see it, the ladies of the Brigade boiling water and spreading newspapers on Raine Paxton's gleaming Hepplewhite dining room table. To complete the picture Luke would be wearing his cowboy hat and jeans. The sweet man had refused to bill her, saying that he never charged professional colleagues. Except that she didn't see any way to exchange value for value. Both Maddy and Luke seemed supremely happy and emotionally healthy.

"And you're stalling, Daniela," she muttered morosely.

No matter how many ways she figured it, she was going to have to ask her father for another loan. Though it went against every scrap of independence she'd managed to cobble together as the lone female in two families of dominant males, it had to be done.

Lyssa needed school clothes and orthodontia and a sense of security that had been badly shaken when they'd lost the only home she'd ever known. It galled her no end, but she couldn't see any other choice.

The loathing she felt for Jonathan Sommerset was primal, a claws-and-teeth kind of hatred so visceral she could feel it vibrating in the walls of her stomach. She had never thought herself capable of violence, but she was perfectly willing to make an exception in his case. Hard on that thought came the image of the lethal gun Rafe wore on his hip as though it were a natural part of him.

Had he killed with that monster gun? she wondered, fascinated despite her anger at the way he'd just disappeared without so much as a wave, let alone an explanation.

Get a woman all stirred up, then just walk away. Not that she cared, she reminded herself with a fierce little mental nod. Rafe had said it himself. What had been between them was ancient history. Except she couldn't quite stop remembering how right it had felt to be in his arms again. For the first time in months she'd felt safe.

Cherished. It would be so easy to believe that he really cared.

That he had come back into her life to save her, just as he'd always done.

Old tapes, she reminded herself firmly. She of all people should know how tenacious they could be. Helping patients first understand and then deal with the lingering affects of past programming was what therapy was all about.

She would just have to do the same thing for herself.

She drew a long shaky breath. Starting now, she told herself as she reached for the phone to call her father.

Case dumped sugar into his coffee, stirring it with his index finger before carrying it back to his desk where Cardoza waited, kicking back in the battered wooden chair.

His face set in grim lines, he sipped coffee from a cracked mug Case had scared up after discovering they were out of disposable cups again. The Fed's good-looking preppy partner was downstairs with Petrov, dealing with the paperwork involved in booking a federal prisoner.

Cardoza had hoped to find the Beretta nine-millimeter used to kill the MacGregor woman when he'd searched the house in Bellingham. Instead, the man had been clean. All they'd found was a Nevada driver's license and a couple of credit cards in his own name. Nothing incriminating at all.

"He's a smooth one, Folsom," Case said as he settled on his own side of the desk. "Even had the booking sergeant preening like a candidate for Homecoming Queen and she's as tough as an old saddle."

Cardoza took a sip, then rocked back a few more inches and balanced the mug on his belt buckle. "Any way you can keep the press off this?"

Case took a sip. Colored water, he thought in disgust. Feldman must have pulled coffee duty again. "I'll do my best, but this is prime stuff." He ran his finger around the rim of his mug, anticipating the stories aloud. "A beautiful, bright shrink who should know better gets suckered by smooth-talking con man who walks away with everything but the clothes on her back. Sex, glamour, a connection to a prominent Oregon family, it's got it all.'' He compressed his lips then sighed. ''Sorry, can't see the press backing off on this one.''

Cardoza's face hardened. ''Yeah, why should they give a damn if they hold an innocent woman up to public ridicule, maybe even destroy her career just to sell papers or grab air time? Not to mention what the notoriety might do to an innocent twelve-year-old who's still dealing with the loss of her dad.''

Case shared the man's disgust. He'd had his face splashed across the TV screen a time or two. The last time had nearly gotten him killed. ''Any idea where Folsom's got his money stashed?''

''No. The wife claimed they were in Canada on a second honeymoon. Drove across so there's no airline record. RCMP is running a check on the banks and brokerage houses in case he slipped away from the little woman to open an account, but I'm not holding my breath.''

Case nodded. ''Guy that savvy has to have a couple of aliases at least.'' He leaned back and propped his feet on the corner everyone knew to keep free for just that purpose. Helped him to think, he claimed. Mostly he did it because the squad's spit-and-polish captain hated it. Hated him, too, though Case had enough citations in his service jacket to make him off limits.

''What about the woman in Bellingham? You got any idea if she was involved?''

''Doesn't appear to be.'' Cardoza took a sip and to his credit managed not to grimace. ''Damn near fainted when I flashed the warrant in her face.''

Case lifted his tie, smoothed it over his chest. ''Wish I could have seen Folsom's face when you whipped back the shower curtain and stuck the Glock in his belly.''

Cardoza's mouth slanted. ''Have to admit it was one of those rare moments that make a cop's day.''

Case hadn't expected to like the guy, but he did. He had all the moves of an arrogant government hard-ass, all right, and enough chilled steel in those green eyes to freeze the meanest street tough in his tracks. But Case would bet heavy there was more heart inside that linebacker chest than the man wanted anyone to know.

Case had spent half his life hiding his own softer side, so he recognized the signs. From the way Cardoza had turned the conversation to the subject of Daniela Fabrizio's well-being almost as soon as they'd shoved Folsom into the back of the vehicle, he was also pretty sure the Fed felt more for the lady than a cop's natural empathy. Case had been there and knew how tempting it could be to take that fatal step past the professional to the personal.

"When are you planning to head back east?"

"Probably after the arraignment tomorrow—unless the judge grants bail." He finished his coffee, then let the chair drop to four legs as he set the mug on the desk.

"Hey, Randolph, call for you on line two," Hal Vincente shouted across the squad room.

"Might be the prosecutor who caught the case," he said as he dropped his feet in order to reach for the receiver. As soon as he heard the voice on the other end, he knew they'd gotten lucky.

Felicia Hall-Jones had a lilting Jamaican accent, the tenacity of a bulldog and a take-no-prisoners mentality. After exchanging the usual banter, Case opened the case folder and ran down the details of the arrest. "He's standing on his rights, used his one phone call to contact an attorney."

"And who might that be, sugar?"

"Addison Tandy." Case saw Cardoza's gaze sharpen. The portly, flamboyant San Francisco defense attorney was as well known for his love of the camera as his willingness to go to virtually any lengths outside blatant malfeasance to win an acquittal.

"Whoo-ee, now that does make things interesting, doesn't it?" Felicia exclaimed in her distinctive sing-song voice.

"My money's on you, counselor."

"Take it to the bank, sugar," she replied before making arrangements to meet Case and the Feds outside court ten minutes early to review his probable cause testimony.

As he leaned back again, Case allowed himself a cocky grin.

"We drew the A-team this go round. A tough-as-nails lady prosecutor named Felicia Hall-Jones. Has the best conviction record in the district."

"What about bail?"

"Says she intends to ask the judge to deny."

Cardoza flexed his shoulders before tossing a sealed evidence bag onto the blotter. Cardoza's initials and those of a Bellingham PD evidence clerk were scrawled across the yellow sealing tape.

Case picked it up and examined the contents. "Nice ring. Where'd you find it?"

"On the alleged Mrs. Folsom's finger. According to a neighbor, it was a reconciliation present. Since it matched the description of the ring in your crime report, I vouchered it for evidence."

Case held the bag to the light and watched the emerald flash green fire. He felt a pang of regret that he would never be able to give his sweet Prue a classy thing like this. "Bet the lady screamed bloody murder, right?"

"Oh yeah." Cardoza's mouth flattened. "Daniela will need to ID it, so I figured I'd take it by her place tonight—unless you have a problem with that."

"No problem. As a matter of fact, if you're ready to go now, I'll give you a lift."

Chapter 8

"First thing tomorrow your brothers and I will drive one of the rigs up to Portland and pack up your things. We'll have you and Lyssa back where you belong by dinnertime."

Eduardo Mancini was prone to outbursts of emotion and his voice reflected every nuance. At the moment Danni heard eagerness and a paternal command mixed with a hint of Sicilian arrogance. "I'll have Rosaria make your favorite *arroz con pollo*."

Clamping the phone against her shoulder, Danni dumped linguini noodles into the boiling water and adjusted the flame. Her father had been unavailable when she'd called earlier. He'd returned her call just as she'd started dinner. As soon as she explained her reason for calling he'd immediately launched into all the reasons why she and Lyssa belonged at home with him so that he could take care of his "girls."

"We've been all over this before, Papa. Several times, in fact. I'm not moving back to the vineyard. Not only do I have my practice and my friends here in Portland, but it would be terribly traumatic for Lyssa to leave her school and her friends."

"You're barely making ends meet, *cara.* That's no life for you." His tone both dismissed her arguments and rebuked her for making them. Danni had heard it all before—too many times. And not just from him. Her father-in-law had been lobbying for her return to the valley since Mark's funeral.

"These particular circumstances are only temporary, Papa, just until the police find Jonathan and recover my money."

"Police, bah! How long have they been looking for that crook? Three months, that's how long. And not one solid lead."

"The Secret Service is…are…" She stopped, considered, then shrugged. "Well, whichever it is, *they're* looking for him now, too."

"You mean those bozos in sunglasses who guard the president? What do they have to do with Jonathan?" She heard the scowl in her father's booming tenor and winced.

"It's a long story, Papa. I'll explain when we come for your birthday."

"But that's a month away, *cara.* Come for dinner this weekend. I'll invite Eddie and Pamela and their girls."

The front doorbell chimed then, and she shot a look at the clock. At the same time she heard Lys's sneakers pounding down the stairs. "I'll get it, Mom," she shouted, her young voice distressingly eager. Every time her daughter heard the doorbell or the phone, she raced to answer. According to her therapist, Lyssa still held out hope that Jonathan was going to return.

Danni's heart went out to her, but she couldn't quite bear to destroy her last fragile hope. Not until it was necessary. "Someone just came to the door, Papa. I'd better go." She waited, then steeled herself. "About the thousand dollars…I need to call the mechanic as soon as possible."

There was a pause, then a defeated sigh. "Do you still have the same account number at Portland National?"

"Yes, the same." She heard the rumble of a deep voice coming from the living room and frowned.

"I'll have the bank transfer the money first thing tomorrow."

"I'll pay you back, Papa, I swear."

"Don't be silly, *cara*. You know I want to help you all I can. You're the one who keeps refusing."

They were heading down a familiar path, one that would only lead to frustration for them both. "I really have to go, Papa. Hi to everyone there. I love you."

Peanut size with delicate features, masses of black hair pulled up in a bouncy ponytail and big brown eyes, Lyssa looked so much like Danni at twelve that for an instant Rafe's heart had stopped.

"Is your mom around?" he asked, watching the eagerness in her eyes fade into suspicion.

"What do you want with her?" she demanded, arching her back in order to look up at him.

"Just to talk to her for a few minutes. Tell her it's Rafe, okay?" A movement to his left caught his eye and he stiffened.

"Rafe! I...wasn't expecting you." Danni came toward him, padding barefoot along the bright hall runner.

Emotion slammed into him like a fist. Part relief that the ghostly pallor was gone. Part worry about how she was going to take the news of Folsom's arrest.

Mostly, though, he thought how touchably soft she looked in a loose-fitting man-tailored shirt the color of raspberries and little white shorts that covered her fanny, but only just. His gaze skimmed the sleek thighs and trim calves, and his mouth went dry. "Would you believe I was in the neighborhood?"

"Probably not," she said, her lips curving. He couldn't quite get a read on her mood, and that made him edgy.

"Mom, do you know this guy?" her daughter asked suspiciously.

"Yes, Rafe is an old friend," Danni said, slipping an arm around her daughter's brave little shoulders to give her a reassuring hug. The two were nearly equal in height but Lyssa's body still carried the softness of childhood, while Danni's was ripely voluptuous.

"Honey, dinner will be ready in twenty minutes. Why don't you wash up now, okay?"

"Are you sure you don't want me to hang around?" she asked, shifting her darkly suspicious gaze from his face to her mom's. "You know, just in case you get dizzy again or…whatever?"

"I'll be fine, sweetie, but thank you for being so considerate. Right now, I need to speak with Rafe alone, if you don't mind."

"Okay, but I'll be upstairs if you need me." As fierce as a little commando, Lyssa shot him a warning look before heading up the stairs. Both amused and oddly proud, he watched her take each step slowly. The amusement fled when he realized she was limping very badly. What was it Jarrod had said? That she'd nearly lost her leg?

Danni caught the direction of his gaze and frowned. "We'll talk in the kitchen."

Before waiting for an answer, she turned and led the way. The view from the rear was even more mouthwatering, he decided as he allowed himself a long, lingering look. Tired as he was, his body responded instantly.

The kitchen was full of rich smells and had a homey feeling that had been missing the night he'd made coffee. Then it had felt cold and empty. Now, with the rays of the setting sun just skimming the tops of the potted herbs in the window over the sink and pasta bubbling on the stove, it felt welcoming, somehow. The bleached pine table was set for two, with colorful china and pretty place mats. The part of him that remembered noisy family dinners and teasing laughter over rice and beans ached.

"I'm not sure I should even talk to you, considering the way you just disappeared," she said as she walked directly to the stove and picked up a wooden spoon to stir the pasta boiling in a large kettle.

Feeling awkward and out of place, he leaned his backside against one of the counters and crossed his arms. "Yes, well, about that—"

"It was rude and inconsiderate, and caused me no end of grief."

Alarm ran through him. "Grief?" he asked cautiously.

She shot him an irritable look over one slender shoulder. "Absolutely. Shrinks are trained to have an insatiable curiosity, you know."

He allowed himself a brief smile. "Kinda like cops."

Steam caused her hair to curl into those sexy little wisps again. His body gave another insistent surge. He blocked it out.

"Exactly. And when someone in your, uh, situation gets a message to call his boss one minute and then suddenly is nowhere in sight the next, a whole carillon of bells starts jangling in my curious little brain."

"I take your point, and I apologize."

She banged the spoon on the pot before lifting the lid on a large saucepan. The mouthwatering smells were coming from that, he decided as his stomach gave a hopeful rumble.

"It wasn't about delinquent paperwork, was it?" Her shoulders were stiff with tension, and her breathing was just a little too rapid. It was because he'd remembered how quick she'd always been to read any kind of evasion in him that he hadn't said goodbye.

"No, it was about Folsom. We found him."

She spun around, the large wooden spoon held like a sword, her face paling as he watched. "Where?"

"In Bellingham, Washington. The computer guys scared up an address and Seth and I staked it out on the chance he'd show up. We arrested him late yesterday afternoon and brought him back to Portland today. He's presently in custody."

Her mouth trembled, then firmed. "Jonathan's actually in jail?"

"He's actually in jail." He hoped to hell they'd thrown him in with some real dirtbags. With a little luck he'd get himself shanked in the shower room and save the government the cost of a trial.

"Did he say what he did with my money?" The hope in her voice had him biting down hard.

"He didn't even admit he knew you—or Jonathan Sommerset."

"The bastard," she said with heartfelt disgust. "I hope he rots there."

Rafe debated how much to tell her now, how much to hold back until she wasn't so emotional. Though she looked almost completely recovered from her bout with the flu, he'd do just about anything to keep her from doing her rag doll thing again. After studying her face, he decided to go with some positive news first.

"It's possible we recovered the ring you reported stolen." He pulled the evidence bag from the pocket of his jeans and held it out to her. "Do you recognize this?"

Shock replaced the moment of curiosity, and her breath hissed in. "Oh Rafe." Eagerly she put down the spoon before taking the baggy from his hand. "Oh God, yes! It's mine. My engagement ring. The one Mark gave me." Her face softened as she rubbed her finger over the glittering stone. "He insisted it had to be one of a kind, so he had it designed just for me. When I saw it for the first time, I thought it was the most beautiful ring I'd ever seen. I still do."

It took him a moment to realize the emotion ripping at his gut was jealousy. He wanted to snarl. He wanted to jerk her against him and kiss her until Fabrizio was less than a pale memory. He wanted *her* with a desperation that burned away years of denial until he felt as though his skin was on fire.

It took effort, but he managed to ice the feelings the way he'd iced other injuries suffered in the line of duty.

"Can I open the bag?" she asked eagerly, her eyes bright now with joy.

"No, sorry," he said with real regret. "It has to be entered into evidence with the seal intact. Otherwise, the integrity is violated."

"Oh yes, of course. I should have realized." She ran her blunt fingernail over his scrawled initials. "I'd planned to give this ring to Lyssa on her sixteenth birthday. A…A present from her daddy. It was the worst, knowing she had nothing left of him but memories. Now, thanks to you, I—" She closed her hand carefully over the bag, then turned away.

Picked up the spoon.

Put it down again.

"I'm making clam sauce. I…" Her voice broke. "Damn,"

she muttered in a shredded voice, her hand going to her tummy. "My p-poor little angel baby. Saddled with a mommy who's an emotional basket case."

"Ah hell," he muttered under his breath as he pulled his hands from his pockets and turned her to face him. Plain tears he could handle, no sweat, he told himself. He was used to tears. Victims cried. Suspects cried. Hell, he'd had partners who bawled their eyes out. What none of them had done, however, is gaze up at him with shimmering sad angel eyes that pleaded with him to make it right.

He cursed fate.

He cursed the Mancini brothers and the bastard she married.

He cursed himself for being a fool for that look.

"It's been a while, but I think I can still manage a hug if it would help."

She stood stiffly for a moment, and then with a helpless little cry, she was burrowing against his chest, her arms hugging him hard and her nose buried in the open collar of his shirt. She fitted against him perfectly, but he'd already known that. From the moment he'd kissed her the first time, she'd been in his blood. A part of him.

Giving up the fight, he tightened his arms and rested his cheek against her silky curls. Closing his eyes, he breathed in her scent, something light and flowery and familiar. Suddenly, in his mind's eye he saw her in the moonlight, her eyes glowing with passion. He saw himself, a boy who touched her with a man's need.

A boy who'd loved too much.

There wasn't much of that boy left in him. Still, he tried to be gentle as he rubbed his hand in slow circles in the small of her back. "You may be a basket case at the moment," he murmured into her hair, "but you're a strong woman, strongest woman I know. Heck, my jaw still stings from that right cross you laid on me."

She made a choked little noise, then drew back to lay her fingers against his jaw. "I don't see any permanent damage." Her eyes were dark with apology, but her voice reflected her determination to keep things light.

Her house, her rules, he thought as he answered with a lazy grin.

"Not all wounds show, Princess." Then, because he'd been making his own rules for a long time now, he tightened his arms and brought his mouth to hers quickly before either of them could think.

God, the need, the wild exhilaration! It jolted him. It frightened him. The hot rush of blood through his veins, the reckless urge to take her fast and hard, thrusting into her again and again until he was free of the anger and resentment and humiliation.

Until he was free of her.

Driven by something primitive and raw and barely under his control, he pushed her back against the counter and fisted his hands in her hair. The muscles of his thighs burned as he rubbed his distended groin against her rounded tummy.

Danni gasped, her world spinning wildly. Desperate to touch him, she jerked his shirt free of his jeans, her palms skimming taut, warm flesh. Eagerly she touched him, feeling needs grow and bunch.

When he teased her mouth open, then plundered with his tongue, the spasm of pleasure taking her was so great she raked her nails across his spine. Beneath her nails, his muscles rippled, then turned hard as his breath hissed into her open mouth. He groaned her name, crowded closer until every inch of those powerful thighs was molded to hers. With every frantic breath she took she was acutely conscious of the insistent pressure of the thick ridge of him against her abdomen.

Pleasure built low in her body until she no longer had rational thought. Helpless to resist, she pulled him closer, until she could scarcely breathe. He lifted one knee, prying her legs apart, then rubbed his thigh against the delta of her thighs.

She gasped, then shuddered as a shattering spasm took her away. He swallowed her cries, then pressed her head against his chest until the aftershocks passed. Boneless, she sagged against him, listening to the fierce pounding of his heart beneath a shirt that was damp with his sweat.

Finally, when her breathing had slowed, he drew back, his eyes hot and hungry on hers. A pulse hammered in his throat and he seemed to be having equal difficulty drawing a steady breath.

"We have unfinished business, Princess," he said hoarsely.

"Yes," she whispered because anything but brutal honesty would be useless.

Something dangerous blazed in his eyes and his voice was suddenly rough and thick with tension. "I could have taken you now, with your daughter upstairs and your pasta boiling on the stove." His thumb stroked the curve of her bottom lip and she couldn't move. "And you would have let me, wouldn't you?"

He was right. Still, she clung to the last little scrap of free will as she slid her hands to his sides and gave his solid midriff a token shove. Keeping his gaze on hers, he moved back slowly, like a man bracing for a blow, but only far enough to allow her to breathe more easily.

"It's...it's a common dynamic," she said, scrambling as fast as she could for safer ground. "Lack of closure often generates feelings of heightened emotion between two people who are essentially strangers."

His mouth quirked. "Emotions, heightened or otherwise, are your business, Princess. Me, I'm more of a bottom-line guy. In this case, I want to be inside you the next time you use those kitten claws on my back."

She felt her cheeks grow hot. "Yes, well, there is a physical element, I grant you."

He flashed that bad boy grin at her, and his gaze was suddenly full of the very devil. "Ah, you want to jump my bones. I promise I won't resist."

He skimmed his palms over her buttocks, then lifted her against him. He was full and heavy behind the fly of his jeans. Try as she might, she couldn't stop the memory of that night from filling her mind. "I didn't say that," she protested, but her body was already turning to liquid heat inside again.

His grin widened. "Still the curious little cat, Danni?"

"I don't know," she said, searching his face for more than the residual signs of sexual passion. "I know I'm not the impulsive girl I was then.'' She sighed. ''A certain recent, deeply regretted decision notwithstanding.''

He brushed his mouth over her forehead. ''You know what I want. I'm willing to give you time to figure out if it's what you want, too.''

She blinked. ''How much time exactly?''

The cagey little note in her voice had him smiling inside. He liked that in her, the determination to surrender on her terms. Because he wanted her complete cooperation when they finally consummated this edgy chemistry they generated without even trying, he steeled himself to give her room to maneuver. But not too much room.

And not too much time. Twenty years was a long time to burn for a woman.

That decided, he allowed his private smile to show on his face. ''Gresham and I are booked on the red-eye tomorrow night.''

She took a deep, shaky breath. ''In that case, you'd better stay for dinner.''

Chapter 9

Lyssa was anything but pleased to find they had a guest for dinner. Like a sulky four-year-old she made her displeasure known by picking at her favorite meal, speaking only when asked a direct question and shooting Rafe sullen looks across the table.

Apparently unruffled, he worked his way through two helpings of linguini and a half dozen slices of garlic bread, then scraped the last of the salad from the bowl after politely asking if anyone else cared for another helping.

Danni was deeply embarrassed by her daughter's rude behavior. Because she understood the emotionally fragile girl's need for stability right now, she was reluctant to chastise her. Instead, she did her best to pretend nothing was wrong.

Rafe helped, asking Danni about her work and the neighborhood. When Danni mentioned that Lyssa had a part-time job helping Liza Savage with her day-care kids, he led Lyssa to talk about the little ones. Her gaze on her plate, Lyssa answered in monosyllables.

"Is Jody having a lot of guests for her party tomorrow

night?'' Danni asked when another silence settled over the kitchen.

Lyssa poked at the pasta with her fork. ''Not many,'' she said in bored tone. ''Her mom says they don't have room for a big crowd.''

Danni took a sip of milk. ''Jody just invited girls, right?''

Lyssa sent her a sullen look. ''She wanted to have boys, but you said no boy-girl parties 'til I'm thirteen. Only it's not fair!''

''Lys, we've been all over this. You're the child, and I'm the mom. I get to make the rules and you get to follow them. It's Mother Nature's way.''

''It's humiliating!'' Lys protested. ''All the other girls have boyfriends.''

At the age of twelve? Danni doubted that very much. ''I'm sorry, but in my opinion twelve is too young to start dating.''

''Everyone's gonna think I'm a retard or something.''

Danni's fork froze halfway to her mouth. ''Lyssa! I won't have you using that word. It's prejudicial and cruel.''

Her daughter's mouth trembled for an instant. Before her daddy's death and her long recuperation, she had been the sunniest of children, a bubbly extrovert that Mark had called Little Chatterbox. Now she was subject to violent mood swings. This one she could definitely do without, Danni thought with an inner sigh.

''Whatever,'' Lys muttered, her face dark.

''Your mom wasn't allowed to date until she was fourteen,'' Rafe commented before lifting his mug to his lips for a long swallow.

''Fourteen and a half,'' Danni corrected. ''And four days.''

Mystified, and interested despite this latest case of the sulks, Lyssa glanced at each in turn before finally settling a wary gaze on Rafe's teasing expression. ''How do you know that?''

''I had to listen to her for days trying to decide what to wear on her first date. It was a Halloween party and she finally settled on Snow White. Looked real pretty in this gauzy white dress. Had a tiara and everything, too.''

Smiling, Danni let the memory play out in her mind. Rosaria had made the dress for her, and they'd argued over how tight to make the bust. Danni had stuffed her bra with socks to fill it out, only to have Rafe tease her so mercilessly she'd taken them out again—after she'd taunted him about not being invited to the party at the Valley Country Club. It was mortifying now to realize what an arrogantlike snob she'd been in those days. She wouldn't have blamed him if he'd tossed her in the river and walked away.

"I had new high heels and I got blisters," she said, apologizing to him with a look. "I've never been so miserable in my life."

"Yeah, well so was everyone else, the way you limped around whining for a solid week afterward."

"I wasn't whining," she said, falling easily into their old pattern. "I was merely explaining why I was hobbling like an old lady."

A smile played around his mouth, softening that hard face in extremely appealing ways. She'd missed him, she realized. Terribly. "Ah, my mistake, Princess."

"How do you know all that stuff about my mom?" Lyssa demanded suspiciously.

Rafe didn't answer, and Danni realized he was letting her describe their shared past in any terms she chose. "Rafe is Enrique and Rosaria's oldest son," she said quietly, drawing Lyssa's quick gaze for an instant before her daughter swung her gaze his way again.

"You don't look Mexican," Lyssa said with a challenging look. "I'll bet you can't even speak Spanish."

Rafe smiled slightly. *"Ah, pero si, señorita, hablo español muy bien. Y tú, hablas español?"*

Lyssa shrugged, her expression turned sullen.

"She knows more than I do," Danni said, chiding her daughter with a look.

Lyssa tilted her head and regarded Rafe through narrowed eyes. "If you're Enrique and Rosaria's son, how come I've never heard of you?"

Danni saw his jaw flex. "Beats me."

"Rafe left the valley when he was seventeen," Danni said because she knew how tenacious her daughter could be.

"How come you left then? Were you arrested or something?"

His face changed. Danni felt a chill sweep through the room. "No, I wasn't arrested. It just seemed like the right thing to do."

"But—"

"If you're finished, sweetheart, you'd better start your homework," Danni interrupted firmly.

Lyssa looked anything but pleased. "You promised to help me pick out an outfit for the party."

"I'll be up as soon as I finish my dinner," Danni said calmly.

"Whatever."

Lyssa got up and carried her plate to the sink. Before she left the kitchen, she turned to give Rafe a distinctly unfriendly look. "My mother's married, and she's going to have a baby and my stepfather will be back soon. He won't like you being here, so you'd better leave."

Danni had had enough. "Lyssa Mary, that was uncalled for! Please apologize to Rafe for being rude."

An angry flush spread over Lyssa's face. "Sorry," she muttered, but the defiant glint in her dark eyes said she was anything but.

"Apology accepted," Rafe said, looking at her steadily, his expression remarkably mild.

Lyssa looked from one to the other, then turned and left.

Rafe waited until her footsteps sounded on the stairs before shifting his gaze to Danni's face. He looked troubled. "Was all that attitude my fault?" he asked, lifting one tawny brow.

"Only indirectly." Danni took in air and let it out slowly. "You heard what she said about Jonathan. She was crazy about him, and she's still in denial about his being a con man and thief."

"How does he explain his stealing you blind, then disappearing without a trace?"

"She doesn't. She just keeps saying that Jonathan must have had a good reason, and when he comes back, he'll explain. Although she hasn't come right out and said it, I'm pretty sure she blames me."

He forked salad into his mouth and chewed. "Is that why you didn't want me to mention his arrest?" he asked after swallowing.

She nodded. "I want to pick the right time."

He gave her a hooded look. "It's bound to make the papers, Danni," he said before taking a bite of bread.

"I know. I'll tell her tonight when I go in to kiss her goodnight." She put down her fork and wiped her mouth with her napkin. "Her therapist thinks she's clinging to Jonathan because she's terrified to lose another father figure." She sighed heavily. "It makes me sick inside to think I actually encouraged him to bond with her. And when he went out of his way to pamper her and spoil her, I was thrilled." Her face tightened. "I would hate him for hurting her, even if he hadn't robbed us blind."

"I assume you told her you'd filed for divorce."

"I tried. She got hysterical, so her therapist and I decided to downplay it until the divorce was final."

Rafe used the bread to sop up the last of the clam sauce. His appetite would have been gratifying if she weren't so worried about Lyssa. When his plate was empty he pushed it aside and reached for his coffee again. Instead of drinking, however, he gazed down at the contents for a long moment before settling those startling green eyes on her face.

"Guess there's no easy way to say this except straight out. There's a possibility your marriage isn't legal."

She stared, her heart thudding. "But...but we went to a justice of the peace recommended by the captain of the ship. He assured us a Mexican marriage was recognized as legal in the States."

"I'm sure it is. But Folsom did use an alias which clouds the issue." He took a sip then, draining the mug before returning it to the mat. "There's something else, too. We found Folsom by running a trace on marriage licenses. Back in '85, he married a woman in Bellingham, Washington. She still lives there." His expression turned gentle. "Unless he divorced her without her knowledge, they're still married."

Her mouth went dry. "What...what did Jonathan say about that?"

"Nothing about his marriage. Told her the arrest warrant was simply a case of mistaken identity. She believed him."

She felt a sharp pang of disgust, most of it directed against herself for being equally gullible. "Why shouldn't she believe him? The Weasel's an expert at lying to women.'' Suddenly she felt the baby give a hard kick, and she uttered a startled gasp.

Alarm shot into Rafe's eyes. ''Are you okay?'' he demanded in a sharp tone.

She gave a shaky laugh. ''The little stinker just gave me a heck of a hard wallop. It's the first time it's actually hurt.''

His gaze dropped to her stomach and lingered. For a moment she thought he looked sad. ''Picked out a name yet?''

''Not yet. Lyssa and I have been going through a book of names. Lys was named for Mark's grandmother so I never really had a choice.'' She took a sip of milk. ''There've been some interesting studies on the impact of a person's name on their personality, and even their choice of profession. For example, one researcher found a statistically significant number of surgeons named Cutter.''

He lifted his brows. ''Folsom is the name of a prison. Think that's an omen?''

''I fervently hope so.'' She smiled. ''Did you know that Rafael means a gift from God?''

His face closed up. ''I was named for Rosaria's oldest brother who was drowned trying to swim the Rio Grande.''

''Stacy MacAuliffe who lives on the other side of Case and Prudy named her oldest daughter Victoria as an affirmation after her ex-husband raped her.'' She stared at the lavender roses in the pale blue vase in the center of the table. ''I want this baby to have a strong name. A...brave name.'' Suddenly self-conscious, she lifted her head. ''Sorry, I didn't mean to get philosophical.''

He gave a little shrug. ''Guess my question would be whose name you're going to put down as the father?''

''Certainly not Jonathan's. I...oh my God, if we aren't legally married, that means this baby is a—'' She stopped abruptly, her face turning hot.

''A bastard,'' Rafe finished for her in a voice without expression.

''Legally, I suppose that's true. Fortunately, being born to a single parent is perfectly acceptable in today's times.'' But was it really?

"Can't help wondering how *El Jefe* will take to having a bastard grandchild, though," Rafe said, watching her with enigmatic eyes.

"He'll be fine with it," she declared firmly.

It was there again, that hard glinting look that shivered through her from the inside out. "Guess it's different when it's his own flesh and blood at that."

"He always liked you, Rafe."

"But not enough to accept me as a son-in-law."

She took a breath. "Would you have married me if Eddie had given you the choice?"

"Yes, I would have married you. And it would have been hell for both of us."

"I know it would have been difficult, but—"

"Not difficult, impossible. All I had to offer you was one third of a bed in a trailer with seven other people."

She frowned. "Don't be ridiculous, Rafe. We would have lived in my house until we finished school."

"No, Danni, we wouldn't. A man provides for his own wife. He doesn't accept handouts." His face shuttered, he got to his feet and picked up his plate. "Finished?" he asked, glancing at hers which was still half full.

"Yes, but I'll take care of the dishes," she said hastily, pushing back her chair. "You're a guest."

His grin flashed, folding those irresistible creases into his cheeks. "I intend to be more than that, Princess." This time the look in his eyes was far too easy to read. Her body turned soft inside, and her breath seemed to shiver through her throat.

It stunned her to discover how vulnerable she was to him, even now. As soon as she'd felt his mouth settle over hers, she'd held nothing back, perhaps because she'd had no warning, no time to erect defenses.

Instinct told her he hadn't planned to kiss her. She could have resisted deliberate charm. No, it hadn't been contrived or, she suspected, even expected, that wild conflagration that had flared between them. Now, however, her body felt incredibly relaxed for the first time in months. Silk inside as well as out.

"I'm not ready to make that decision, Rafe," she said, for her benefit as well as his. "I may never be ready."

"I've waited twenty years. Guess I can wait a little longer." His grin flashed again, as potent as wine on an empty stomach. "But not forever."

For sex, not marriage, she thought as he turned to carry both plates to the sink. When she didn't move, couldn't move, he shot her a glance over his shoulder.

"Go talk to your daughter, Danni," he ordered quietly. "Right now, I suspect she needs you even more than I do."

"Jody's mom let her get a whole new outfit just for the party," Lyssa muttered dejectedly as she tossed another rejected top onto the mound of discards on the bed. "All the other girls will probably have on new stuff, too. Everyone's seen everything I own about a million times."

"What about this one?" Danni asked a little desperately as she took a silky chartreuse blouse from the back of the closet. "Look, it's still got the price tag on it," she added triumphantly. "No one can possibly have seen it."

Lys dismissed the pretty top with a disgusted look. "That's because the color makes me look putrid." Lys sat down on the edge of the bed and stared up at her angrily. "I'm not going unless I get something new."

Sighing, Danni returned the top to the closet before turning to face her unhappy daughter again. "Sweetheart, I wish you could get a dozen new things, I really do, but we just don't have the money right now."

"You could ask Grandpa Mancini or Grandpa Fabrizio. They have lots of money."

"I could, but I won't," Danni said firmly. She'd drawn the line herself. Only in the case of an emergency like the need for transportation or money for Lyssa's medical care would she ask for help. It was a matter of pride, and since that was about all she had left, she didn't intend to squander it on trivialities.

Lyssa's face turned red as her Italian temper let loose. "You just want to punish me because Jonathan loves me better than you!"

Danni stared. "What are you talking about?"

Her eyes glistened with angry tears and her mouth trembled. "He said I was his own special girl, just like Daddy always said."

"Perhaps you were," she said carefully. "But he still left us."

"You must have done something to make him go away."

"Of course I didn't, Lyssa. I loved Jonathan. Or the man I thought Jonathan was. But he was lying—"

"He wasn't! You can't make me believe that! You must have said something to him. Something mean and hurtful." Her voice broke, and the tears overflowed. Angrily, she dashed them away. "I hate you for driving him away!"

Even though Danni realized that it was healthy for her daughter to vent her emotions, the violence of Lys's feelings shook her to the core. Where had this come from? "Lyssa, listen to me, you're upset, but—"

"He's probably tried to call me and you won't give me the message because you're jealous."

Danni took a step forward, only to have Lyssa leap from the bed and move out of her mother's reach. Danni stopped and dropped her arms to her sides.

"Of course I would tell you, but he hasn't called either of us," she said, digging deep for the patience and understanding Lyssa needed right now.

"How do I know that?" Lyssa lashed out, her eyes flashing. "How do I know you're not the one who's lying?"

Her legs were suddenly unsteady, and bile scoured her throat. She swallowed, but the sickening taste remained. "Because I've never lied to you," she declared in a low soothing tone designed to defuse the anger.

"Then tell me where he is!" The desperate note of pleading in Lys's voice reminded her of how young and vulnerable her daughter really was.

Aching inside, she took a deep breath, determined to tell Lyssa the truth, but the words dammed in her throat. It was the wrong time to tell her about Jonathan's arrest. First she needed to prepare her.

"Lyssa, honey, I know this is difficult for you to accept, but

Jonathan isn't the person you thought he was. In fact, he was even using an assumed name. His real name is Jacob Peter Folsom, and he's conned a lot of other women before me.''

"I don't believe you!" Lyssa shouted, the anger surging back. "You're lying!"

"No, she's not, Lyssa," Rafe said from the open doorway. There was steel in his deep voice that had Lys's eyes widening. "Your mother is only trying to spare you more pain."

Danni realized what he was about to do, and lifted her hand to stop him. "Rafe, don't," she pleaded quickly. "She's upset."

"If she wants to be treated like an adult, she'd better start behaving like one instead of throwing a tantrum like a spoiled brat."

Lyssa's jaw dropped before she rounded on her mother. "Are you going to let him talk to me like that?"

Danni's own temper spiked, but she managed to keep it from showing. Later, when this was all over, her daughter definitely needed an attitude adjustment. "Lyssa, please. Rafe's only trying to help."

Lyssa's face was scarlet and her eyes were filled with a desperate kind of fury. "He doesn't belong here. Tell him to go away, Mommy."

Danni felt her stomach lurch, and drew a quick breath as she gave Rafe a beseeching look. "Maybe you *should* go."

Irritation crossed his face, giving it a harsh look. "You don't need this kind of grief right now, Danni."

"Please, Rafe. Let me handle this my own way."

Rafe took in Danni's shadowed eyes, and knew what it was to feel both frustration and tenderness. The first he dealt with on a daily basis. All cops did. It was the latter that shocked him. He hadn't even known the man he'd become was capable of tenderness.

"Twenty minutes," he said, giving in with great reluctance. "After that, I'm handling it my way whether you agree or not."

Rafe was standing at the front window, looking out at the lights of Vancouver, Washington, on the other side of the river. In his hand was the ubiquitous mug. The man seemed to live on coffee, she thought wearily. As she stepped into the living room he turned a searching gaze her way. "Well?" he demanded impatiently.

Danni didn't bother to hide her resentment of his highhanded behavior. "I told her. She didn't take it well, but I finally got her calmed down. I came down to make her some hot chocolate."

"I'll do it. You sit down before you collapse."

"I'm not about to collapse," she exclaimed angrily. The need to vent was stronger than her will to resist, she realized as she took another quick breath. "Ever since you walked into this house last Friday night you've done nothing but issue orders and expect everyone around here to say 'how high should I jump, master'?"

His expression turned sardonic. "Not you, Daniela. If you're not hanging over the john or folding up like some kind of melodramatic heroine, you're letting your daughter treat you like garbage, like no mother should ever be treated. So, yeah, somebody needs to take charge. Since I don't see anyone else stepping forward, I guess I get the job by default."

That stung. She refused to let it show. "Point taken," she said coolly. "Now, if you're quite done, don't let the door hit you on the way out, Agent Cardoza."

His grin flashed. She told herself she was immune. "That lady of the manor thing you do so well might work with some guys, Danni, but I remember how the Princess begged the peasant boy to make her a woman."

She sucked in hard, and her face grew hot. Tears of humiliation pressed her throat. "Did you enjoy it, Rafe? Having me beg?"

Impatience crossed his face. "I'm damned tired of getting slammed because I wanted your first time to be a lot more special than that would have been." His jaw tightened. "God knows, if I had it to do over again, you never would have left that pond a virgin."

She glared at him. "That wasn't my choice," she muttered. "I was willing."

"Believe me, honey, I remember!"

She saw the gritty frustration on his face and realized she was only wasting precious energy arguing. "Oh go ahead and do whatever you want to," she muttered, sinking into her favorite corner of the sofa. "When you're done, however, we're going to get some things straight, you and I."

His mouth thinned. "Count on it."

Bypassing the living room, Rafe took the hot chocolate directly upstairs. Lyssa's room clearly belonged to a younger child who would appreciate the frilly curtains and canopy bed. A doll collection occupied the top two shelves of a built-in bookcase encompassing one entire wall. The lower shelves were filled with children's games and books.

The lights in the room had been extinguished, but there was enough light pouring through the door for him to see Lyssa curled into a fetal position beneath the pink-and-white checked comforter. Cheek buried in the pillow, she glared at him as he approached.

"I wish Jonathan had shot you and run away when you tried to arrest him," she said in a fierce little voice.

Rafe ached for the kid. Disillusionment was a bitch and a half. "You're entitled to wish anything you want, sweetheart."

"Don't call me that! I hate you."

He put the cup and saucer on the table next to a lamp with a fringed shade. "You won't believe this now, Lyssa, but there are some people in this world who are pure evil. They don't care about anyone or anything but their own wants and needs and pleasures. The man who married your mother is one of those people. He'll say or do anything to get what he wants. He used her and he used you to fill his own pockets. He's done it before and if we don't find a way to lock him up for a long time, he'll do it again."

Her face darkened. "You're right, I don't believe you."

"I'm sorry about that." He hesitated, then sat down on the side of the bed. With a little cry of protest, she scooted to the far side of the mattress. He refused to let her see his annoyance. "Your mother loves you very much, Lyssa. You are the most important thing in the world to her, and that's the way it should be. But she's also under a great deal of stress right now. I don't know if anyone told you how sick she was on Friday night.''

"It was just the flu," she grumbled. "She was already feeling better when I got home.''

His patience thinned, but held by a thread. "She's going to have a baby. That takes a toll on a woman even under the best of circumstances. And your mom's not as young as she was when she had you, which makes it even rougher on her. She needs your help, not more stress.''

Guilt crossed her face, and she closed her eyes. There was more he figured needed saying, but he remembered Danni at this age. Getting her to admit she might be wrong on the first try had been damn near impossible, so he'd learned to coax her into it, little by little.

"Given how smart your mom is, I figure you're no slouch in the brains department. So why don't you think about all your mom has been through these past couple of years and see if you can't figure out some things you could do to make it easier on her?''

She didn't react. He realized he was disappointed. So much for his wise old uncle act, he thought as he got to his feet.

"Good night, *niña*," he said quietly. "Sweet dreams.''

"Go to hell," she muttered before pulling the covers over her head.

Telling himself he was damn glad Lyssa wasn't his problem—and never would be—Rafe headed downstairs. Braced for the blast he figured was coming, he didn't know whether to be relieved or disappointed when he arrived in the living room to find Danni curled up into the sofa cushions, sound asleep.

He rubbed his hand over his heart, then realized what he was doing and shoved it into his pocket instead. Because he wanted to settle down beside her and cradle her in his lap, he turned instead and walked toward the kitchen.

Committed to truly being off duty for a few hours at least, he'd left both his cell phone and his beeper in the briefcase along with his weapon. Frowning, he took the card with the motel's number from his wallet and punched out the numbers on the wall phone.

"Room 112, please," he said when the switchboard answered.

Seth answered on the second ring. Rafe heard a ballgame in the background. "Gresham, here."

"I'm bunking out tonight. Pick me up at Dr. Fabrizio's at seven tomorrow."

"Got lucky, did you, *compadre?*"

"None of your damn business, and if you don't want to end up guarding some congressman's dog for the next twenty years, you'll pretend we didn't have this conversation."

"What conversation?"

Rafe waited to chuckle until the line went dead. The kid had potential, he thought as he switched off the light and left the kitchen.

It was the usual middle-of-the-night call of nature that woke Danni a little past midnight. Her neck was stiff and her arm had fallen asleep. She wiggled her fingers, then winced when pins and needles ran through from the fingers to her shoulder.

The living room was dark, but Rafe had left the light on in the entry before he left. He'd obviously draped the duvet from the bed upstairs over her as well. Moving slowly, she uncoiled her legs and dropped them to the floor.

She saw him then, stretched out in front of the fireplace hearth on the priceless Oriental rug, one of the pillows from her bed tucked under his head. One hand was splayed on his belly, the other buried beneath the pillow. He'd removed his loafers and crossed his big feet at the ankles. His head was cocked toward her as though he'd been watching her as he fell asleep. His expression was grim.

The lion asleep but not at rest, she thought whimsically as she got to her feet. Though she was absolutely certain she hadn't made a sound, his body tensed and his eyes flew open. "Are you all right?" he demanded without a hint of sleepiness in his tone.

"I have to wee."

His mouth relaxed. "Ah. Guess that happens a lot now, huh?"

"Every three hours like clockwork." She padded off to the powder room, feeling his gaze following her.

He was looking at Morgan's masks when she returned. He'd turned on one of the end table lamps and folded the duvet. "You feel up to talking before you go upstairs to your bed where you belong?"

She shook her head. "I'm too tired to yell at you tonight."

His mouth slanted. "Okay, I'll take a rain check. In the meantime, you need to know that Folsom's arraignment is scheduled for tomorrow morning, ten o'clock in federal court. Randolph and Gresham and I will be there, along with the prosecutor."

She felt a rush of satisfaction. "And me, I'll be there, too. I want The Weasel to know how much I loathe him for what he did."

Rafe watched her mouth firm and her chin come up. His little brown-eyed scrapper. An unfamiliar emotion moved through him. "Are you sure you're up to it?" he asked, watching her.

"Oh yeah, I'm up to it." She frowned. "I'll need to call the patients scheduled for the morning, though, and reschedule their appointments for later in the week. I'll have to check my book but I think my first appointment is at eight."

"Seth's coming to pick me up at seven. We'll take you and Lyssa out for breakfast."

Her gaze sharpened. "What do you mean, seven? Surely you don't intend to stay?"

"No choice. Seth has the wheels." His grin started in his eyes and spread with a sensuous slowness to his lips. "Don't worry, Princess. I'll bunk down here. This time."

"This time and every time," she muttered, only to see those eyes flash with wicked laughter.

"Want to bet?"

She shot him a dark look. "Go to hell, Cardoza," she muttered before stalking out.

"Like daughter, like mother," she thought he said as she swept up the stairs.

Chapter 10

The transport van stank. The prisoners scheduled for court appearances were crammed three in a seat, watched over by two brutally muscled, hard-faced marshals with shotguns. Jake Folsom sat close to the rear, jammed against the van's side wall by a hairy, tattooed Hell's Angel twice his size who smelled like puke.

Shoulders wedged sideways, Jake stared straight ahead. Some men broke under the humiliation. Some fought back, only to end up pissing blood from bruised kidneys.

Unlike a lot of the fish in the tank, Jake knew the game. The marshals wanted a model prisoner? No sweat, Jake Folsom was a damn role model.

He had been a snot-nosed kid picking pockets and snatching purses when he'd discovered he could con social workers and cops alike by turning himself into whatever they wanted him to be. They wanted to see him as a sad, neglected kid so they could feel like heroes riding to his rescue, that's exactly what he'd given them. They'd wanted a reformed delinquent to prove the big bucks they'd spent on intervention had worked, hell, he could play that easy. A woman wanted a man to love her for her brilliance or her personality instead of the size of her breasts, fine by him.

He didn't have a read on the judge yet, but he would. The jurors, though, that might be a challenge.

Rage seethed like hissing snakes in his belly whenever he let himself think of the humiliating scene in Arlene's prissy pink bathroom.

His mind darkened. That stupid cow. She was almost as much to blame for what happened as Cardoza. How many times had he told her not to open the door to strangers? For her own safety, he'd said so she wouldn't get suspicious. Did the dumb bitch listen? Hell no, just opened the damn door and invited the Feds inside like they were honored guests.

He'd made a mistake by not making an excuse to remain behind in Canada as he'd planned. For peanuts, too. The measly fifty grand she'd recently inherited from her great-aunt. Less than the cost of the S-class Mercedes "Michael Carlyle" had on order with a dealership in Vancouver. Once he'd wiggled out of this charge, he intended to make her pay—after he'd cleaned out her savings account.

Before he split for Canada, he'd take care of Cardoza. The Fed was a dead man walking. Only the time and place of his execution had yet to be decided. The Fed's own .45 would be the means, the same one the grinning SOB had shoved into his gut. His belly was still black and blue.

It hurt to move. It hurt to breathe. Jake had passed an edgy sleepless night in that noxious hellhole cell planning the sequence and placement of each shot. He knew enough about anatomy to keep the bastard alive a long time. Long enough to reduce him to begging—not for his life, but for the *coup de grace*. It was then he planned to shoot the bastard in the throat, then walk away, leaving him to choke on his own blood.

After that he would take care of Daniela—and that marked-up brat of hers.

"Ever been to court before?" Seth asked Danni as the three of them rode up to the second floor in the elevator.

"A few times to offer expert testimony."

She wrapped her icy fingers a little tighter around the strap of her shoulder bag and tried to ignore the nerves making her heart pound and her mouth dry. Next to her, large and comforting and protective, Rafe glanced down and smiled. Clean shaven, with his thick hair glossy and well brushed, he looked polished and confident in his suit and tie. "You doing okay?" he asked quietly.

"So far," she said as the car stopped and the doors slid open. The oatmeal she'd forced down for the baby's sake had congealed into a lumpy ball in her stomach, and her legs felt wooden.

"My money's on you, Princess." Rafe slipped his hand under her elbow as they exited and kept it there as they headed toward the small knot of people halfway down the long, wide corridor.

Case was there, she realized with a little flurry of gratitude, looking reassuringly competent and appropriately professional in a conservative blue suit. Next to him stood his shaggy bear partner whose name she'd forgotten, looking rumpled and grumpy in a truly ugly green-and-beige plaid sports jacket and wrinkled brown trousers.

The third person in the group was a willowy African-American woman with close cropped hair bleached nearly white and strongly defined features. Nearly as tall as Case in her three inch heels, she'd dressed for both impact and chic image in a superbly tailored bronze-and-black houndstooth check jacket over a black silk shell and a pencil slim black shirt. An expensive looking briefcase was slung over one elegant shoulder.

Danni read her as a power player who knew how to use her exotic beauty and height as a weapon to both intimidate opposing counsel and hostile witnesses while at the same time bedazzling male jurors. On the other hand, Danni knew, less favored female jurors might resent her for the very things their male counterparts found so fascinating.

Danni felt both reassured and worried as she sneaked a peek at Rafe's face. Sensing her gaze, he glanced her way—and winked. She felt a bubble of laughter rising to her throat and

ARTS
GAME

YOURSELF IN...

Play **LUCK**

when you play
...then contin
with a sweeth

1. Play Lucky Hearts as instruc
2. Send back this card and you
   novels. These books have a
   Canada, but they are yours t
3. There's no catch! You're unde
   ZERO—for your first shipme
   of purchases—not even one
4. The fact is thousands of read
   Reader Service™. They enjoy
   the best new novels at disco
   love their *Heart to Heart* subs
   recipes, book reviews and m
5. We hope that after receiving y
   choice is yours—to continue
   invitation, with no risk of any

- ◆ **Exciting Silhouette® romance novels—FREE!**
- ◆ **Plus an exciting mystery gift—FREE!**
- ◆ **No cost! No obligation to buy!**

YES!

I have scratched off the silver card. Please send me the 2 FREE books and gift for which I qualify. I understand I am under no obligation to purchase any books, as explained on the back and on the opposite page.

With a coin, scratch off the silver card and check below to see what we have for you.

SILHOUETTE'S

LUCKY HEARTS GAME

345 SDL C6QT

245 SDL C6QP
(S-IM-OS-06/01)

NAME   (PLEASE PRINT CLEARLY)

ADDRESS

APT.#   CITY

STATE/PROV.   ZIP/POSTAL CODE

Twenty-one gets you 2 free books, and a free mystery gift!

Twenty gets you 2 free books!

Nineteen gets you 1 free book!

Try Again!

Offer limited to one per household and not valid to current
Silhouette Intimate Moments® subscribers. All orders subject to approval.

▼ DETACH AND MAIL CARD TODAY! ▼

The Silhouette Reader Service™—Here's how it works:

Accepting your 2 free books and gift places you under no obligation to buy anything. You may keep the books and gift and return the shipping statement marked "cancel." If you do not cancel, about a month later we'll send you 6 additional novels and bill you just $3.80 each in the U.S., or $4.21 each in Canada, plus 25¢ shipping & handling per book and applicable taxes if any.* That's the complete price and — compared to cover prices of $4.50 each in the U.S. and $5.25 each in Canada — it's quite a bargain! You may cancel at any time, but if you choose to continue, every month we'll send you 6 more books, which you may either purchase at the discount price or return to us and cancel your subscription.

*Terms and prices subject to change without notice. Sales tax applicable in N.Y. Canadian residents will be charged applicable provincial taxes and GST.

If offer card is missing write to: Silhouette Reader Service, 3010 Walden Ave., P.O. Box 1867, Buffalo, NY 14240-1867

SILHOUETTE READER SERVICE
3010 WALDEN AVE
PO BOX 1867
BUFFALO NY 14240-9952

BUSINESS REPLY MAIL
FIRST-CLASS MAIL   PERMIT NO. 717   BUFFALO, NY

POSTAGE WILL BE PAID BY ADDRESSEE

NO POSTAGE
NECESSARY
IF MAILED
IN THE
UNITED STATES

wondered if he'd been deliberately trying to put her at ease. She suspected that he had and was grateful.

Spying them approaching, the prosecutor placed a slim hand on Case's arm and drew his attention to them as well. "It's a good day in the neighborhood, boys and girls," Prudy's sometimes moody, always intense husband said with a cocky grin that registered one notch below Rafe's for testosterone power. The four cops shook hands and Rafe officially handed over her ring as evidence. Case gave Danni a brotherly hug before introducing the federal prosecutor.

Felicia Hall-Jones had a firm handshake and a brisk, nononsense manner. In contrast, her throaty voice had an exotic island lilt that Danni found charming. "Dr. Fabrizio, I assume Agents Cardoza and Gresham have explained that this is merely a hearing to present probable cause for the charges against the defendant and to record his plea," she asked after the two of them had exchanged pleasantries.

Danni nodded. "Will the judge let him out on bail, do you think?"

Ms. Hall-Jones shrugged. "A toss-up. I'll present Folsom as a flight risk, his attorney will cite his good character and lack of previous convictions, etcetera. Judge Bonaventure tends to lean toward the side of the good guys, but not always."

"Well, if it isn't the lovely Ms. Hall-Jones," a voice boomed, rocketing off the thick walls like a cannon shot in a phone booth.

The man deliberately making his arrival known to all and sundry had a prodigious Orson Welles belly as well as the temperamental actor's flair for making dramatic entrances. Of average height, he had carefully styled iron gray hair, hypnotic blue eyes and a perfect tan. His navy pinstriped suit screamed custom tailoring and the well-tended hand he extended toward the prosecutor sported a diamond pinkie ring that fell easily into the category of a major rock.

Danni's first impulse was to dismiss him as a bloated buffoon—until she saw the nearly imperceptible narrowing of the prosecutor's shrewd eyes. The dislike between the two was nearly palpable. Ms. Hall-Jones didn't strike her as a woman who squandered her emotional energy on lightweight adversaries.

"Counselor," the prosecutor said with a polite smile as she allowed her hand to touch his briefly—and with a subtle distaste that the other man caught instantly, though he recovered quickly.

"You are looking ravishing as always, Felicia," he said, lifting a well-shaped brow that seemed almost feminine. "I do envy you that lovely bone structure."

Her self-possession unruffled, Ms. Hall-Jones reached out to flick an imaginary speck of lint from his lapel. He wore a pink carnation in his buttonhole and a diamond tiepin that was nearly as large as his pinkie ring.

"I thought you only trolled for high-profile capital cases these days, Addison," she said with a smile that was subtly shaded toward derision.

"Alas, homicides are on the decline thanks to such stalwart members of law enforcement as these." He swept Case and his partner a condescending look before settling his gaze on Rafe.

It was subtle, the change that came over Tandy. The merest flicker of an eyelash, the slight tightening of facial muscles. Even his nostrils flared, like a hyena catching the scent of a lethal predator. His voice when he spoke, however, was affable. "Agent Cardoza, we meet again."

"Looks that way, Counselor." Rafe's voice held only icy contempt. His eyes, too, were about as friendly as a winter dawn.

Tandy managed a credible smile. "You seem to have recovered without any ill-affects."

"Count on it."

Recovered from what? Danni wondered, but before she could ask Rafe to explain, Tandy shifted his attention her way. "Addison Tandy, at your service ma'am. And you are?"

"Dr. Daniela Fabrizio," Ms. Hall-Jones said before Danni had a chance to answer for herself.

Recognition flashed in the attorney's eyes an instant before his lips scythed into a smile. "A very great pleasure, Doctor. I've been looking forward to making your acquaintance since speaking with my client early last evening."

"Mr. Tandy," she said politely, but with no warmth.

Smile fading, Tandy dropped his gaze to her midsection before returning it to her face. There was a ruthless cunning behind the showy exterior, she realized. And a cruel cast to his thin mouth.

"Am I correct in assuming you intend to claim the child you're carrying is my client's, Doctor?" His tone was pleasant enough, she'd grant him that. His choice of words, however, had the men surrounding her instantly on guard.

"I wouldn't go there if I were you, Tandy," Rafe warned in a tone that was barely above a whisper, and yet the hair on the back of her neck suddenly shivered.

"It's not a claim, Mr. Tandy," she said, refusing to be intimidated. "It's the truth."

His mouth smiled once more, but his eyes had a calculating glint. "I certainly wouldn't presume to doubt a woman of your impeccable reputation and family background, Dr. Fabrizio." He nodded and started to turn away. He paused, however, as though struck by an afterthought, and glanced again at her belly. "If we do find ourselves going to trial, however, I would be remiss if I didn't ask the judge to order a paternity test."

He left her speechless.

Rafe had no such problem. The name he called Tandy was graphic—and, in Danni's opinion, completely appropriate. She only wished she'd said it first.

The anteroom off the courtroom was little more than a box with a table and three straight-backed chairs. A vent in the ceiling provided the only ventilation. Alone and still chained, Jake cast an impatient glance at the wall clock that was the only adornment on the beige walls. There were still forty minutes to cool his heels until court convened. To distract himself, he tapped one foot against the floor, the cheap prison clogs making a slapping noise against the terrazzo floor. With each movement of his foot, the shackles rattled, fueling his growing anger.

He heard a quick tap on the only door before it opened, admitting his attorney.

"About time you got here, Tandy," he snarled as the marshal closed it again. "I've been in this stinking shoebox for almost an hour."

The fat lawyer looked unruffled as he deposited his attaché case on the table, then pulled out a chair. "Regrettable, but unavoidable," he said as he took out a handkerchief and wiped the seat before settling his elephant ass.

"I'll make this short and sweet, Mr. Folsom. I've reviewed the government's evidence and I've met the star witness." He allowed a hint of a smile. "Dr. Fabrizio is a prosecutor's dream. Attractive, beautifully dressed, poised, with honest brown eyes and the face of a Madonna. The kind of woman a man just naturally wants to protect, even when he's figuring out how to get her into bed."

"A damn wedding ring is how. It's all or nothing with that bitch."

Tandy looked as though he'd just caught a whiff of something foul. "Be that as it may, sir, bottom-line, with her face and her testimony, this case is a slam dunk—for the opposition. Your only chance to avoid prison time is to plea bargain."

Panic rose before Jake pushed it down. "Bull. I watched the Michelson trial on court TV. You made mincemeat of that mealy-mouthed blond bitch who cried rape."

Impatience crossed Tandy's face. "Don't be naïve, Folsom. Juries don't take kindly to counsel badgering a woman who's expecting a child, especially one who's claiming to have been victimized by that child's father."

Jake went cold inside. "What do you mean, expecting a child?" His voice came out too loud and too shrill, a break in his control that added to his rage against the woman trying to destroy him.

Tandy's face changed. "You mean you didn't know she was pregnant?"

Jake shook his head. "Last time we spoke on the phone she said something about having a wonderful surprise waiting for me in London." His mouth thinned. If he'd known, he would have found a way to make sure the brat wasn't born alive.

Conscious that Tandy was watching him, he schooled his features to reflect an honest dismay. "I had no idea. I swear it. If I'd known, I would have found a way to work things out."

Tandy studied him with eyes that missed very little. Jake kept his poker face in place and thought about summoning a tear or two. Apparently satisfied, Tandy pursed his lips and drummed his fingers as he reflected. Finally, his gaze sharpened.

"Look, why don't I have a private chat with that delicious Ms. Hall-Jones, see if we can do some horse-trading?"

Jake kept the sudden spike of hope carefully hidden. "What kind of horse-trading you have in mind?"

"A plea of guilty to one count of bigamy and an offer of reasonable restitution in exchange for a suspended sentence and probation."

It was tempting, Jake realized. Few states even bothered to bring cases of bigamy to trial, but this was a federal case. Still, even federal prosecutors liked to notch easy wins.

He could plead poverty, ask for time to raise the payback money. He'd make sure the judge liked him. Hell, he could charm anyone out of anything when he set his mind to it. Everyone but that bastard Fed with those green eyes that bored into him like lasers.

"Make the deal," he said, his spirits lifting. "I don't want my child born while I'm behind bars." It was a lie. He'd didn't want the child born period.

Tandy looked pleased as he rose. No doubt mentally counting the remainder of his fee—which he'd play hell getting— Jake thought as the fat bastard lumbered to the door and called for the marshal.

The conference room near the elevators seemed to pulse with tension. Danni sat at one end of the table, the prosecutor at the other. Between them, four large, grim-faced men listened silently as the prosecutor relayed Tandy's offer.

"On the one hand it would save you the trauma of testifying," Ms. Hall-Jones said, her expression carefully neutral. She hadn't seemed particularly surprised when Tandy had requested a prehearing conference. Nor had she expressed an opinion of the plea bargain Tandy had proposed. She had simply explained the proposal on the table.

"And on the other hand?" Danni prodded when the prosecutor remained silent.

"On the other hand, the scumbucket walks away with a measly slap on the wrist," Case's partner grumbled in a graveled voice.

Though Case remained silent, his expression showed that he agreed. Seth, too, seemed unhappy with the proposal and allowed his feelings to show clearly on his handsome face.

"Detective Petrov is essentially correct," the prosecutor said in her musical accent. "If Folsom reneges on his commitment to make restitution, the court can have his probation revoked and order him to serve his full sentence."

Danni considered, then frowned. "How much prison time would he have to serve for bigamy?"

"Best case scenario, eighteen months. Realistically, half that."

Next to her Rafe tipped back his chair, his gaze fixed on a spot on the wall opposite. Long blunt fingers laced over his flat midriff, he appeared relaxed, even disinterested. She knew he was anything but.

Mark would have already made the decision for her, she realized. Dutiful wife that she'd been, she would have meekly acquiesced. Last night she'd accused Rafe of being arrogant and controlling. But maybe he was simply taking care of her again. Her big, sweet protector with a heart of gold.

Her face softened as she called his name. Turning his head, his oddly brooding gaze sought hers. The impact was immediate, a shimmering feeling of awareness on so many levels. "Aren't you going to offer your take on this?" she asked.

His mouth flattened. "Cut him loose and he'll rabbit before the ink is dry on the probation agreement."

She took a careful breath. "The woman who...died, she wouldn't have let him plea bargain, would she?"

She saw the truth in the depths of his silvery green eyes. "This has to be your decision, Danni." His voice had a rough burr of understanding that warmed her heart. "There's some-

thing I want you to consider carefully before you make it however.''

"What's that?''

"If you reject this offer, and Folsom is released on bail, odds
are he'll try to shut you up before you can testify the way he
did Alice. The only way to protect you and Lyssa is to hide
you someplace where he can't get to you. It could mean weeks,
maybe months in seclusion.''

She felt a quick stab of fear. "I never thought of that,'' she
admitted in a strained voice.

Seth leaned forward to say, "Rafe's right, Doctor. Folsom
is as ruthless as they come.''

She turned her attention inward, to the small precious child
Folsom had given her. Could she really take the stand and
testify against her baby's father? More significantly, could she
put this child and Lyssa at risk for the sake of a principle? Out
of a sense of morality and justice that a goodly segment of
society considered outmoded?

It was time she stopped caring what others thought or wanted
or told her to think or want or do. It was time the Princess
stepped out of the fairy tale and into the real world. Her jaw
firmed, and a calm spread through her.

"No deal.'' She meant to look at the prosecutor when she
voiced her decision. Instead she found herself looking directly
into Rafe's beautiful eyes.

The flash of admiration she saw there was almost as comforting as a hug.

The hearing had been an anticlimax, a ritual repeated so
many times it seemed almost like a play performed by rote by
actors bored with their chosen roles.

On the other hand, Judge Paul Bonaventure exactly fit Danni's
idea of all a jurist should be. In his late forties or early fifties,
he had lean, aesthetic features dominated by an impressive Ro-
man nose and a resonant tenor voice. Seated at the bench which
offered both majesty to his office and a superior vantage point
from which to observe both participants and spectators, he'd
exerted total control, both emotionally and procedurally.

Even Tandy lost some of his studied flamboyance. Or perhaps he'd feared the judge's reaction. Given Judge Bonaventure's austere countenance and no-nonsense demeanor, she doubted he tolerated histrionics in his courtroom.

In what seemed like a dry-stick caricature, both counsels played the expected parts after which the judge set bail at five hundred thousand dollars. After much consulting of schedules, the trial was set for the first week in August. Tandy had asked for an additional month, but Ms. Hall-Jones had cited Danni's advancing pregnancy as an argument against delay. The judge had ruled in her favor.

Unable to come up with the ten percent required by the bail bondsman, Jonathan had been taken back to county jail. Before he'd been shackled and led away, however, he'd given her a long searching look, his eyes full of bewildered hurt. *I love you,* he'd mouthed before the marshal had prodded him to move along. She'd nearly been sick.

It had been a masterful performance, however, one the prosecutor had noted with some alarm. After arranging a date for the middle of June to go over Danni's testimony, Ms. Hall-Jones had departed in a burst of energy and verve, leaving behind a lingering hint of electricity and Opium perfume.

Now, nearly an hour later, Rafe and Danni sat in her favorite corner by the window in a family owned café near her office, having lunch. Seth had begged off, preferring a visit to Portland's famous Powell's Books which occupied a full city block in the heart of the downtown district.

It was still early, and the regulars had only begun to drift into Allegro's. Mama Allegro's eldest son, Tito, cooked on Fridays. Recently dumped by his girlfriend, he'd taken to playing vintage Billie Holliday through the superb speakers tucked unobtrusively in Mama's forest of prized lemon and pomegranate trees. Now and then Tito's voice singing along with the fabulous Billie could be heard drifting from the kitchen.

It was a great place to be on a sunny Friday afternoon.

Danni normally left feeling pampered and relaxed. Today, however, she was too wrung out to do more than pick at the chicken and avocado salad Rafe had pressed her to order.

"I wondered how I would feel when I saw him again," she admitted, poking at a cucumber slice with her fork. "I expected to feel anger, but for a moment, when I saw the chains and that horrible orange suit, I actually felt sorry for him."

Rafe had been wound tight most of the morning. He'd managed to keep most of his concentration on the proceedings, but a part of him had been actively observing Danni and her reactions. He'd been worried sick she wouldn't be able to handle the stress. With only a few wobbles here and there, she'd held solid. He'd made the mistake of thinking she'd finally seen Folsom for the scum he was.

It was raw fear he felt now, fear for what her soft heart might lead her to do. Fear that led him to use his voice like a razor to slice through those rosy illusions. "For a smart woman you can be incredibly naïve, Doctor," he taunted.

Even before he finished, her head shot up so fast her thick glossy mane swung wildly against her neck. Dark eyes snapped to his and seethed. "I beg your pardon," she grated through a tight jaw. A pulse hammered at the base of her creamy throat. It was the same spot where his lips had teased her into a low moaning sob less than twenty-four hours ago.

Wired as he was, it was an easy step from wanting to shake her into facing reality to simply wanting her. It clouded his mind, this need he had for her. It made him edgy and impatient and vulnerable. It made him push past tenderness to real anger.

"Letting yourself feel anything but disgust for a man like Folsom is just plain stupid, Daniela. Worse, it's like handing him a knife, then baring your throat to the blade."

Horror crossed her face before she drew it back. "I know that, Rafael. I was merely sharing my feelings with a friend." Her mouth took on a stubborn line. "A *friend* who is very lucky he isn't wearing my salad at this very moment."

He froze, his mind scrambling to take in the sudden glint of laughter in her eyes. "Hell," he muttered, feeling like an ass. He did his best to shore up his crumbling dignity with a scowl. It was about as effective as the cold shower he figured he'd be taking as soon as he got back to the motel.

Chapter 11

Seth was already in the room when Rafe returned a little past one, his carry-on bag open on the bed he'd used. It was nearly full, the contents shoved in so haphazardly Rafe actually winced. With eight people stacked into four rooms of a single wide trailer, neatness had been a must. It was a habit he'd never shaken.

"How about we grab some dinner in one of the seafood places by the river before we head to the airport?" he suggested as Rafe unclipped his weapon and dropped it onto his own bed.

"Sorry, partner, I'm having dinner with Daniela."

Seth's patrician brows shot up. "Damn, you work fast."

Rafe methodically emptied his pockets onto the built-in dresser. "If you call twenty years fast."

Seth tossed his sneakers into his bag. "No offense, but this morning at breakfast I got the distinct impression the daughter isn't your biggest fan."

"I'm working on that." He stripped off his suit coat and hung it up. "She was smitten with you, though," he said as he unbuttoned his cuffs. "Even laughed at your lousy jokes."

Seth took a jumble of underwear from the drawer and stuffed it into his bag. "Everyone laughs at my jokes, but you. Might make a man doubt himself, except everyone knows Rafe Cardoza doesn't have a sense of humor."

Surprised, and a little irritated. Rafe shot him a look. "Tell one that's funny instead of corny and I will."

The kid grinned. "Any idea how strong Fabrizio's gonna hold on testifying if Folsom reaches out to her?"

"She'll hold."

Looking thoughtful, Seth set the bag next to the door, then flopped like a loose-jointed puppet into one of the chairs. "Assume you arranged with Randolph to get a heads up if Folsom makes bail?"

Rafe pulled off his tie. "Yeah, but I'm thinking of staying over a few days."

"Probably be a good plan, yeah." Seth stretched his arms over his head and yawned. "Want me to stick around, too?"

"No, but keep yourself loose and your phone charged."

"So how's the party?" Danni asked when Lyssa called around seven.

Since the accident, Lys was obsessive about checking in often when she was away from home. It was reassuring to Danni as well.

"It hasn't really gotten started yet," Lyssa said, raising her voice to be heard over the rock and roll pounding in the background. "Only a couple of the girls have shown up so far."

"It's early." Danni clamped the phone between her shoulder and ear in order to insert the pearl teardrop into her other earlobe. The heirloom earrings had belonged to her mother's grandmother first, and then her mother. Now they were all she had left of the family pieces she'd cherished. She still had them only because she'd worn them on the plane to London.

"So what are you doing tonight?" Lyssa asked.

"Rafe invited me to dinner as a thank you for feeding him last night."

"He just wants to sleep with you! I could tell from the way he was looking at you."

A frantic guitar riff assaulted her eardrums, making her wince. "Lyssa, men often look at women that way. A strong sex drive is hardwired into them in order to perpetuate the species. It's nature's way. But wanting and doing are two different things."

"I don't like him," Lyssa said stubbornly. "And I don't want you to go out with him."

Danni bit off a sigh. "I absolutely respect your feelings, sweetie, but this is a decision for me to make alone."

"I knew it! You want to have sex with him, too, and I think it's disgusting!"

"My sex life is my business, Lyssa, and I don't intend to discuss it with you."

Danni heard what sounded like a sob before Lyssa hung up on her. She disconnected, then stood with the receiver in her hand, worrying her lip. Part of her thought she should call Lys back and talk this out immediately before it had a chance to fester. Another part knew that her daughter needed time to work things through. She was still waffling when the doorbell rang.

By the time she made it downstairs, she was as giddy as that starry-eyed girl who'd slipped out for a midnight adventure with a green-eyed charmer with magic in his smile and a body that made her mouth water.

It's just dinner with an old friend, Danni, she reminded herself firmly as she reached for the doorknob. She took a moment to smooth a nonexistent wrinkle from the loose fitting yellow silk chemise, part of the communal maternity wardrobe that had come to her by default after Liza's tummy had outgrown it. Then, with her armor firmly in place she pulled open the door.

"Right on time," she said briskly.

His grin flashed. "Two minutes early by my watch."

He had changed from his suit to tailored gray slacks and a pale blue Oxford cloth shirt with a button-down collar. His hair was clean and shiny and, as usual, any style had been left to chance.

She started to invite him in, then froze. He'd brought her

flowers, snowy white peonies in a nest of silvery lace. "Oh my," she said softly, staring helplessly at the shimmering blossoms.

He shifted, his jaw tightening. "Some guy on the corner had these for sale cheap," he said, all but shoving them into her hands.

Unable to resist she buried her face in the fluffy petals and breathed in a honeyed fragrance that made her senses swim. Her mother had planted peonies on the day she'd found out she was pregnant with her fourth child. The child that was Danni.

White peonies for the daughter she'd always longed for. With this same heavenly smell that wafted through the open windows in the summer. As a child she'd lain in bed and pretended it was her mother's perfume she smelled. Had she told Rafe that? She couldn't remember.

Slowly, she lifted a bemused gaze to his. The sensuous gleam in his silvery green eyes had those soft little ribbons of desire winding around her heart again. "You aren't by any chance trying to seduce me, are you, Agent Cardoza?" she challenged when her breath steadied.

"Absolutely." His lips curved into a lazy grin that had a sly little hook at one end. "How am I doing so far?"

It was the grin that kept her from grabbing him by the front of that starched blue shirt and hauling him inside. "I'll let you know after dessert."

Lifting a hand he touched one of the blossoms. "Sure you don't want to have dessert first?"

Feeling young and free and very sexy for the first time in months, she allowed herself a slow, sly smile of her own. "Not a chance, Agent," she declared, letting her voice go sultry. "I'm eating for two now, and baby has a yen for something sinfully rich and gooey tonight."

He sighed. "Guess I can hang on a little longer."

At least she wouldn't be a pushover this time, she told herself firmly as she challenged him with a look. "If I don't agree to go to bed with you, do I have to give these back?"

"Absolutely."

Laughter bubbled past the lump in her throat. "Aunt Gina was right—you are a bad influence on me."

"God, I hope so." Without waiting for an invitation he stepped over the threshold, forcing her to move backward. He closed the door and locked it before turning her way again.

"Do come in," she muttered, but her heart was already racing. She felt the heat of his body and a coiled kind of tension running through that lean powerful body. His skin carried the scent of a recent shower and the wind. Clean, honest scents, with no pretension.

Crowding her a little, yet careful not to crush the flowers she held like a shield against her breasts, he reached up to touch her mother's earring. "Funny, I've always pictured you in pearls," he murmured as he slid his hand along the curve of her jaw. Rough callused skin against soft and pampered. Excitement shivered through her. "Even that night by the pond, with your hair wild and your nails ripping my shoulders bloody, you never lost that regal look."

She frowned. "I never...I wouldn't *rip* you.

"Want to see my scars?" he challenged with a grin.

"I'll pass, thank you."

Grin fading, he settled his hands on her shoulders. "You marked me good that night in more ways than you know," he said in tight, angry tone that belied the heat in his eyes. "No other woman has ever made me burn the way you did."

Her mind stuttered. "Oh Rafe, I wish—"

The phone shrilled, drawing her quick startled gaze to the hall table where she'd put it before opening the door. "That might be Lyssa," she said before turning to answer it.

Frustration tightened his face. "I'll put these in water," he said, taking the flowers from her.

"There's a vase under the sink," she said as she picked up the phone. Before she could answer, he ducked his head and kissed her so fiercely her mind went blank.

"Hold that thought," he said with a cocky grin before heading for the kitchen.

She was smiling as she answered.

"Hello, love. Missing me, I hope?" It was the same resonant

purr that had whispered words of love in the darkness. Now the very sound sickened her.

Her breath hissed in. Her heart thudded painfully. "Don't call me that," she ordered sharply. "I'm not your love. I never was."

"Ah, you wound me deeply, darling Danni."

Her fingers clenched tighter around the portable receiver. "Believe me, I'd like nothing more."

His laughter was an obscene joke. "This is all a mistake, Daniela. I was in a financial bind and I was too embarrassed to tell you. But I swear I intended to pay you back every cent."

"Save your breath, Jonathan. Or should I say Jacob Folsom."

"I can explain—"

"Don't bother. I'm hanging up—"

"I put that brat in your belly, Daniela. Nothing you can do or say will change that."

She went cold. "Wrong. My baby was fathered by a man who never existed."

"Oh he exists, all right. Daniela," he declared in an oily tone that had her stomach roiling. Worse were the crude gutter words he used to describe their wedding night. Forcing her mind away from the ugly images, she drew a steadying breath.

"It's tempting to hate you, Folsom, but you're simply not worth the energy it would take."

His soft laughter was more chilling than the filthy words. "If it's a boy, I hope you'll name him Jacob after his father. Jacob Peter Folsom, Junior. Has a nice ring to it, don't you think?"

Rafe was stabbing the last stem into the vase when he heard her enter. Feeling like a kid showing off for his best girl, he turned to give her a good look at his handiwork.

It took him a full half second to realize she looked stunned. "Danni? Is it Lyssa?" he demanded, already moving.

"No, thank God. Not this time anyway." She drew a shaky breath and even managed a smile. "You'll never guess who that was," she said, her voice thin. "Or maybe you would, come to think of it."

He went still. "Folsom?"

She nodded. "I didn't realize prisoners could make calls."

Rage was a hard, twisting knot in his belly. "Fact of life, prisoners can do damn near anything they want."

Because she looked dangerously brittle, he kept his movements slow and easy as he took her in his arms and tucked her head beneath his chin. She made a soft little moaning sound as she settled against him, her arms tightening around his waist. He felt the rounded contours of her belly, the fullness of her breasts. The fear she was trying hard to master.

"Tell me what he said, Danni," he ordered when some of the rage settled. "Exactly what he said."

"He…he said he'd give me until tomorrow to withdraw the charges. Otherwise—" She broke off, her breath shuddering in and out as she fought to steady her voice. "Otherwise, he intends to sue for joint custody of both this baby and Lyssa."

He should have seen that coming. That he hadn't filled him with a sick shame. "It's an empty threat. Danni. He's just trying to spook you."

"He succeeded all right." She huffed out a humorless laugh. "You were right, Rafe. He's evil. Pure evil."

He was that and more. " He won't win, Danni. Not this time."

"But that's just it, the way things are now, the jurors might not believe I didn't sign that power of attorney. He's a masterful liar, and women just naturally gravitate to him. I saw it on the ship, the way they hung on every word. And if there are women on the jury, they might side with him over me."

"They'll believe you, honey. You have no reason to lie. And Hall-Jones is a tiger in kitten clothes. She'll fight for you with everything she has." Because he knew next to nothing about comforting a grown woman, he rubbed her back the way he'd done with the babies when they needed soothing.

"His voice was so…smug!" she burst out. "I could tell he was enjoying himself."

He kept his smile inside. "Be a shame if he found himself

thrown in a cell with a bunch of meat-eating bikers, wouldn't it?''

"Is that possible?" she asked in a little flurry of excitement. "I mean could someone actually arrange that? If he—or she—were so inclined?"

He was definitely inclined. "*Someone* could, yeah. If he didn't mind breaking a few rules." He pressed a kiss into her soft hair, the promises he'd wanted to make locked deep inside.

"Do you know anyone like that?"

"You want the list in alphabetical order?"

Choking a laugh, she drew back. "You're a menace, Rafe Cardoza."

He dug for the hell-raising grin that hid a multitude of feelings better left unnamed. "Bribe me with another of those soul kisses, Princess, and I'd fight the devil himself."

"It's tempting, but no."

Grin fading, he lowered his head slowly, his thick wheat-colored lashes flickering as his intense gaze roamed her face. "No to the kiss, or no to the bikers?"

She'd known his temper and his resentment and his sweetness. Suddenly she wanted his heat. The raw sexuality that seemed to pulse out of him with every breath. It was primitive, this need to explore those power sculpted muscles with her mouth and her hands. She burned to rub her breasts against his hard chest and feel his thigh rubbing against the hot ache between her legs. Most of all she wanted to watch his body swell and harden and know that he wanted her. She licked her lips, and his eyes grew dangerously turbulent.

"Time's up, Danni," he commanded hoarsely.

"Yes to the kiss," she whispered, tilting her head up. "Yes, yes, yes."

Chapter 12

With a heartfelt groan, he scooped her off her feet and into arms that were both possessive and steely.

"This is getting to be a habit," she grumbled, putting her arms around his neck.

He glanced down, his eyes crinkling. "Stop wiggling, or you'll end up on that sexy fanny."

Before she could answer, he lowered his head and kissed her until her senses scrambled. When he lifted his head again, she murmured a little protest that had his mouth slanting.

"Patience, honey. I've waited a long time for this. I'm not about to rush it."

"Promises, promises," she muttered, but she snuggled closer.

Why this man? she wondered, kissing his ear. What was there about him that made her feel wanton and free? Why did her body respond to his like tinder to flame?

Her mind could cite dozens of reasons why a relationship would never work. Logical, practical reasons. He was tough and cynical and driven by God only knew how many demons.

She cried at camera commercials and felt sorry for criminals, even though she knew better.

As soon as he touched her, none of that mattered. She wanted him desperately. Tomorrow she would deal with the emotional blow-back. Tonight she wanted to be a woman instead of a lady. To feel all that raw power inside him slam into her. To feel his body shudder helplessly beneath her hands. Closing her eyes, she drew in the soapy scent of his skin and felt her body sigh with a longing she could no longer fight.

When they reached the bedroom he let her slide down his body slowly, shuddering when her belly rubbed against his engorged groin. "Don't move," he grated, holding her tight against him. His muscles were hard and straining as he waited out the punishing urge to take her with one fast, deep thrust.

Her fingers kneaded his back impatiently. Her breath was moist and hot against his chest, wetting the shirt he'd bought after tracking down those damn flowers she'd always been crazy about. He'd felt like an ass, carrying those fluffy things around, but damn, the starry-eyed look on her face had been worth it.

He closed his eyes and distracted himself with images of his body plunging into a deep dark pool filled with ice water. Gradually his heart stopped its frantic hammering and the searing pressure eased. When he was in control again, he loosened his hold and drew back. Her lashes fluttered open, and her lips parted as she sighed his name.

He had no words, only needs so desperate, so deeply felt they bordered on savage. "I lived in hell for years wishing I'd taken what you offered that night, Princess," he admitted, his voice rough with feelings he only half understood. "You have a hook in me. I don't like it, but I can't seem to shake free."

Her lips curved. "I've thought about this moment for years," she murmured. "Even when I was married to Mark, I wondered if it would be different with you."

Conflicting emotions pulled at him. He didn't want to think of her with Mark. He didn't want to think of what might have been. This was what mattered now. This prowling need to thrust into her, deep and hard, until she felt only him. Knew only him.

"It's been a long wait, Princess," he murmured an instant before bringing his mouth down on hers.

It was exactly what she wanted, his mouth hot and desperate on hers, his hands tangled in her hair as he made her head spin and her body burn. His mouth, so hard when he was angry, so hungry now, branded her with one drugging kiss after another.

Her breath hitched as he slid his mouth to the spot behind her ear. Sensations rained through her, slow rippling needs and sweet shimmers of heat. Too needy to wait, she tugged at his shirt, ripping it free of his trousers. A desperate moan broke from her throat as she fumbled with his belt buckle. When it slipped free, he covered her hand with his.

"I'm not getting naked alone," he said, his gaze skimming down to her breasts. Instantly heat spread over the swollen fullness, searing her skin and puckering her nipples.

Excitement raced through her bloodstream like her father's best vintage. "According to Emily Post, guests always go first," she managed, her voice thickened with so many needs, so many longings.

His gaze narrowed. A faint sheen of sweat covered his brow. Beneath the soft fabric of his trousers, his body was still heavily engorged and rigid. "No way. Not until I see some skin."

She was suddenly terrified. "I'm not sixteen any longer," she said, trying for a light touch.

His eyes grew dark and intense. "Ah, honey, if you're worried I'll be disappointed, I have to tell you there's no way that can happen."

She felt his gaze burning into her as she fumbled to unbutton the front of the chemise. It fell open, revealing her plain cotton nursing bra. As she stepped out of the dress, she felt her body tremble.

"So beautiful," he whispered, his eyes glowing. His hands shook as he slipped his fingers beneath the straps, sliding them over her shoulders. His hands were rough, rasping over her skin. Sensations shivered and built beneath the surface as he kissed her shoulder, then slid his mouth lower. Moisture pooled between her thighs as a restless heat built. Whimpering, she reached for his zipper.

Her fingers brushed his rigid flesh and he jerked. His fly fell open and his body surged free. He was thick and large, hard and rigid beneath softest velvet.

Inside her needs were building, like a restless pressure spreading like ripples outward from her womb. Her skin was hot and itchy, and her breasts felt swollen.

Her mouth went dry as she closed her fingers around the length of him. With a low, guttural moan that seemed to come from some deep and dark place inside, he hurriedly unhooked her bra and her breasts spilled free.

"Heaven help me," he whispered reverently as he filled his palms.

Slowly he bent to swirl his tongue over an aching nipple. Her womb contracted, and her body yearned to feel him inside her. Muscles rippled beneath her skin.

"Now," she whispered through a tightening throat. "Please, Rafe, make love to me now."

He moaned, then kissed her hard before quickly stripping. He jerked back the covers while she stepped out of her panties.

"Come here, sweetheart. Let me love you."

He drew her down onto the pale sheets and covered her with his body. Eagerly, she parted her legs. He skimmed his hands over her belly, her thighs, trailing his fingers over the tender flesh, finding moist heat.

She gloried in each touch, each sensation, her mind splintering, her body responding of its own accord. It felt so good, the solid weight of his big chest against her breasts, the press of hard thighs, the heat pouring from his skin, searing hers.

His body straining, his skin burning, he thrust one finger into her. He groaned when he found her wet. Lost, he slid his hands beneath her buttocks and lifted her. He thrust into her slowly, feeling the hot moist passage expand to accept him.

She shuddered, her breath sighing out. Hands fisted in the sheets, she tossed her head side to side, her desperate cries of pleasure driving him toward the brink. He gritted his teeth, struggling to hold back.

"More," she demanded desperately. "Harder. Let me feel you."

He thrust faster, and felt her tremble. She licked her lips, her face tense, her brow pleated from a desperate need. "Let it go, sweet," he grated as his body begged for release.

Just when he thought he couldn't hold off any longer, she shattered, her breath escaping in a low keening cry that drove him over the edge. His mind splintered into a thousand colors as pleasure crashed through him. She let out a helpless little sob, and then she was shuddering again.

Still buried deep inside her, he eased down next to her and pulled her against him. Sated and drowsy, he brushed her hair away from her heated face, then kissed her gently. The need to cherish her was strong inside him, and his throat was suddenly thick with words he couldn't say, promises he couldn't make.

He kissed her again, with tenderness this time and something that felt like sadness. Her lips curved in a drowsy smile.

"I was right," she murmured. "You really are formidable."

He laughed, then drew the sheet over their sweat-damp bodies before cuddling her close. She let out a little sigh of pleasure and kissed his shoulder before her lashes fluttered down.

Closing his eyes, he stroked her arm with lazy fingers until her breathing slowed, then evened. Only then did he let himself sleep.

He woke her with a kiss flavored with coffee. She opened her eyes to a lovely lethargy—and the sight of a well-built, gloriously naked man setting a tray on the night table.

"What's that?" she asked, feeling a little shy now.

"Dinner." He handed her a neatly folded cloth napkin that he'd obviously taken from the drawer in the kitchen. "Mama's version of a Spanish omelet." His grin was a little crooked. "Without the peppers. You must have run out."

She laughed. "Baby doesn't like them."

His gaze flickered to the small mound beneath the sheet, and something infinitely sweet flashed between them before he sat down next to her. He'd turned on the bedside lamp and his skin seemed to glow like burnished bronze. Because she could, she laid her hand on his thigh and felt the muscle contract. In the past she'd always felt the need to shower after making love. But now, somehow, the lingering scent of musk seemed absolutely right.

Sex in nature was raw and sweaty and messy. And sometimes violent, she thought as she ran her tongue over the inside of her swollen lips.

"What time is it?" she asked because he was between her and her clock.

"Nearly ten."

"It's a good forty minutes from here to the airport," she reminded him with a pang of regret. "If you don't leave soon, you'll miss your flight."

"I'll catch another one."

She smiled. "Obviously a man who sets his own schedule."

"When it's appropriate." He smoothed her hair away from her shoulder, then bent to kiss it. "Are you okay?" he asked as he lifted his head.

She smiled drowsily as she played with the hair on his chest. "Very okay."

"Sore?" He curled his free hand over her hip.

"A little," she admitted, turning her attention inward. It was a sweetly intimate ache, she realized. An affirmation that for a time they'd been as close as a man and woman can get. Now only the possessive weight of his hand connected them. She mourned a little.

"How about you?" she asked as she ran her gaze over the hard contours of his chest.

His mouth softened. "Honey, if I felt any better, I'd be wearing angel wings." He looked so proud of himself she burst out laughing.

"More like devil's horns," she said, adoring him with her eyes. "But such a handsome devil."

His grin flashed, replacing the deep gouged lines bracketing his mouth with a rogue's dimples. But it was the tender light in his eyes that had her heart fluttering.

"Since we've already had dessert, how about an appetizer before dinner?" he suggested, his voice dipping into a musical drawl.

Her body quickened, and suddenly her body was no longer sore. "Depends on the appetizer," she murmured, but his mouth was already slanting over hers.

They finally ate the reheated omelet around eleven, then showered together, playing in the water like a couple of kids. She'd forgotten that he was ticklish and did her best to torment him. He retaliated by backing her up against the slick tile and kissing her until her legs were shaky and she was forced to cling to him to keep from sliding down into a little puddle of pleasure at his feet.

Accepting her surrender with a cocky grin that wound down inside her like a heartfelt moan of pleasure, he soaped every inch of her, his hands slow and thorough and very skilled. She reciprocated, eager to touch and explore each sinew-roped muscle and solid plane. His skin was slick and hot, roughened in spots by golden hair, his buttocks hard, his belly ridged.

To her surprise—and definitely his, he admitted with a crooked grin—he ended up fully aroused again. It had been both hilarious and wildly erotic as he hoisted her there in the shower, with the water beating down, and her legs locked awkwardly around his waist.

Afterward, both still a little dazed, they dried each other off. While she dried her hair, he took the dishes back to the kitchen.

When she emerged from the bathroom wearing only her robe and a splash of her Chanel No. 5, he was already in bed with the sheet drawn to his waist, his knees drawn up, his back propped against the lacy pillows. His chest was bare, his hair tousled, his eyes a little sleepy.

A well-worn duffel bag sat on the floor near the closet door. He hadn't asked to stay. She hadn't invited him. Like their friendship it was simply assumed.

His eyes heated as she slipped out of the robe and tossed it onto the foot of the bed. "What time is Lyssa due home tomorrow morning?" he asked, lifting the sheet so that she could climb in next to him.

"Noonish," she said arranging the remaining pillows against the headboard before settling in next to him.

It seemed completely right, somehow, to snuggle up next to that strong, warm chest and feel his arms close protectively around her. "She and Jody have a kick-boxing class at ten," she explained, slipping her thigh over his. Beneath her ear she could hear his heart. "Jody's mom offered to drop her off after."

"Kick boxing?" He sounded incredulous. "A little thing like Lyssa?"

"Mmm. Her physical therapist thought it would help with her coordination and strength. Turns out she's a natural. Her instructor's absolutely convinced she was a ninja assassin in a previous life."

He chuckled. "Way she looks at me, I can believe it."

Danni yawned. She felt as though her insides had melted, so content was she. "It's not you personally. She'd look that way at any man she thought was interested in me."

"Damn, and I thought I was being subtle."

She laughed. "Oh you were. Especially that night in the kitchen."

"Yeah, well, I might have slipped up a time or two." He stroked her back, his movements slow and lazy. His face was more relaxed than she'd ever seen it. "You're heady stuff, lady."

"So are you." She sighed. "I swore I was going to live the life of a nun from now on."

She ran her fingers through the soft golden hair covering his pectoral muscles. Half-hidden was a rough puckered line where his chest had been sliced open. Her fingers lightly traced its length and he stiffened.

"Does that hurt?" she asked apologetically.

He captured her hand and kissed it. "No, but it's still sensitive."

"What happened?"

His face closed up. "I made a mistake."

"You were shot?"

He nodded. "The same man who got Alice MacGregor tried his best to take me out, too."

Hiding her shock, she raised up far enough to press her lips against the obscene scar. "I'm sorry."

The tension came from deep inside him, tightening his muscles and turning his jaw white. "Alice MacGregor would still be alive if I hadn't screwed up." Though quiet, his voice had an edge of self-contempt that was painful to hear.

"You're convinced it was Folsom, aren't you? The person who shot you?" Even as she said the words, images formed of this strong chest spurting blood as bullets slammed into him. Fear was a chilled blade in her own heart. Fear for him. Fear for her and Lyssa and for the baby.

He curled his fingers around her hand and tucked it against the scar that would always remind him of the price Alice paid for his lapse of attention.

"Maybe Folsom pulled the trigger, maybe he didn't. But Alice died because I made the mistake of thinking that just because I gave her an order she would follow it."

"What order was that?"

He hated talking about that morning. Hated even to think about it. So many times in the hospital he'd gone over and over every detail, every move, every decision. It still shook out the same. Despite his training, despite his experience, he'd let his emotions cloud his judgment. His guilt was like a constant ache deep in his gut. It sometimes faded, but it never quite went away.

"First day we were in the safe house, I laid down the rules. The curtains stayed drawn. The doors stayed locked. I made sure she didn't have her cell phone. If the doorbell rang, she was to ignore it. Even if she was sure it was one of us, she wasn't to go near the door. I explained why. I asked if she understood. Yes, she said. Of course she understood. Even got prickly about it." He felt his throat getting painfully tight. He'd told his story so many times it had started to feel like begging for forgiveness.

"What happened?"

What happened, Rafe? Damn it, we had it covered. How did he get to her?

How? Too damn easily.

Like a video on slow motion that morning played out in his head. The splash of sunshine on the worn kitchen counter as he diced peppers, the radio playing drive-time rock, the smell of brewing coffee.

The shrill sound of the doorbell.

The split second delay when he went from thinking that Seth was ten minutes early to raw terror. He'd got to her too late.

Sorrow exploded like shrapnel inside his chest.

"One morning, while I was in the kitchen making breakfast, she opened the door and died."

His voice was so terribly controlled. But there was so much he wasn't saying. So much he needed to say in order to heal. Because the wound was still raw. God knew, she'd heard enough terrible stories to sense the effort he was making to keep it all shoved down inside.

Helping people heal was as much a part of who she was as his badge and that awful gun were a part of him. But there was more to Rafe than a man doing a dangerous job. So much more.

The sensitive boy who'd soothed her tears and talked his mother into mending a beloved doll was still inside that powerful man's body. A man capable of holding her head while she retched and waking her every few hours to make her swallow the medication that would lower her temperature and soothe her aches, then bully her into drinking foul-tasting liquid because Luke said she needed it.

"Rafe, you can't blame yourself if she disobeyed your orders. Yes, it was tragic and a waste and all the things people say and feel when an innocent person is killed for no good reason. But she has to bear some responsibility for what happened to her."

His anger flashed, a whiplash cutting toward her. "Spare me the shrink talk, okay? I've heard it all before."

"But you didn't listen, did you?"

"It was my fault, damn it! Alice was scared and lonely. We

talked about books, movies, played gin. Things you do to pass the time. I knew she was starting to feel things for me she shouldn't, and I knew I had to put some distance between us. I asked for relief, but half the available agents were out with the flu. I could have pulled rank, but I figured I could deal with it for a few more days. Then the night before…'' His jaw turned to stone and he closed his eyes. "I waited one day too long."

Danni felt herself go pale. "You slept with her?"

His gaze seared her. "No, damn it! I didn't sleep with her. I explained…tried to, anyway, that what she was feeling wasn't love but gratitude." Anger draining, he raked his hand through his hair, his expression tortured. "Have you ever heard of the Stockholm Syndrome?"

Of course, now she understood, she thought, nodding. "The growing identification of a hostage with his or her captor. Like Patty Hearst and the SLA. Often those feelings are mistaken by the hostage as love. It's often the same with patient and therapist. I've had to refer patients out a time or two myself."

He took a ragged breath. "Even though she was a bright woman, Alice wouldn't listen. She was so sure what she was feeling was real. Nothing I could say changed her mind. That night, after I, uh, turned down the offer she made me, she cried herself to sleep."

Alice was a good woman. A decent woman who loved kids. She'd trusted him and he'd let her down. He'd thought long and hard about turning in his badge. Maybe when Folsom was locked in a cage, he still would. Until then, he needed the authority the job gave him to make sure the bastard paid.

"I'm sorry, Rafe," Danni said softly, laying her hand against that tight jaw. Her voice was gentle when he wanted it to be harsh and accusing. He wanted to lash out the way he'd lashed out at the agency shrink and damn near everyone else who'd tried to absolve him.

"Danni—"

"No, don't close me out, please, Rafe. I know it's a cliché but it's also true that no one is perfect." Her lips curved into a rueful smile. "Lord knows I've proven that in spades recently. Maybe, if I didn't have Lyssa and this new little one to think about, I'd let myself wallow in guilt and regret, but I don't have that luxury. So I had to find a way to forgive myself. You can do the same.''

He felt the gentle barb bite deep. ''You don't pull your punches, do you lady?''

Her eyes pleaded with him and emotion seemed to shimmer from her. ''Not when I care as much as I care about you.''

Caring he could handle. Caring he could return. And did, he realized with a depth that came as close to love as his cynical heart could manage.

He took a breath and then because his chest was tight, took another. Because he needed to touch her, he ran his fingers through her hair and the springy curls caught on calluses rubbed deep in his palms by the work he'd done for her father. She leaned into his hand, and he cupped her cheek.

''If Folsom makes bail, promise me you'll accept protection for you and Lyssa,'' he said gruffly.

He saw the refusal flicker into her eyes, saw her banish it. ''Protection, yes,'' she said quietly. ''But I have to make a living, Rafe. I can't go off and live in seclusion for two months.''

It was enough for now. If it became necessary, he'd find a way to convince her, even if he had to enlist the help of her father and that brother of hers. Hell, he'd hog-tie her and throw her over his shoulder and haul her off to a cave if he had to.

''If you're finished wearing me out, Wonder Woman, how about we get some sleep?''

Chapter 13

It was dawn when he woke to find himself fully aroused and wanting her. It surprised him some to realize he'd slept deeply, without the usual tangled dreams. He told himself it was because she'd worn him out.

She was still asleep, curled against him, one hand relaxed on his chest. Her hair was tickling his chin, and each little breath warmed his neck. Her breasts were pressed against him, full and soft, and her scent was in his head, something classy suited for a princess. There was a hint of musk on her skin now, an earthy scent than ran just below a man's consciousness.

It made him smile to remember how the elegant Dr. Fabrizio had shattered under his touch. And yeah, maybe it made him feel a little smug.

He didn't consider himself a stud like Gresham, but a man didn't get to be nearly forty without having some memorable moments. Last night, when she'd come apart, he'd felt invincible. With his sweat shining on her skin and her lips swollen and rosy from his, she'd been his Danni, the girl who held his heart.

It was tempting to think they could go back to those feelings. The innocent trust they'd shared. The uncomplicated friendship. He'd told her things no one else knew. How he planned to go to college so he could get a good job and buy his family a nice house. How he wanted to be married forever like his folks and have at least six kids of his own. Kids with his blood. A connection to the future because he had no past.

The little hoyden who'd rarely sat still longer than it took to tie her sneakers or wolf down a fast meal had sat quietly next to him on the riverbank, a fishing pole in her hand, listening to him for hours. Not just with her ears but her heart, the way she'd listened last night.

Linc, Seth, others had damn near begged him for months to get past that bloody morning. He'd blocked them out. With her big brown eyes full of compassion and a steely determination to rival his own, Danni had slipped past the land mines in his head to plant a seed. Like a cool hand on a hot forehead she'd soothed him somehow.

The guilt was still there, but a lot of the sharp edges had been blunted. He was a long way from forgiving himself, but the tenacious little mule had jolted him into opening the door. Might even have given him a start on the peace he craved.

Several times he'd awakened when she'd left him to pad into the bathroom. She'd been half-asleep when she stumbled back to bed. She'd snuggled close, then kissed his shoulder, patted his chest as though to comfort him and then ordered him to go back to sleep. It had given him a glimpse of what it must be like to be someone's husband. No, not someone's husband. Danni's.

A familiar feeling of loss ran through him.

Whatever they had now was a mix of leftover feelings and sexual attraction. He wanted her the moment he'd seen her struggling with those grocery sacks with her face damp with the rain and her big eyes sparking outrage.

He'd fought it. But he hadn't been able to get past the fact that she made him feel things he'd denied for years. Want things he'd learned to live without. Just being around her made him edgy in his soul, and it wasn't a comfortable feeling.

In fact, it bordered on desperation, the kind that made a man want to pound his fists against something hard until they were bloody and raw and hurt so much he couldn't feel anything else but the ache.

A few days, a week, whatever time he could justify was all they had. All they would ever have. It wasn't what he would have chosen, but he'd learned to play the hand he'd been given. A man who lived one wrong move from death learned to live in the moment.

Right now, this moment, making love to Danni was what mattered, he thought as he brushed his lips across hers. She stirred, then smiled. Her lashes fluttered, but remained closed.

"I was dreaming about you," she murmured, her voice slurred. A wave of tenderness crashed through him. He wouldn't think about the other men who'd had the right to kiss her awake. Or of the baby in her womb.

The baby he'd once longed to put there twenty years ago, even as he'd fought not to plunge through her maidenhead. He would only think of now and the magic they made together in this bed.

"What were you dreaming, honey?" he asked, his voice thick with feelings he didn't dare acknowledge.

"Hmm." Her fingers toyed with his chest hair, raking over his skin. His muscles contracted helplessly, and her lips curved in pure female satisfaction. "We were at the pond and you were trying to leave me again."

"Couldn't be me, honey. I learn slow but I do learn."

"So do I," she said in a purring voice that shivered through him.

"Is that right?"

"Hmm." She ran her hand down his body, her fingers trailing fire. He fought to keep the groan inside, but when her fingers curled around his engorged body and squeezed, his breath exploded in a harsh cry.

"I'm not leaving this time, not this time," he vowed as he rolled her onto her back.

But he would, Danni thought as his mouth crashed down on hers. And she would have to let him go. Again.

* * *

Two hours later, Danni sat at the kitchen table in a pool of sunshine, enjoying her second cup of raspberry tea. Rafe was loading the dishwasher, the muscles of his long, lean back stretching and contracting in a fluid, efficient rhythm. It could have been a ballet, or perhaps a martial arts exercise, so perfectly coordinated were his movements.

There was nothing more adorable than a steely-eyed cop doing dishes with a towel tucked into the low slung waistband of his jeans and his thick sun-bleached hair disheveled, she decided, her heart doing a slow sweet roll.

Suddenly, his gaze swung her way. It was unsettling, the rush of giddy excitement running through her as his hard mouth slanted into a slow, supremely smug grin. It irritated her no end that he knew exactly how he affected her. He'd always known.

"Finished with that mug, honey?" he asked, his gaze brushing over the mug in her hand to rest on her breasts. She felt the impact of those green eyes all the way to her womb. It unsettled her to realize she was in real danger of falling in love with him again. Or perhaps she already had.

So far she had managed to keep herself from examining her feelings too closely for fear of what she would find. Afraid her thoughts would show on her face, she dropped her gaze to the mug. It was all but empty. Perversely, she tightened her grip. "No, actually I'm not," she declared in a little burst of defiance.

Rafe heard the lick of irritation in her voice and was pleased. Danni was a strong woman. She'd suffered a blow that had all but destroyed other victims in her situation, but she'd managed to hold on to her sweetness. And her compassion. If she was glaring at him, it was a good bet she was on the mend.

To punish her a little for getting to him in ways that no other woman ever had, he skimmed his gaze down the length of that curvy little body, taking time to enjoy the elegant line of her throat, the hint of cleavage where the lapels of her honey colored shirt met in a deep vee. When his gaze skimmed the ripe little belly, his heart bled a little.

"You have any plans for today?" he asked as he measured soap into the receptacles on the door.

"Yes, three loads of laundry, followed by a rousing game of Russian roulette with my bills."

The proud jut of her chin warned him not to offer sympathy. Instead he offered an alternative. "How about playing hooky and going to the coast for a picnic after Lyssa gets home?"

He saw her hesitation and sweetened the pot. "We both could use some downtime, Princess. A couple of hours to stuff ourselves with junk food and bake in the sun."

A wistful look crossed her face. "God, that sounds wonderful, but—"

"But what?"

"It's just that the beach might not be the best idea. Lys is still self-conscious about her scars."

"She shouldn't be. They're hardly noticeable."

"To Lys they are. I suspect they're all she sees when she looks in the mirror." She smiled. "These days I tend to obsess about other women's waistlines. One or two times I've even glared at a particularly skinny specimen."

She would, he thought, resisting a smile as he closed up the dishwasher and set the dial. Over the sudden rumble of the water, he tugged the towel from his waistband and wiped the counter before returning the towel to the rack. "I like your little tummy, Princess," he said, letting his gaze linger there. "It's curvy, just like the rest of you."

Surprise shone for an instant in her eyes. "If you're trying to get on my good side, it's working, darn it," she said in glum tone.

He figured it was safe to laugh now, and did as he poured the last of the coffee into his mug, then switched off the coffeemaker. "I assume she's had reconstructive surgery?" he said before taking a sip.

"Several times. The surgeon thinks one or two more operations will complete the process." She drained her mug before carrying it to the sink. He took it from her, opened the dishwasher and tucked it inside before buttoning everything up again.

"Sounds like it's been rough," he said as he restarted the machine.

"The first year after Mark's death was sheer hell." Shadows chased through her eyes. "Lyssa is a gutsy kid though. Sometimes I think she supported me more than I supported her."

"I suspect you supported each other." And the pain of watching her child suffer was still raw inside, he thought as he pulled his watch from his pocket and strapped it on.

"I'm trying to decide if I should let her attend the trial."

He glanced her way. "You know that as a witness, you won't be able to be with her if she does attend, don't you?"

"Yes, Ms. Hall-Jones explained the process. But my father will insist on being there and probably my brothers. Lys will be safe with them. They're even more protective of her than they were of me."

"I doubt it." The sardonic edge to his voice had her glancing up. His face had gone hard, and the lazy glint was gone from his eyes.

She hesitated, then decided he would never be more receptive than now. "Rafe, instead of going to the coast, let's go down to the vineyard."

"No, Danni."

"You're their son, and they still love you, I know they do."

His mouth turned cynical. She hated it, she realized. The Rafe she knew was sweet and loving and kind. "Yeah? Just how do you know that?"

"Because I'm a mother. I know how I would feel."

"Lyssa carries your blood. My mother was a teenage slut who threw me away and never looked back."

"Your mother is the woman who nursed you from her own breast and rocked you back to sleep when you had bad dreams and saved pennies so that you could go to college."

He frowned. "What are you talking about?"

"Rosaria's dream jar. She kept it on the top shelf of the pantry. I saw her putting money in it once, and she told me that was the reason she sold her salsa at the crafts fair every spring, to fill up the jar so you could go to college."

He didn't believe her, she realized. But he wanted to. She let him see the truth in her smile. "She loved all her children, she said. But you were her answered prayer. Her gift from God.

She wanted to give you everything you wanted." She rested her hands on his chest. "She's getting older, Rafe. She misses you. It would mean so much to her to see you."

His jaw tightened. "I'll think about it."

She knew the buttons to push. His love for his mother, his strong sense of gratitude, his deep vein of honor. She could push and he might listen. In her heart she knew he wanted to go home. But it had to be his decision. She'd manipulated his emotions once before and everyone had suffered. So this time she would let him make his own decisions.

Still, it wouldn't hurt to give him a few nudges here and there. "Okay, no coast, no vineyard," she teased as she touched the scar at one corner of his mouth. "I know someone who could lend us some rods and tackle. If I promise not to hook you again, will you take us fishing?"

Lyssa had been less than enthusiastic—until Danni had suggested she invite Jody to come along. The place Luke recommended was on a bend of the Willamette, about twenty miles outside the city. Though secluded enough for privacy, it was close enough to the parking area to make for an easy walk.

It was a beautiful spot, surrounded by lush vegetation and towering trees. Sweet William and blackberry vines grew in wild profusion along the narrow path, and the air was alive with the sound of bees.

Deliciously warm now after the morning chill, the air was flavored with the mingled scents of rain-washed leaves and wind. Overhead, the sun was butter-cup yellow, lazily slipping in and out of meandering clouds the texture of cotton candy.

They'd eaten first—fried chicken and potato salad and iced lemon bars Rafe had picked up at a deli near his motel. Outgoing and bubbly, Jody had been immediately smitten with Rafe, which had irritated Lyssa no end.

While Lys sulked, Danni had listened in rapt attention as Jody managed to find out that Rafe had started his career guarding President Reagan and had even ridden with him at his ranch. He'd just finished his two years on the protection detail a few days before the former president had been shot. The frustration that crossed his face had touched Danni deeply. He cared, she realized. And he took his responsibilities very seriously.

Now, as the sun started its downward slide toward afternoon, the girls were wading in the shallows along the shore, skipping rocks toward the other side while she lay curled on her side, watching Rafe fitting Luke's fly rod together.

Looking large and enticingly male, he wore a khaki muscle shirt and running shorts. Every time he shifted position, the hard muscles of his thighs flexed and contracted, sending little ripples of reaction through her. Her body was definitely telling her what it wanted. At the moment she was trying very hard not to listen. To occupy her hands, she opened the container of cookies.

"Want one?" she asked when his gaze flickered her way.

"Just a bite." He leaned forward and opened his mouth, his eyes suddenly dark and questioning on hers.

She broke off a piece and brought it to his lips. His hand captured her wrist as she started to withdraw. With his gaze still on hers, he licked a smear of icing from her index finger, his tongue hot and rough against her skin.

"Thanks," he said, releasing her.

"You're welcome," she replied politely, her stomach doing slow rolls beneath her floppy maternity T-shirt. His eyes told her he was feeling the same frustration. She forced herself to look away.

"Okay, let's catch us some fish," he said, rising to walk barefoot over the sand into the water. "Lyssa, how about you go first."

"I don't want to," she replied sullenly.

Jody looked at her curiously. "Don't be a dweeb, Lys. It's fun. My grandpa taught me ages ago."

Lyssa flicked Rafe an unfriendly look. "Fish are yucky."

"That's what your mom said," Rafe told her with grin. "Until she decided she was going to catch a bigger fish than me."

"I did, too," Danni told Lys smugly. "He was *not* happy."

Lyssa looked torn. Finally she shrugged. "Whatever," she grumbled, but she moved toward Rafe instead of the shore.

"Careful, the rocks are slippery," he said, holding out a hand. Lyssa hesitated, then put her hand in his. When the water was nearly to her knees, he stopped. "See that dark patch of blue just past midstream? I have a hunch that's where the wily ones hang out."

"Just don't expect too much, okay?" Lys grumbled but Danni heard a hint of excitement in her tone.

"Okay." He slipped behind her, his arms coming around hers. His voice was patient as he coached her through her first attempt.

Danni remembered how it had been for her. The warmth of the sun on her back, the feeling of his strong chest against her back, the rumble of his voice against her ear. Back and forth, feel the snap in the wrist, put the fly upstream, then let it drift with the current.

"He's out there, *niña*, just skimming along the bottom, that lacy tail fluttering just a little, waiting for you to dip that pretty little fly right in front of his nose."

"I don't see anything," Lyssa whispered, her voice hushed.

"Keep lookin' at that patch of dark blue water. Let yourself become part of the river."

Panic tightened her features, making her scars stand out. "I can't do it," she protested.

"Sure you can. It just takes practice." Moving slowly, he slid his hand over hers, curving the thin rod in a wide arc to the right and behind. And then, suddenly, the line arced out. The fly hit the water, sending out circular ripples. Danni held her breath, and then suddenly the line pulled taut, bending the slender rod.

Sheer elation broke over Lyssa's face. "I feel it, Rafe!" she shouted. "We caught a fish!"

"Not me, *niña*. This guy's all yours," he praised. His grin proud as a doting father's, he helped her land the prettiest steelhead Danni had ever seen.

It was just past 4:00 p.m. when Jake Folsom walked through the door to freedom. The clothes he'd put on when Cardoza had arrested him were stiff with sweat and wrinkled after being stuffed in a bag in the jail property room.

They hadn't let him shower since yesterday morning, and the disposable razor they'd given him had chewed up his face. First thing when he hit the street he'd buy decent threads, then scrub the scum off his skin in a hot shower. He hated feeling like he'd slept in a pile of garbage. He'd done enough of that as a kid.

A blinding glaze of red covered his eyes as the memories of the she-bitch whore who'd made his life hell pulsed through him. He'd been five the first time she'd locked him out overnight. He'd been fifteen the last time she'd tried it. He'd used her own butcher knife on her. Gutted her like the stinking fat pig. Squealed like one, too, she had.

It still got him high, just thinking about it. A smile creased his tired face as he nodded at the guard at the desk who merely looked bored. In the crowded waiting area near the rear entrance Arlene leaped up from the chair where she'd been waiting, and hurried toward him. He gave her the grateful smile she expected before gathering her into his arms. A lumpy sack of potatoes would have felt sexier.

"Oh baby, you feel so good," he lied into her mousy hair. "More than anything else, I hate involving you in this nightmare." He allowed himself to shudder in her arms and felt them tighten. Revulsion ran through him. Only a few more weeks, he reminded himself as he nuzzled his face against her neck. "If I could have spared you this, I would have, but there was no one else I trusted."

"It's so unfair, Jacob," she declared with what sounded like a sob in her voice. "There's definitely something wrong with our legal system when a respectable man like you can be arrested simply because you happen to resemble a criminal."

He drew back, then glanced around. "Let's get out of here, babe. I want to take a shower and then make love to you until I feel human again."

Tears flooded her pale blue eyes. "Our motel is only a few blocks from here. Mr. Tandy made a reservation for us in a hotel downtown, but you know me and those fancy places, so I asked him to find us a more modest place. It's not fancy, but the sheets were clean and it was only a third of the price. I hope you don't mind, sweetheart."

Feigning affection, he put his arm around her shoulders and

gave her a squeeze. "That's my girl, always so sensible. It's what I love best about you, Arly."

She slipped her arm around his waist. "Oh, Jake, I'm so happy that you came back to me." A shy smile crossed her pasty dumpling face. "I'm only half alive without you."

He thought about the Beretta tucked into one of his bags in the Bronco. He hadn't decided yet whether or not to kill her before he left for Canada.

Rafe was unlocking the door to his motel room when his beeper went off. It took him a moment to place the number. When he did, his blood iced.

Inside, he tossed the key onto the dresser with one hand and reached for the phone with the other. Face grim, he punched out the number, then ran his hand through his hair as he listened to the ringing on the other end. The oily smell of fish still clung to his fingers.

Lyssa had actually smiled at him a couple of times on the drive home. Chalk up one for his side. Not all that much in the scheme of things, but it was better than a slug in the gut.

"Randolph residence." Instead of the brusque baritone he expected the voice that came across the line was light and airy—and decidedly not male. "This is Chloe speaking."

He wondered which of the two copper-haired charmers in the picture on Randolph's desk she was. The one with the two missing front teeth, or the one who had her dad's grin? "Uh, is your daddy available, honey?"

"May I say who's calling, please?"

Randolph was one lucky man, he thought as he gave his name. His brows drew together as he tried not to think of the daughter he and Danni might have had together. He suspected she would have looked a lot like Lyssa. Might have had something of him, too, though that would have just been a sweet bonus. Just knowing she was a part of him would have been enough.

"Rafe?"

"Yeah. Something tells me I'm not heading back to D.C. any time soon."

"The wife put up the bond. Fifty thousand cash. I just got the word. He's been out about three hours."

The word Rafe used was foul.

"My sentiments exactly," Randolph said in a tight voice.

Rafe pulled out the chair and sat down to untie his sneakers. "Any idea where he is?"

"Not a clue. I put in a call to Felicia. As soon as she gets a local address from Tandy, I'll let you know."

"I'm a good twenty to thirty minutes from getting back to Danni's. Can you cover for me there until I can make it?"

"Already figured on it."

"Rafe, you darling man! Thank you so much for the birthday flowers! Lincoln was quite wonderfully jealous when they arrived."

Margie Slocum was by her own admission as plain as a mud hen on a bad day, with a boy's figure and a brilliant mind. She even wore thick glasses. Linc was crazy about her. Because he loved Linc like the big brother he never had, he couldn't help adoring the woman who had brought peace to Linc's tortured soul.

"Jealous enough to buy you that Jag you keep hinting about?" he teased as he rubbed a towel over his shower damp hair.

"Not yet but I did get a lovely lobster dinner and the cutest little black silk nightie. When are you coming back, darling? I'd love to show it to you."

"Over my dead body!" Linc growled in the background.

Margie giggled like a woman half her age. "Lord, but I love those testosterone surges."

Laughing, Rafe tossed the towel over the shower door, then tucked his cell phone against his shoulder in order to pull on his skivvies. "If the big guy's done nibbling on your neck, can I have a word with him?"

"For you, dearest Rafael, anything." He heard the smile in her voice and fought off a pang of envy. "You take care of yourself, okay?"

"Yes, ma'am." He heard something that sounded definitely X-rated before Linc's graveled voice boomed down the line.

"Find someone else to send those damn flowers to, Cardoza. Cost me a bundle saving my ass."

"About that black nightie—"

"Forget it, Ace," Linc said, laughing. But when he spoke again, his voice had turned serious. "I saw the flash about Folsom's arrest. Good work."

"Yeah well, he just made bail."

"Damn. What about the witness, what's her name?"

"Daniela Fabrizio. She doesn't know yet. I just found out. The local cop on the case happens to be her next door neighbor and he's sitting on her until I can get there."

"What kind of a set up does she have at her place?"

"Workable, but not ideal." After switching off the light, he walked out of the bathroom. "It'd be my preference to hole up in a safe house as far away from Portland as possible, but no way will she go for that."

"Have you given Gresham a heads up yet?"

"Not yet. I was hoping you could arrange for him to use one of the advance planes to get back here quick." Field agents only got priority on the Secret Service Gulfstreams when the protection types weren't using them to prepare for VIP trips.

"Should be doable. No major trips are scheduled by either the president or the vice president until July. Unless you hear different, he'll be there by morning."

"Thanks." He pulled on his Wrangler jeans, leaving the fly open as he sat to pull clean socks out of his duffel. "You want me to have him call you?"

"Might save time if I call him. Give me his cell phone number."

Rafe rattled it off, then added, "Ask him to stop by my place and pack a bag for me. Enough for a couple of weeks. Mrs. Peebles across the hall has my key. She knows him, so it shouldn't be a problem."

"Anything else?"

"We're going to need some extra firepower and backup from the local office. Guy in charge, Henderson, wasn't all that eager to offer assistance when we asked to borrow a vehicle. Seemed to think he should have gotten the call on this one."

"I'll take care of it." There was a pause before he added gruffly, "Rafe, do me a favor. Don't take any foolish chances, okay? Margie would never let me hear the end of it if I let anything happen to you."

"I'll do my best," he said before hanging up. Two minutes later he had his weapon on his hip, his duffel over his shoulder and was out the door.

Case Randolph and his feisty, copper-haired wife, Prudy, had been having tea with Danni in the living room when he'd arrived. Case had already told Danni about Folsom's release on bail.

It was clear that she was upset, but so far she was holding up amazingly well. Seated next to her mother on the sofa, Lyssa sat frozen, looking as though she couldn't quite understand what all the fuss was about.

It had been his decision to lay out the procedures for both of them at the same time. As he'd suspected, Danni had refused to let him move the two of them to a safe house. To his immense relief it was the only protest she'd made.

"Seth and I will move in here." He caught Lyssa's startled look and grinned. "I figure he can take one of the bunks in the boys' room."

He felt Danni's gaze and meshed his gaze with hers. "Which bunk will you take, the upper or lower?" she teased, her eyes skimming down his body. He felt his skin growing hot.

"I plan on bunking down on the sofa in the den."

Lips still slightly swollen from his kisses curved, but she remained silent.

"At night there'll be one of our guys sitting out front, another in the alley in the back. A tech crew will be here tomorrow to install security lights."

Danni looked startled. "Rafe, I don't own this house, remember? What if the Paxtons don't want security lights?"

He offered her a reassuring smile. "Then we'll uninstall them when they're no longer necessary."

A worried frown formed between her brows. "This is getting complicated."

"It's necessary, Danni," Case Randolph spoke up quietly.

"I agree," Case's wife added firmly—and for once dead serious. "I've been a nurse long enough to know that anything that *can* happen usually *will* happen—and when you least expect it."

Danni sighed. "I know when I'm outnumbered."

Rafe sent the Randolphs a grateful look that won him a guarded look of friendliness from Mrs. Randolph and a look of commiseration from the man himself.

"Seth or I will take care of the marketing and any other chores. Lyssa, Seth will accompany you to school and bring you home."

She looked both intrigued and annoyed. "The kids will think I'm a retard or something."

"Lyssa!" her mother chided.

"Sorry," the girl muttered.

"He'll stay outside the classroom, but he'll walk with you from one to another."

"Couldn't he sort of hang around but not, like, actually be with me?"

"We'll see," he conceded, figuring Seth could handle that his own way.

"What about me?" Danni asked. "I don't intend to neglect my patients because of that miserable weasel."

Rafe risked a grin. "You get me, Doctor. Where you go, I go."

Danni slept alone—and hated it.

Like a giddy schoolgirl she hugged the pillow he'd used, her face buried in the goose down, inhaling the scent that was uniquely Rafe. She wanted him desperately.

She wouldn't let it be love.

There were too many years gone by, too many ghosts, too much pain. But there was affection and friendship and pleasure. So much pleasure. She felt a pulse start deep inside, and rocked back and forth, trying to ease the need for him.

Was he missing her, too? she wondered. Instead of sleeping tonight, he intended to stand watch. He'd been brewing coffee when she'd come upstairs. His weapon had been on his hip and there had been a look in his eyes that had both frightened and thrilled her.

Once, when she'd been home with the flu, a friend from her first period algebra class had smuggled in one of her mom's steamy romance novels. For the next four hours, the two of them had huddled under the covers, reading about a marauding Viking warrior named Hauk and his English captive, the lovely—and deliciously fiery—Lady Alys.

Even as a child she'd always had an especially vivid imagination and the writer had been a gifted wordsmith. Not only had Danni seen the firelight flickering over the warrior's steely muscles and massive, wound-scarred chest, but she'd smelled the musk of his sun-bronzed skin and felt the slow gliding of his sweat-slick body down the length of her own.

Rafe was her very own Hauk. A bronzed, golden-haired warrior with the soul of a poet. Smiling, she slid down between the sheets and was turning to snap off the lamp when the phone rang. Automatically she answered, only to have Folsom's voice rip through her.

"Drop the charges, Daniela. Otherwise, dear sweet Lyssa will end up an orphan."

"You bastard," she cried, her voice shaking. "You can't scare me."

"Can't I, Daniela? Perhaps I should kill Lyssa first, just to prove I mean business." He hung up before she could reply.

Rafe had just opened a mystery novel he'd found on the bookshelves in the den and was preparing to see how fast he could figure out the killer when he heard the phone. He made it to the extension in the den just as the caller hung up.

Furious at her for ignoring his order to let her machine take the call, he took the stairs two at a time. Her door was ajar. He didn't bother to knock.

She was sitting up, her face waxen, her eyes huge. "Oh, God, Rafe, this time he actually threatened to kill me." Her lips trembled. She pressed them together until she'd regained control. "When I told him he didn't scare me, he...he threatened to kill Lys.'' Her fingers turned white where they clutched the sheet.

His heart bled. ''Don't, sweetheart,'' he pleaded as he slipped in next to her and pulled her onto his lap. ''He wants you to fall apart. You can beat him if you stay strong.''

''I'm so tired of feeling strong,'' she whispered, her voice shredding. ''I feel like I'm crumbling inside.''

He smoothed her hair back, then kissed her forehead. ''Then lean on me for now, honey,'' he ordered, his voice thick with words he couldn't say and promises he couldn't make. ''Let me take care of you.''

''I wish I'd never taken that cruise,'' she cried, her eyes full of misery.

''No, you don't, honey.'' He cupped both hands over her belly. ''This little one wanted to be born and chose you as her mama. Once she's born, you'll forget all about the man who was little more than a sperm donor. When she looks up at you, you'll only see Lyssa and maybe if you look hard enough, Mark.''

She pressed her hands over his. ''How did you get so wise?'' she asked in a shaky voice as she turned to kiss his jaw.

''Not wise. Just a guy who cares about you.''

He pulled her head against his shoulder and rocked her the way Rosaria had once rocked her babies. Twenty minutes later she was asleep.

Still he held her, his hand gently combing through her hair. He would die for her, that was a given. It was his duty, his reason for getting up every morning. But this was personal, holding her. Comforting her the only way he knew how. Letting the warmth of his body drive the chill from hers.

It would never go away, he knew now, the hunger he felt for her. She was imprinted on his soul.

That day at the Greyhound station, he'd thought nothing could hurt more. He'd been wrong. The day that he left her again, that would be worse.

That would be hell.

Chapter 14

Jake drove like an old woman all the way back to Portland from the Seattle-Tacoma airport. The last thing he needed now was some county mountie running a make on him after stopping him for some traffic violation. Although the car was registered in the name of Michael Carlyle, he had his real ID in his wallet.

Four days with Arlene in a fleabag motel had shortened his temper and thinned his patience. A dozen times he'd been tempted to wring her scrawny neck and be done with it, but the sixth sense that had served him so well had him holding back. When he disappeared again, he figured they'd waste a lot of man hours sitting on her place again.

Like he'd be that stupid, he thought, his lips curling in disgust. Cops were so predictable. It was a wonder they solved as many crimes as they did.

Spying a rest stop ahead, he signaled a lane change and eased the Bronco onto the exit ramp. He needed to brush his teeth, get the taste of Arly's goodbye kiss out of his mouth. Another hour, he'd be back in Portland.

The place he'd rented under the name of Michael Carlyle

was in the exact opposite end of town from the room he and Arly had found together. He would get his mail there—while he would be safely hidden somewhere else.

Sweet gullible Arly, she'd shelled out plenty for his cell phone and new clothes. Every time she'd balked, he'd simply tossed her on the bed and given her what she craved.

Lord, he was glad to be rid of her, he thought as he locked the Bronco and walked toward the men's room. The exhaust from her Toyota had still been in the air when he'd caught a cab to the airport.

When she'd called him on his new phone to tell him she'd made it home safely, he'd been driving past Olympia. Stupid bitch had believed him when he'd claimed to miss him. Like she hadn't even known that every time he'd been pounding her into the mattress it had been Daniela's body he'd imagined beneath his. And Daniela's throat he'd longed to snap when he'd climaxed.

As he pushed open the restroom door, he felt a jolt of excitement. Maybe he'd kill Cardoza first, then rape her before he killed her, he thought as he unzipped his trousers.

By the time he was back on the road he had already revised his plans and was mapping out the steps needed for success. The first, of course, was finding the bitch. Find her, he found Cardoza.

He would start with the DMV.

A smile curled his lips as he thought about the small satchel packed full with thirty thousand in small, unmarked bills. It had been intended for traveling money, but there was plenty left over for bribes. After that, as the man said, the rest would be all downhill. To Rafe Cardoza's own private hell.

Danni brought the guided visualization to an end, then waited a beat to let Cindy's system settle. "At the count of five you will be wide awake and feeling refreshed," she continued in the same soothing tone. "The count is one and you're coming up. Two, you're beginning to stir. Three, you're moving your arms and legs. Four, you're aware of your surroundings. Five, your eyes are opening and you're wide, wide awake and feeling great.''

Cindy Habiz opened her big Orphan Annie eyes and stretched her arms over her head. "Wow, that was intense," she said, her small features more relaxed than Danni had ever seen them. "I feel wonderful. I might just be able to take the kids and move to that shelter soon."

"Why not today?"

Cindy's expression clouded. "Abdul's talking about maybe going to one of those counseling groups for abusers, you know?"

"Cindy, he's been talking about that for a year."

"I know, but this time he's serious."

Much as Danni wanted to continue, she knew Cindy wasn't ready to make the break with her abusive husband. Still, she was much closer than she'd been six months ago.

"So who's the gorgeous hunk in the waiting room?" Cindy asked as she sat up and fluffed her cinnamon-colored hair.

"A friend."

"Must be a real good friend, seeing as how he's been sitting out there the last three times I've been here."

"It's complicated to explain." Danni flipped open her appointment book and picked up her pen. "Same time next Friday?"

"What else?" Cindy got to her feet and collected her purse and umbrella. It had been raining for three days solid, and Danni's temper was beginning to fray.

"I'll walk you out." Danni stood, her expanding girth making movement awkward.

"How's the little one?" Cindy asked, casting an envious look at Danni's swollen belly.

"Growing. And it's definitely a little girl. The ultrasound was clear as a bell."

Rafe looked up as the door to the inner office opened. He had taken to bringing his laptop with him, but when she asked him what he was working on that seemed to absorb him completely, he made some joke about a Solitaire tournament.

Rafe walked Cindy to the door, then locked it behind her. "Tired?" he asked as he took Danni into his arms.

"A case of cabin fever, I suspect." She lifted her face for a kiss. He obliged instantly, covering her mouth with his. Her heart did an eager flip-flop as he cupped her buttocks, angling her pelvis against his.

"A case of some kind of fever, anyway."

"Any idea what would cure it?" she challenged, rubbing against him like a cat. He groaned and his body hardened.

"That's a good start."

Because they couldn't make love at her place with Lyssa in the next room and Seth sleeping on the pull-out sofa in the den, they'd taken to lingering after her last patient.

Danni came to think of it as their time. It had become the highlight of her increasingly tense days. "You feel so good," he whispered against that sensitive spot behind her ear.

"So do you." She rubbed her breasts against his chest, feeling his breathing increase.

He ran his palms up and down her arms, then drew back to unbutton her blouse. "It's driving me crazy, being near you twenty-four hours a day without being able to touch you."

It was so wonderful to feel his hands roaming her body, his fingertips sliding so intimately over her breasts until they were engorged and aching. Deep in all the moist, intimate parts her body hummed and warmed and yearned.

Little by little, between kisses and sweet words, he undressed her completely, taking his time, lingering over her breasts before feathering his strokes lower.

"Baby's getting bigger, honey," he murmured, smoothing his big hand over the swell of her belly. The pleasure was so intense she trembled. He returned his attention to her mouth, and between kisses, undressed himself. When he drew her down onto the sofa, she sighed with pleasure and anticipation.

Instead of covering her with his body, he knelt next to the sofa. She reached for him, only to have him grab her hand and kiss the tips of her fingers. "Patience, sweet."

She closed her eyes and let him lead. Soon she was awash in pleasure, his callused fingers unbearably erotic sliding over her belly, pushing through the soft curls covering the mound between her legs.

It thrilled her when his mouth turned possessive and then demanding. She met demand with demand, curling her hands over his shoulders, sliding lower, exulting in the strength of his corded biceps, the wide power of his forearms.

His breathing rasped harsher as his own desire built. She felt his heat, his struggle for control. Her own breathing quickened, became labored as the pleasure built. Heat raced over her throat and into her breasts.

"Do you want me inside you now?" he asked, his voice thick.

She opened her eyes and saw the grimace of pleasure pain that tightened his arrogantly drawn features. "I want you," she pleaded, opening her legs.

With a groan he rose and straddled her. Taking her hands, he drew them over her head, then eased down until the thick tip of his shaft was pressing intimately against her. He thrust slowly, then drew back, his rigid body sliding against velvet walls. He thrust deeper, shuddering as he drew back. Sobbing, she arched up, seating him completely, then began working her hips.

She opened her eyes and saw him watching her. The look in his sage-green eyes was dark and edgy and full of turbulent emotion. So much emotion. Her breath stopped, then hissed out as she writhed, desperate for release. He followed her lead, thrusting harder until she cried out. He caught her cries with his mouth as she shattered. And then his mouth was next to her ear and his voice was thick and slurred as he whispered her name.

"I want to love you, Danni mine. I want that so much." And then with a shudder that shook both of them he found his own release.

It had taken a while and a few greased palms, but Jake found out where she lived. He'd even driven by a few times to get the lay of the land. It was a nice little house, but worlds away from the upscale digs on the hillside in Lake Oswego. Rented now, like poor folks.

It gave him a jolt of satisfaction that was almost sexual.

Princess, her old man called her. Had her believing it, too. Looking down her nose at him when he suggested they do more than the usual missionary position between the sheets.

A real cold fish she'd been. Too bad he had to marry her before he found it out. Had him panting after her like a pimply kid, she had, too. He should have known the way she was holding out for a wedding ring.

It had been the flawless emerald glittering on her finger that had decided him. Now that emerald was locked in the Portland PD evidence room, waiting to send him away for a good portion of his remaining years.

"Think again, Princess," he muttered, his fingers caressing the barrel of the sweet little Beretta resting on his thigh.

Disappointment churned in his gut like bad meat as he realized it wouldn't be here where she died. Too few ways to escape and too many potential witnesses in those tidy white houses.

No, he would have to find a way to lure her into the open. Turning on his blinker he turned on to the street dividing her house from the three in the next block, driving past slowly. No one was home yet. Daniela was at her downtown office, another place he'd rejected for the same reasons. And Lyssa was at school.

Lyssa! An obscenity escaped his thin lips at his own stupidity. She was the key. Get to her, use her to lure her mom away from that bastard Cardoza for only a few seconds, and he'd blow them both away.

Feeling elated, he shoved a Sinatra CD into the Bronco's cassette player and sang along with Old Blue Eyes. All he had to do now was pick his own private killing field, then figure out a way to get around the tap that had to be on her phone.

"Soon, Princess," he promised, tossing back his head and laughing in sheer relief.

"Mom, if I promise to be real careful not to spill anything, can I wear your yellow silk blouse tomorrow night? Jody says it'll be rad with my white bell bottoms."

Danni took a sip of milk before smiling across the table at her daughter. "Okay, but get one little speck on it and you're in big trouble, kiddo."

"I'll be careful, I promise."

Rafe glanced at Seth and lifted a brow. Seth gave his head a nearly imperceptible shake. Obviously he was in the dark, too. "What's happening tomorrow night?" Rafe asked, shifting his attention to Lyssa again.

"Just the most awesome Acid Aliens concert on the planet," she said before popping a cherry tomato into her mouth. "Me and Jody have seats in the third row."

Damn. "Where, exactly, is this concert?"

"At the Rose Garden. Jody's mom is taking us, so Seth can have the night off." She turned to give him a smile. "You could ask Miss Fishbein out for tomorrow night like you keep saying you want to. She asked me all about you yesterday after class."

"Shh," Seth teased. "Don't out me to the boss, okay?"

She giggled happily. "Bummer, sorry about that."

Rafe gazed across the table at her shining eyes and knew he was about to lose all the ground he'd been slowly gaining during the four weeks he'd been living in Danni's house.

"I'm sorry, Lys," he said with real regret. "I can't let you go to a public concert right now. It's too dangerous."

Her happiness turned to shock. "But that's not fair!" she protested, her face flushed. "Me and Jody have been planning this for ages."

Danni turned anxious eyes Rafe's way. "Surely he wouldn't try something in the middle of a crowd?"

"That's the problem, Danni. We can't control the situation, which makes it an unacceptable risk."

"I don't think Jonathan is dangerous at all," Lyssa cried, her eyes flashing. "I think you just made it up so mom will let you hang around."

"Not true, Lyssa," Seth jumped in before Rafe could find the patience he needed. "I would have made the same decision as Rafe. It's our job to protect you and your mom. Sometimes that means making the hard choices, but the alternative can be far worse."

She blinked lashes almost as long and curly as her mom's. "Maybe it's just a mistake." As a compromise, it was paper thin, but it was a start. "Maybe you just *think* Jonathan wants to hurt Mom and me."

"I hope it is, but we can't take that chance." Seth covered the hand she'd tightened into a little fist next to her plate with his. "Put yourself in our place, Lys. What if you were convinced that some miserable piece of…that *someone* was going to try to kill your mom. Wouldn't you do everything in your power to try to protect her?"

Mouth drooping, she struggled to find a way around the ruthless logic. Rafe felt for the kid. It had to be rough, living with the memories of her father's death. "I guess," she conceded grudgingly. "Only it's like, Acid Aliens is my favorite group, you know? And I used all the money I made helping Liza to pay for my ticket."

"How about this? When this is over, I'll find out where they're playing next, and we'll all go, you and me and Jody and your mom." He shot Rafe a look. "We'll even take the old guy."

"Do we have to?" she grumbled, and Danni winced.

Seth chuckled. "Ah, c'mon, Lys, cut him some slack. It's rough playing dad to this strange family we have here."

"Especially since he's learning on the job," Danni added, her gaze filled with tenderness as she lifted her nearly empty glass of milk in a toast. "To you, Rafael. Our own gift from God."

Early morning fog curled upward from the gorge, mingling with the sweat pouring through his pores as Rafe ran along the cliff path, his feet pounding the hard-packed gravel, his muscles begging for relief. To his right the mighty Columbia tumbled and tore toward the Pacific. Rafe felt the same turbulence surging inside.

It had been a mistake, moving into Danni's house. With every day that passed he found himself having to fight harder to remember why it would never work between them.

Because it seemed to be working damn well. Even Lyssa had gotten over her anger and seemed more relaxed around him. She'd even begun to tease him about his lousy luck at Monopoly. So far he'd been skunked in twenty-three straight games.

He'd told himself he wasn't going to get attached to the kid. For her sake as well as his. He might as well have been shouting into the wind for all the good it did. That afternoon in the river, when she'd looked at him with the joy of victory shimmering in eyes exactly like her mother's, she'd set her hook into him but good.

At least she hadn't started treating him like a dad. That he knew would cause no end of complications. Because he wasn't her dad and never could be.

Smart little thing, she knew that as well as he did. She'd seen through him from the start. He was just a guy pretending to be tough who wanted to sleep with her mom.

"Of course I'm not avoiding you, Papa," Danni said, rubbing the knot at the back of her neck. "I've just been busy."

"You got your car fixed, *cara?* The mechanic did a good job?"

"Yes, fine."

His voice turned cagey. "So you and Lyssa will come down early next Saturday so we can spend time together before the fiesta begins?"

She glanced up to see Rafe watching her from the doorway of the den. "I'd like that, Papa, but—"

"No buts, *cara.* It's been nearly six weeks since I laid eyes on my Princess. Besides, it's bad luck to refuse a man his fondest wish on his birthday."

She bit her lip, then made a decision. "Of course, we'll come early, Papa. I wouldn't miss helping Aunt Gina obsess over every miniscule detail for anything."

With Rafe's gaze boring into her she managed to say goodbye without making any more promises. Her hand shook slightly as she hung up, but she figured he was too far away to notice.

"Save the glare for someone who doesn't know what a soft heart you have hidden beneath that rampaging tough guy exterior," she said, leaning back in Morgan's butter-soft chair and crossing her arms.

He actually turned red although his jaw remained white where the muscles were strained taut. "Have you listened to anything

I've been saying, Doctor Fabrizio?'' he demanded in a voice that was dangerously soft. ''Or has that hard head you have hidden beneath all that soft hair finally turned to pure stone?''

She felt her backbone snap into a straight line. ''The only time Lys and I missed one of Papa's birthday bashes was the year Mark died. This year especially we need to feel that connection with family tradition. Besides, there's no way Folsom can know where we're going unless he follows us, and you're too careful to let that happen. And even if he did follow us, the vineyard is just about the safest place we could be.''

Those thick tawny lashes narrowed until his eyes were mere slits. Instead of lessening the lethal impact of those remarkable green eyes, however, it seemed to magnify it exponentially. ''Tell me, Doctor, what brilliant piece of logic led you to that conclusion?'' he demanded, biting off his words.

''Simple arithmetic, Agent. Four Mancini males, three Fabrizios, four Cardozas—well, five, if we count you which I certainly do—plus countless other vineyard workers against one weasel.''

She'd seen him lose his temper only once—when he'd caught one of the seasonal workers beating his ten-year-old son. Though he'd been only fourteen and only half the man's weight, he'd backed him up against the bottling shed and torn into him. The man's terror had been so great Danni had felt it yards away.

At the moment he had his temper under rigid control, but she felt it strain to explode. ''Run that count again, only subtract one Cardoza. Seth will handle this particular detail. I'm taking the day off.''

He turned on his heel and disappeared, leaving her feeling as though she'd just survived a train wreck.

Lyssa kept the cell phone under her winter sweaters on the shelf in the closet when she was at school. As soon as she got home, however, she slipped it under her pillow where the ringing would be muffled.

She had been thrilled when Jody had given it to her in algebra class, explaining that Jonathan had knocked on the back door of her house when her mother had gone to have her hair done and begged her to slip the phone to Lys when Seth wasn't watching.

He said the police are likely recording all the calls on your regular phone, Jody had explained, looking as guilty as sin as she glanced around to make sure no one was eavesdropping. *Listen for his call at eleven every night,* she had added, then giggled. Lys had felt like some kind of secret agent when she'd slipped the cute little phone into her purse.

At first she'd been so happy to hear his voice. He sounded so sad that her mom hadn't believed him about his business being in trouble and all. Lyssa understood how he needed her money to keep from going bankrupt, so why didn't her mom?

He was doing great now and wanted to pay her back, only Rafe had cooked up this plan to earn himself a promotion by proving Jonathan was a crook.

But my sweet Lyssa believes in me, don't you, baby? he kept asking over and over, like it was really important. So she told him that she did. Which had been true at first, but now, she wasn't so sure.

With a sigh, she closed the history book she wasn't really reading before flipping onto her stomach. Resting her chin on her hands, she stared at the tiny pink rosebuds in the wallpaper, trying to decide what she really thought.

It wasn't easy figuring out adults. With her friends, it was pretty easy to tell when someone was lying, but like Jody said, grown-ups had a lot more practice perfecting their act.

The thing was, she was beginning to have this funny prickly feeling in her stomach as soon as she heard Jonathan's voice. Like her body was hearing stuff her mind wasn't. Kind of like ESP, she figured, letting her mind wander for a minute to the program she'd seen once on the Discovery channel. How some people can pick up signals like radio waves that tell them things. Like the sudden burst of panic she'd felt right before Dad's Jag had started skidding.

The feeling she got from Rafe was different. Even when he was being all bossy and mean, she always felt safe when he was around, kind of like a part of him was holding her in his arms. It was the same feeling she got from Mom, only different, too.

Did that mean he was right about Jonathan wanting to hurt her and Mom? She and Jody had talked about it a lot since Jonathan had started talking about the two of them figuring out a way so he could talk to Mom alone, without Rafe hanging around.

Jody liked both of them, but she liked Rafe better. But that was because she had a crush on him. Jody didn't think it was right to trick her mom, but Jonathan made it sound like she'd be really hurting Mom if she didn't help him. Like if Mom still loved him, Lys would be the one keeping them from being a family again.

Only how could Mom love him when she and Rafe were always touching and smiling and laughing together when they thought she wasn't watching? Seth claimed Rafe hadn't ever been married and never really got serious about the women he took out back in Washington.

Only Rafe didn't act like he wanted to be her dad the way Jonathan did. Lyssa wanted a dad more than anything. Sometimes she missed her real dad so much she wanted to die so she could be with him. She'd been with him in the light for a long time before the angel told her she had to go back to her body because it wasn't her time.

Now she was beginning to have that same scary feeling, like maybe she shouldn't have told Jonathan about them going down to the vineyard for Grandpa Mancini's birthday on Saturday.

He'd seemed so excited when she'd told him. It was perfect. Now all he had to do was figure out a way to get Mom alone. He would need her help, and she'd promised, but now she was feeling kind of guilty about the whole thing. She was still trying to puzzle things through when the phone rang. She took a deep breath, then drew it out and answered.

"How's my pretty girl this evening?" Jonathan asked, his voice loving like always. Only the prickles in her belly were worse all of a sudden.

"Okay," she said, cupping her free hand around the receiver to keep anyone from hearing.

"I've figured out where we can meet," he said, sounding like he was smiling. "I have it all worked out. And you, my baby girl, are going to play the most important part of all."

Chapter 15

Something wasn't right.

It had been niggling at him for a week now, this feeling that he was missing something important. But what?

He ran over the precautions he'd taken one by one, examining each one for possible flaws. It was solid, damn it. All of it. Still, he'd taken to checking with both surveillance teams before buttoning up the house for the night. They were seasoned pros, both of them, if a little young.

Danni and Lyssa had gone upstairs around 10:00 p.m. Seth had watched the playoff game between the Blazers and Pacers before turning in around midnight.

Habit had him checking on his partner before he headed back into the den. With his hair mussed, and face relaxed he looked a lot like his brother, Carlos, who was the oldest of Rosaria's natural children.

A hard knot formed in his gut as he remembered the awe he'd felt when Enrique had put the new little baby boy in his arms a few minutes after he'd been born. Because he was their special son, he was to be his baby brother's godfather, the man he'd worshipped had told him before putting his strong arms around them both.

His eyes burned as he remembered the pride that had filled him at that moment. It felt good to be special, he'd thought as he made a vow to God to protect his *hermano* with his own life.

Carlos would be thirty-two now. A man who likely had sons of his own. Did they even know they had an uncle who loved their father very much? he wondered as he reached down to tug the afghan closer to Seth's stubborn Yankee chin.

He snapped off the lamp the kid had left burning before turning to walk back to the den. He had just tugged off his shirt when he heard a soft tap on the door he'd left ajar.

"Rafe, can I come in?"

Surprise ran through him when he heard Lyssa's voice. "Come ahead, *niña*," he said, his curiosity hitting the red zone.

She was dressed for bed in an oversize Acid Aliens T-shirt in a gaudy green color he was pretty sure glowed in the dark.

"Thought you'd be asleep hours ago," he said after a quick look at the antique wall clock. "One in the morning's pretty late for a girl who has kick-boxing class in the morning."

"I couldn't sleep," she mumbled, pressing her hands together in front of her. Protecting herself from him? he wondered. Or trying to keep herself from flying into pieces?

"Something I can help you with?"

She shrugged, her gaze darting from the desk, to the overflowing book cases, and then finally to the floor. Anywhere but at him. He was beginning to feel the telltale burning in his gut that told him something was about to go sideways unless he paid close attention.

"Want to give me a hint, or should I just pick a subject at random?" he teased when she continued to stand there looking like a puppy expecting a scolding but desperately hoping for a hug instead. He had to anchor his hands on his hips to keep from grabbing her up and cradling her close.

Her silence had him biting off a sigh. What now, slick?

Women liked guys to bare their soul, right? Maybe he couldn't do it with Danni, but Lyssa already hated him, so he had nothing to lose and everything to gain.

"Lyssa, I know you're not real sure about me and why I'm here, but I swear on all I hold sacred that I'd volunteer to take a beating rather than hurt you or your mom."

A clam gave away more than one half-grown girl. Some guy was going to have his hands full with this one in three or four years.

"She said you're her friend," she said finally, looking anything but convinced.

"I am. There was a time when I thought maybe I'd be lucky enough to spend my life with her. Your dad ended up having that honor, but she's still very special to me. And so are you because you're one very special girl."

"You're just saying that 'cause you know my Mom wants us to get along," she whispered in a hurt voice that went deep inside him.

"I meant every word, sweetheart. I know what it's like to wake up in a hospital bed in a world of hurt, scared I was going to die one minute and praying that I would the next. It had to be a thousand times worse for you, Lyssa. I know how much courage it took for you to come back from that, and I can't think of anyone I respect more."

Her skinny shoulders heaved but she glanced up, more like a peek, he thought, only when her gaze hit his chest, her expression changed and her head came up fast. "What happened to your chest?"

He glanced down at the railroad track scar running from sternum to navel. Did it really look all that bad? he wondered, brushing his hand over its length. "I got shot. The doctors had to open me up to keep me from bleeding to death."

"They did that to me too, only it was my stomach." She frowned. "Who shot you?"

"My money's on your good friend, Jonathan Sommerset." He took a chance and walked over to give her a real good look at the damage a bullet can do. "Lyssa, I know you don't want to believe me, but he's no good, sweetheart. He's killed at least once before, only we couldn't prove it."

She stared at his scarred flesh, the freckles sprinkled across her nose standing out as her skin visibly paled. "He told me you weren't doing your job and that's why that lady got killed, only he didn't shoot her the way you said he did. He swore on his mother's grave that you were trying to make him take the blame on account of you got in trouble for not catching the real killer.''

Rafe kept the staggering shock buttoned inside but he had to take a minute before he could trust his voice to remain calm. ''Sounds like you and…Jonathan have been having some real interesting conversations.''

Her chin drooped lower. ''He calls me at night.''

''Does he?'' He shot a glance at the phone. Since that one slip, Danni had let the machine answer. Since six, when he and Danni had gotten home, it had rung several times. He'd listened to the messages before passing them on. Two had come from ladies in the neighborhood, one had been from a patient. The fourth had been from Eddie.

''Did you talk with Jonathan tonight, honey?''

She nodded. ''He gave Jody this cell phone to give to me in algebra class. I keep it in my room.''

It hit him then, what had been bothering him. ''The other night when I heard you talking when I passed your room, and you said you were practicing a part in a play for drama class? You were talking to him then, weren't you?''

She nodded again. ''I'm sorry I lied, but I knew you'd take away my phone. And tell Mom.''

He risked a grin. ''You got that right on both counts.''

''You can yell at me if you like. I deserve it.'' Anticipating the blast, she squared those brave little shoulders, and the urge to hug her was almost more than he could handle. But he made himself stand perfectly still. His gut told him she was still trying to decide if she could trust him not to hurt her. Much as he hated doing nothing, the decision had to be hers.

''Guess I could yell, yeah. Only that would just make us both feel bad, and I can't see any useful purpose to that, can you?''

As brave as a soldier facing court martial, she looked him squarely in the eyes and shook her head. ''Once when Daddy yelled at me, I threw up all over his new shoes.''

Rafe eyed the loafers he'd just spit shined that morning before giving her a rueful look "That settles it for me. We'll skip the yelling and go straight to the part where you tell me what you and Jonathan talked about."

The amusement that had crept into her eyes disappeared instantly. "Mostly he asked questions, about what Mom did and where she went. He wanted me to find out if she was going any place special, like to see Dr. Jarrod or for a walk, stuff like that. He didn't like it much when I told him you and Seth always took a different way when you took us places. And sometimes you used different cars, too. But then he got real excited when I told him about going down to Grandpa's on Saturday."

Rafe noticed that she was beginning to look a little wobbly. He wasn't feeling all that steady himself. "Lys, if you wouldn't mind, I'd like to finish this sitting down. It's been a long day for this beat-up old body."

She looked startled, but she padded to the couch and sat down. He was careful to keep some distance between them as he did the same. Moving slowly, he stretched his arm along the top of the cushion and gave into the yawn that was always there, waiting when he was chronically short of sleep.

"So what's this plan Jonathan's come up with?" he prodded when she remained silent.

Eyes as big as silver dollars, she stared at him. "How did you know he had a plan?"

He shrugged. "Why else would you pick tonight to brave the lion?"

She frowned. "What lion?"

"Me, honey." He tried to gentle his voice and his smile. "Or maybe I'm the big bad wolf?"

She studied him silently and so intently he actually had to stop himself from squirming. "I think you're more like a lion than a wolf, especially if you let your hair grow."

"I wore it that way once. Drove me crazy, always in my face or making my neck hot, so I took to tying it back in a little tail when I worked. Your mom liked it that way, so I put up with the hassle."

She cocked her head like an inquisitive little bird. "Why did you cut it?"

"Went into the Army. This mean-as-a-grizzly drill sergeant explained real polite like that soldiers weren't allowed ponytails. Seemed to think it was wimpy or something weird like that."

She laughed and he felt like pumping his arms in the air and shouting. Instead he reached over to tug on a soft curl. "Now that you found out the lion doesn't bite brave young ladies with pretty brown eyes, how about you tell me all about Jonathan's plan?"

It took him most of the night to work out the details from every angle, but by dawn when he shook Seth awake, he had a solid plan. The two of them had gone through two pots of coffee, trying to think of everything that could go wrong. By the time they'd run out of possible screw-ups, he called Linc's private number.

It both humbled and gratified him that Linc had cut short a meeting with the Secretary of the Treasury to take his call. Now, almost twenty minutes later, he stood in front of the den window, watching a couple of jays splashing each other in the birdbath, laying out the details in logical order. "I know it's risky, but with the right planning and personnel, it's workable," he said when he'd finished.

"Why use the daughter? Why not the mother?"

"For one thing Dr. Fabrizio is more than six months pregnant. For another, I can't take the chance she'd refuse."

"In other words you're dead certain she would refuse to put her daughter at risk."

Rafe winced. Trust Linc to cut through the bull. "Something like that, yeah."

Linc's sigh was weighted. Not a good sign. The scar tissue on Rafe's chest started to throb. "Legally, it's not entrapment since you're acting on a tip from an informant, so we're clear there."

Rafe heard that big "we" and the knot in his gut eased off a fraction. Feeling Seth's gaze boring into his back, he turned to shrug.

"We know where he plans to come at you, so we can scout it out in advance, see if there's enough cover, maybe construct some kind of blind if we have to. Our people would have to be in place before first light on Saturday, just in case.''

He heard Linc blow out air, a sign that he was thinking. Linc tended to think aloud, one of the few habits of his mentor Rafe had never adopted.

More intuitive than linear in his thinking, he was more comfortable working everything out in private first. The few times he'd thought about it, he figured it was because he couldn't afford to make mistakes like his brothers and sisters who blurted out the first thing that came to mind. But they knew they were keepers. Him, he'd figured he was only a part of the family as long as he didn't piss anyone off. As it turned out, he'd been dead right.

"I agree, it's workable, but only if he shows up with a weapon,'' Linc summed up. "Even if he's armed to the teeth, you have to catch him in the act of pointing his weapon at someone before we have something the prosecuting attorney can use.''

"I know him, Linc. He's pulled off so many cons without taking a fall he's got himself convinced he's smarter than God. Certainly smarter than the dumb cops. Way I see it, he'll not only pull his weapon, he'll grandstand long enough for our guys to take him down.''

"Only if he thinks he's totally safe. The way you have this set up, everything depends on a twelve-year-old girl playing her part perfectly. Any hint that it's a setup, the whole thing explodes. A witness under our protection gets hurt—or God forbid, killed—and the Service will take a bad PR hit. Not to mention what it will do to us personally.''

Linc was only saying out loud what Rafe had agonized over for most of the night. "Lyssa's young, but she's got a warrior's soul.''

"You'd better be right about that, old son, because your life—and hers—depends on it.''

"I'll work with her. She'll stay frosty.''

"About that, I'll have to defer to your judgment.''

Triumph cascading through him, Rafe turned to give Seth a nod. His partner pumped his fist and grinned. "About personnel," Linc continued briskly, "do you have the people you need out there or do you want to name your team?"

"I was thinking of the guys who worked the MacGregor case with me. They have a stake in putting Folsom away, too."

"Good idea. I'll pull the list and cut the orders. They'll be in Portland by tonight. Anything else?"

Rafe rubbed his hand over his chest. "Yeah. I'd like you to run the show on Saturday personally. From the field."

The silence was deafening. Then Linc cleared his throat. "Margie will likely skin me alive if she finds out, but given the fact she just flat turns me on when she's spitting mad, why the hell not?"

It took Rafe a moment to pull in the emotion that had closed his throat. "I owe you one, boss."

"You can repay me by staying alive."

Folsom had told Lyssa to expect his call on Thursday night to go over the final plans one more time. Her door was open a crack when Rafe went upstairs at ten forty-five under the pretext of taking a shower. Seth had challenged Danni to a game of Scrabble in order to keep her from coming upstairs too soon.

He knocked, then nudged the door open at her invitation. Dressed in that same green shirt, she sat cross-legged on her bed clutching a stuffed Tigger with one missing eye and a ragged ear.

"Scared?" he asked as he sat down on the edge of the bed.

She nodded. "A little."

"Remember he expects you to be excited, not scared, because you want your mom and him to get back together again."

Her gaze skittered away from his. "I guess you think I'm pretty dumb, believing him like I did," she muttered, tugging on the tiger's ear with nervous fingers.

He took her hand pressed it between his. "Not even close, *niña*. In fact, I think you're pretty terrific. I even bragged on you to my boss who said to tell you he can't wait to meet you."

Her mouth softened. "Really?"

"Really." He kissed her hand before letting her go. "The

best thing to do is let him do most of the talking. It's okay if you sound worried. Tell him you're afraid I'll get mad at you if that would help.''

Dropping her gaze again, she played with Tigger's long tail. ''Rafe, do you still want to marry my mom?''

Talk about a no-bull lady, that was Lyssa. He tucked his amusement behind the poker face that twenty years of practice had perfected until it was second nature. ''It's not a question of wanting, Lys,'' he navigated carefully. ''It's more like bad timing.''

She glanced up. ''What do you mean?''

What was it with females anyway? Always asking the tough questions at the worst possible time. Stifling a sigh, he glanced at his watch. It was nearly eleven. Still, he took a moment to think of the best way to lay it out so she would understand.

''When your mom married your dad, I felt so bad that I'd lost her that I had to make myself stop loving her or go crazy. It took a while, but I finally did it.'' He hated remembering the brooding, bad tempered jerk he'd been then.

''Did Mom love you, too?''

That was a question he'd had to stop asking. ''I don't know, Lys. What I do know is that she loved your dad a lot. That kind of love never dies.''

Unhappiness settled over her like a veil. ''When she called me from Acapulco, she said she'd fallen in love with a wonderful man and that I would love him, too.''

Was she simply doing what her mother told her? he wondered. ''Men like him are like chameleons, honey. First they figure out what kind of man appeals to the woman they want to impress, and they make themselves seem like that man.''

She hugged the tiger closer. ''Maybe he knew I wanted a dad and so he pretended that's what he wanted, too, only he didn't really.''

He nodded. ''You're one smart cookie, you know that? Probably end up with a bunch of letters behind your name like your mom.''

She struggled not to look too pleased, but finally gave up and grinned. ''I want to be a lawyer, like Daddy. I—''

The phone rang, and panic splintered the smile in her eyes. "Don't leave, okay?" she begged as she scrambled to find the phone under her pillow.

"Don't worry, I'll be right with you all the way. You can count on it."

The phone rang again. Looking pale, but determined, she took a deep breath—and answered.

By Friday night Danni was worn out.

During the last month, the baby had managed to get her days and nights mixed. While Danni was awake, she slept. As soon as Danni dropped off, she came away, kicking and tumbling around for hours at a time.

Grateful that it was Seth's turn to make dinner, she'd retired to the den for another disheartening session of bill paying. Or lack of same, she thought as she signed her name to the pitifully small check to Oregon Health Sciences University Hospital.

She had just slit open the next envelope in the stack when Rafe came in carrying what looked exactly like two bullet-proof vests.

"No way," she declared as he dropped them on to the couch as he passed.

"Non-negotiable, honey," he said before bending to kiss her.

Desire raged through her like a fever she was reluctant to cool. Every time he touched her it was better than the last. When she wasn't with him, she was thinking about him. When he smiled at her, she felt giddy. When they made love, which had been every afternoon this week, it had been magical. Though it was galling to admit, she had developed a serious addiction to Rafe Cardoza.

"Those things look hot and heavy," she said when he drew back. "And they're ugly."

"They're all three, and you'll hate wearing it. But you will, or you'll stay home."

He shoved aside a stack of bills before angling one lean hip over the corner of the desk. Beneath his threadbare jeans, his thigh muscle bunched, testing the seams. Her palm itched to stroke all that wonderful power. Because she knew she would want more, she busied herself opening envelopes.

"I'm not your prisoner, Rafe. You can't make me stay home," she declared, glancing up to add emphasis to her words.

"I can and I will." His tone was mild, but the look in his eyes told her he meant every word. Worse, he had absolutely no doubt he would win any contest between them.

Pride had her shifting to glare at him. "Don't pull that caveman stuff with me, Cardoza. I'm not some wilting violet who faints whenever you go into your 'Me Tarzan, you Jane,' act."

His eyebrows shot upward, and his eyes crinkled. "I counted three metaphors in that statement, honey. Maybe we should call Guinness, see if that's a world record."

It wouldn't do any good to lose her temper since a tirade would only serve to put her at a disadvantage. Worse, she suspected he would actually laugh. "Is that where you were last night, picking up flak jackets at Army surplus?"

"Miss me, did you?" He lifted a hand to toy with a lock of her hair. She refused to jerk away, but she'd be damned if she would lean into his touch.

"Of course," she declared smugly. "Without you landing on Park Place every third turn, I had to actually work to beat Seth and Lys."

"I'm just lulling you into a sense of false security."

"That is so patently wrong it boggles the mind."

"Now that sounds real promising, sweetheart." He flashed her a grin so ripe with sensual meaning it made her weak inside. "Since you have to strip down to try on the vest anyway, how about getting all the way naked together?"

"There are children in the house," she reminded him, but the corners of her mouth kept wanting to turn up.

"Yeah, but Seth has to learn the facts of life someday. Might as well be now."

"I meant Lyssa and her baby sister." She rubbed her tummy for emphasis.

"Her *sister* has been listening to us get it on for weeks, honey. Who knows, she might even have a real up close and personal view."

She fought not to laugh. "You're terrible, you know that?"

"Yeah, but you're crazy about me anyway, aren't you?" Though he was teasing, she sensed another emotion mixed in with the humor.

Suddenly her heart was pounding. "Absolutely, utterly besotted," she said with a resigned sigh. "It's horribly embarrassing, but what can I say? I'm a sucker for green eyes and dimples."

He stood suddenly and spun her chair until it faced him. "We can build on that," he said, one of those dimples winking at her. This time he pulled her up against him before he kissed her.

Since it was a five-hour drive from Portland to the area of the vineyard near the California border, Rafe and Linc decided to have the team spend the night in Ashland. At 0600 they assembled next to the van in the parking lot of the motel. Five steely-eyed men in forest camouflage, all expert marksmen, well-trained, well-armed, each with a score to settle.

Linc had taken them through every possible contingency. By 0630 they would be in position. It would be a long day. As Linc zipped up the windbreaker with SECRET SERVICE imprinted on the front and back, he checked the sky.

The weather forecast was for morning overcast followed by clearing. It was supposed to be in the mid-seventies and sunny. A perfect day to bag a killer. Or a terrible day for a friend to die.

His bags were already stowed in the back of the Bronco, his cash in a money belt beneath his loose-fitting sports shirt. His passport and ID in the name of Michael Carlyle were locked in the glove box. Anything that would identify him as Jacob Folsom had already been mailed to the postal box he'd rented in the name of M. Carlyle in Vancouver, BC.

He'd parked on the shoulder a half mile south.

Now he waited, seated on a beach chair inside the round metal culvert next to a paved pullout on a narrow county road exactly six point four miles from the main gate of the Mancini Vineyard. It was a little past noon, and he had just finished the salad and cold chicken sandwich he'd picked up in Ashland on his way through. He was alone except for a couple of noisy crows.

The place was perfect for an ambush. If he'd designed it himself, it couldn't have been better. Backed by the foothills of Mount Ashland, the area was mostly scrub trees and brush. Though the pullout was paved, the surrounding area was overgrown with thick salal bushes and blackberry canes. Even if someone were to drive past, he would be screened from view until their vehicle drew abreast. The few drivers who'd passed hadn't even glanced his way.

During the last week he'd made three trial runs, parking for an hour the first time, longer during the second and third trips. While keeping careful note of the number and kind of vehicles that passed, he went over the plan again and again in his mind.

According to Lyssa, they usually left the vineyard around four in order to make it back to Portland by nine. As soon as she spotted mile marker seventeen, she was to complain of stomach cramps. As soon as the pullout came into view one mile later, she was to shout for Cardoza or whoever was driving to stop the car. Pretending that she was going to vomit, she was to jerk open the door and stumble to the edge of the pullout. Naturally her doting mother would run to help her. Like a trained dog Cardoza was sure to follow.

It was five running strides up the incline leading from the culvert to the level. He'd timed himself three times. Less than a second, and he would be face-to-face with Cardoza.

He'd toyed with the idea of shooting from cover. But that would spoil his enjoyment. Almost as much as he wanted Daniela and her brat dead, he wanted to see the shock come into the SOB's eyes when he shoved the Beretta into his gut.

He would destroy Cardoza's kneecaps first, to incapacitate him mostly, but also because his research had told him a shattered knee was incredibly painful. After that he would blow away the other Fed. Because he was a man who understood priorities, he would kill Daniela and her brat next.

Cardoza would crawl before he died. On his belly, like a dog, dragging his crippled legs, begging to die.

Oh yes, it was going to be sweet, he thought as he twisted the cap off a bottle of water. He could hardly wait.

Chapter 16

She wore the darn vest.

It wasn't quite as heavy as she'd expected, but it was miserably uncomfortable. The baby certainly didn't seem happy to find herself being squeezed by layers of bullet-proof "stuff."

To her surprise, Lys had sided with Rafe. *Chill, Mom,* she'd ordered before slipping into hers with what seemed like astonishing familiarity—as though wearing a bullet-proof vest was something she did every day like brushing her teeth. For the first time the two men had worn vests as well. Standard procedure on a trip like this, Seth had tossed off between ravenous bites of Rafe's Spanish omelet.

Now seated in the back seat of the silver Mercedes Rafe had requisitioned from the available vehicles especially for the trip he and Lyssa were huddled together, playing one of her video games while the frantic guitar riffs and screeching lyrics of Acid Aliens pumped through the rear speakers. She'd grown used to the atonal cacophony, but she'd expected Rafe to protest. When the first clanging notes had screamed through the sedan's elegant interior, he'd looked pained but hadn't said a word.

It was turning out to be a day of surprises, she reflected as the familiar sights along the I-5 corridor from Portland to Ashland whizzed past the tinted windows.

The most gratifying had been the presence of Rafe himself, looking very much like the boy she remembered in faded jeans and a faded blue work shirt rolled tight against his biceps. Stone-faced, and unapproachable, he'd simply climbed into the driver's seat, slipped on a pair of aviator sunglasses, and clicked his seat belt into place. Since then, he'd spoken in monosyllables—and only when asked a direct question.

"I'm glad you decided to come," she said, looking his way.

He flicked her an impatient look as he pulled onto the exit ramp for a rest area. "Don't blame me if this turns into a train wreck."

She masked her own anxiety behind a teasing grin. "When did you get to be such a pessimist?"

"Right about the time when your brother smashed his fist into my face."

Lying prone in a patch of buffalo grass that made his nose itch, Linc peered through his field glasses at the man half-hidden by a thicket of blackberry canes near the mouth of the culvert.

It never failed to amaze him how false the public's perception of a vicious criminal could be sometimes. Jacob Folsom was a case in point. A man meeting him at a cocktail party would immediately peg him for an investment banker or maybe a midlevel diplomat, both of which he'd pretended to be during his various scams. Even now, seated in a filthy culvert, he was the picture of sophistication and confidence, occasionally drinking bottled water or getting up to stretch his legs.

An angry knot formed between his graying brows as he thought back to the expression that had come over Folsom's handsome face when the judge in the MacGregor case had dismissed the charges against him for lack of evidence.

That had been the real Jacob Folsom, Linc reflected. That vicious curl of a lip, the glint of pure malice in dead blue eyes, the quick burst of laughter as that fat toad Addison Tandy had shaken his hand.

"Give my regards to Agent Cardoza," he'd said as they'd met in the hall a few minutes later. "Tell him no hard feelings."

Linc knew better. Beneath the striking good looks and urbane manners was a stone-cold killer.

"Hey, that's the gate on the Mancini label," Seth said, leaning forward to peer between the bucket seats as Rafe drove under the ornate wrought-iron arch that perfectly framed the sprawling white house on the hill.

Surprised by the pride she felt, Danni glanced over her shoulder to explain, "My father designed it himself on the back of a comic book when he was only ten. He claimed he always knew he'd been born to make wine and didn't see any need to waste time trying to be anything else."

Grinning, Seth settled back against the butter-soft leather upholstery. "Sounds like my old man. He always knew he was going to be a filthy rich ne'er-do-well playboy like his father and grandfather before him. I doubt he wasted much time either."

"How come you haven't followed in his footsteps?" she teased.

"Who says I haven't?" he countered, flashing her a Groucho Marx leer.

Laughing, she returned her gaze to the front. From the corner of her eye she saw Rafe's jaw harden.

"So what kind of grapes are those in this field here?" Seth asked a moment later.

"I'm not sure," Danni admitted, frowning at the neat rows. "It's been a while since I rode the fields with Papa."

"Those are hybrid Chardonnay," Rafe said, his face set in grim lines.

"Yeah? How can you tell?"

"Soil content of that particular field's perfect for Chardonnay. *El Jefe* hybridized his own variety."

Surprised yet again that Rafe could remember such a small

detail, Danni glanced back at Seth again. "Chardonnay has always been one of Mancini's best sellers."

"Having killed a few bottles of same in my day I'm not surprised. It's as good as any low-end Chardonnay I've ever tasted."

"Don't let my father hear you refer to his pride and joy as low-end or you're liable to end up outside this same gate with a bruise the size of his boot on your backside."

Seth acknowledged that with an apologetic smile. "I take it *El Jefe* is your father?"

She nodded. "Roughly translated, it means the big boss." She glanced in Rafe's direction. "That's right, isn't it?"

"First thing a peon learns growing up here is never to contradict a Mancini on Mancini land." The sardonic edge to his voice had her teeth grinding together. Seth noticed and telegraphed his understanding.

"Some of the men also call him *El Patrón*," she went on, determined not to let Rafe's bad mood spoil hers. "I suspect they sometimes call him other things as well, especially when he's in a temper."

"You got that right," Rafe said under his breath, but Danni heard. She grieved for the years he had lost. With the exception of the miserable months after he'd disappeared from her life, she had experienced nothing but happiness and comfort on this land.

"Some digs, Doc. Looks exactly like a movie set," Seth declared with awe in his voice as the Mercedes made the sweeping circle leading to the parking area in front of the detached four car garage.

It did at that, Danni thought, trying to see her home through his eyes. Freshly painted only last summer, the century-old house gleamed like newly fallen snow in the sunshine. Bright green shutters graced the north facing windows. A new metal roof the color of slate was the only thing that had changed since her childhood. Even the petunias spilling from the tubs on the front porch seemed the same.

Once a traditional boxy farmhouse with a steeply pitched roof, it had undergone numerous changes over the years. A room here, a wing there, all without more than a nodding concession to symmetry or grace. And yet, the whole was more beautiful than its parts.

Like friendship or a good marriage—or a loving family.

"Oh poop, Uncle Vito's already hanging the piñatas," Lyssa exclaimed as Rafe parked next to her papa's beat-up GMC pickup, then killed the engine.

"Looks like you're just in time to help, sweetie," she said as Lyssa hurriedly freed herself from the seat belt. Seth was already climbing out on his side, his gaze unobtrusively scanning the area. His weapon was displayed prominently at his side as was Rafe's. Today, for the first time both he and Rafe had clipped their badges to their belts.

Eyes sparkling and impatient, Lys threw open the door and started to climb out, only to freeze suddenly. "Is it okay to take off the vest while we're here?" Danni noticed she directed her question to Rafe.

"Yes, *niña*. You can take off the vest now." Turning his head, he gave her a smile full of so much tenderness Danni's heart seemed to stop dead. "Just make sure you don't misplace it, okay? I had the devil's own time finding one to fit you."

"Okay." Then she was out of the car and running in her own lopsided way toward the side yard where both workers and family were preparing for the fiesta which by tradition started at 2:16 p.m., the exact moment of her dad's birth sixty-eight years ago.

As she watched, the side door opened and Rosaria came down the steps carrying a large yellow bowl covered in foil. As soon as Rafe saw her, his hands clenched white around the steering wheel.

"She's gotten so much older," he grated in a rough voice. "I knew, and yet in my mind she was still the same as the last time I saw her." His pain was nearly palpable. Tears filled Danni's eyes and clogged her throat.

"It might lessen the shock if I told her you were here before she actually saw you," she said quietly. But even as she said the words, one of the women arranging the food on the long trestle tables drew Rosaria's attention to the Mercedes.

She looked puzzled for a moment before catching sight of Lyssa who had already removed her vest and was carrying it toward the porch. Breaking into a wide grin, Rosaria hurriedly set the bowl on the nearest table before hurrying toward them.

Rafe's shoulders jerked before taking on a stiff line. He hesitated, then opened the door and climbed out, straightening slowly to his full height. As soon as Rosaria saw him her steps faltered and she went deathly pale.

"Rafael? Is it really you, *Mi hijo?*" she whispered as he went toward her.

"Hello, Mama," he said quietly, those brutally large hands curled into loose fists at his sides. Whatever happened, he would accept it with the same steely steadiness that was part of him now. But when his mother's hands lifted toward his face, he flinched. Instead of a blow, however, Rosaria caressed his face with those work-worn hands.

Rafe's hands trembled as they covered hers. His throat was so tight it ached, and his heart was a trip hammer. Her face had new lines, and the thick black hair that always smelled of herbs was threaded with gray. But her eyes still shone with the soft light he remembered as they searched his face.

"So many years I prayed to the Blessed Mother to see you again before I died," she whispered in the same soft, musical voice that had soothed countless troubles.

"Me, too, *Mamacita*," he admitted, his voice breaking. His chest heaved, and then she was in his arms, her sobs shaking both of them. Through the blur of his own tears he saw Danni hurry past on her way to the house. As she passed, she tossed him a brilliant smile through the tears spilling down her cheeks.

It was then that he knew he'd never really stopped loving her.

Sandals slapping the Mexican tile of the entryway, Danni marched down the hall leading to the glassed-in porch at the back where the men of the family went to smoke the smelly cigars Aunt Gina refused to have in the house proper.

Someday she might look back and laugh herself silly at the sight she presented—eyes blazing, hair flying, her belly straining against the ugly blue vest. At the moment all she had was a violent urge to wring her brother's neck.

"Eddie Mancini, where are you?" she demanded as she jerked open the door to the porch.

Caught in the act of lighting a cigar, her brother nearly choked on the smoke as he shot to his feet. "It's about time you got here, little sister," he exclaimed at he opened brawny arms to accept her hug.

Instead, she doubled up her fist and planted it as hard as she could squarely in the center of his prominent Mancini nose. Something crunched as pain jolted up her arm all the way to her shoulder, then ran down again. Blood spurted as Eddie let out an outraged bellow, his eyes glazing over with shock.

"What the hell was that for?" he demanded, putting his hand to his face.

"That's for what you did to Rafe, you miserable excuse for an older brother," she shouted, fairly quivering with so many emotions even she was hard pressed to sort them out. Predominant, however, was a bottomless feeling of loss.

"What are you talking about?" Eddie shouted back.

"I know all about it, Edward. How you and Mark and my two other interfering brothers threatened to turn his family off Mancini land if he didn't leave town and never come back."

Guilt flashed across his face as he jerked his handkerchief from his back pocket. "Who told you that?" he hedged before pressing the folded hanky to his nose.

"Remember the Secret Service agent I told you about? The one who was prepared to die in order to keep Lys and me safe?"

"Yeah, some guy from the East named Gresham."

"Gresham's his partner. *Rafe's* partner."

Beneath the burned-in tan, Eddie's face turned the color of putty. "I can explain, *cara*."

"Explain to us as well, *Eduardo*," her father ordered coldly from the doorway.

Danni's heart stuttered when she saw that Enrique stood next to Papa, shock imprinted on his seamed face. The same shock that chilled her father's dark eyes.

"It's not what you think," Eddie began, only to wince as his rapidly swelling nose caused his voice to thicken as well.

"Is it true, what Daniela has just said about you and Rafael?" Enrique demanded, his customary diffidence forgotten.

Unable to meet the honest eyes of a man who'd given him only kindness and affection for the whole of his life, Eddie took the handkerchief from his mangled nose and pretended to study the blood that had turned the cotton scarlet.

"Our good friend Enrique had asked you a question, Eduardo. We are both waiting for your answer." There was something in her father's voice that Danni had never heard before. It took her a moment to put a name to it.

It was shame.

After drying his mother's tears, and his own, Rafe had shucked off the vest while at the same time explaining how he'd come to be back on Mancini property. She was both shocked by the news that Danni and Lyssa were in danger and grateful that he was watching out for her.

Part of God's plan, she had said with a certainty that never failed to make him uneasy. If his life had been part of a divine plan, it was a good bet he was at the bottom of the favorites' list.

Then, after making sure Seth was keeping an eye on things, he'd led her to a wooden bench in a secluded part of the garden near a flowering plum he'd helped Enrique plant when he'd been six. Barely taller than he'd been then, it now towered over them.

Now, twenty minutes later his mother was running out of breath and family news. They spoke in Spanish as they always did when they were alone. His was a little rusty, but it came back quickly. Even so Rafe was hard pressed to keep up with twenty years of changes. It was as though he'd been swept into some kind of parallel universe where the names were the only thing that had remained the same.

"Paloma is a nurse now, married five years to a fine man who is soon to be a doctor. They have two beautiful *niñas,* Rosalie and Ramon and a beautiful house in Sacramento where he is going to medical school. She wanted to be here today, but one of the babies has an ear infection.''

Paloma had been a chubby two-year-old hellion when he'd left. Now she had babies of her own? God, it wasn't possible, was it?

Carlos had three sons, all of whom he would meet today when they returned from Ashland where they'd gone to put a down payment on a home of their own.

Alfonso and Miguel were also married, both to Anglos. More devoted to their careers than adding to her flock of grandchildren, but good women both of them, Mama had hastened to assure him, despite the resignation flavoring her words.

''And you, Rafi, you've grown into such a beautiful man. My heart stopped when I saw you standing there, so tall and strong, with the face of the golden Aztec prince of the legend. I'm so proud of you, my precious son.''

The praise unsettled him. ''Tell me about Connie, Mama. Did she ever become a teacher like she dreamed?''

''*Pero, si.* Graduated at the top of her class at Southern Oregon. She teaches English literature at the high school in town.''

It didn't seem real to him. Connie had been a leggy nine-year-old with scabby knees and a mischievous sense of humor. ''How many babies has she given you to spoil?'' he teased, smiling more easily now.

''Stubborn girl, she is still unmarried.'' Her sigh was heavy. A mother's burden, it conveyed as clearly as a shout. ''Ah, but she has started seeing a teacher from the junior college. She has promised to bring him today so that we can meet him. She will be so happy to see you.''

''Will she, Mama?''

''Of course. What happened was so many years ago. The anger fades.''

But not the pain, her expression added, tearing off a chunk of his control.

''Tell me about you, *Mamacita*,'' he asked, taking her hand in his. ''Are you happy?''

''Every day God grants us is precious, Rafi, so I am content." Her gaze narrowed, searching his face as though looking for something only she could see. "But you are not, I think," she said finally with sorrow in her voice. Thoughtfully, she shifted her gaze toward the house. "Perhaps God has given you and Danni another chance."

"She's not in the market for another husband, Mama." He found himself reaching into his breast pocket for a cigarette before he remembered he'd stopped.

"She was sad for a long time." Her gaze came back to his. "I don't know why you left, *hijo*. But you have always been kind and loving, so whatever your reason, I know it was not dishonorable the way Eddie claimed."

Incapable of words, he simply took her hands in his and kissed them the way Enrique sometimes had when his own emotions overwhelmed him.

"Talk to him, Rafi. He's suffered, too. Sometimes at night he gets up and walks to the spot along the bank where he taught you to fish. I know he's thinking of you then."

He drew a breath. "There's nothing I can say, Mama."

She touched his face. *"Por favor, Rafi. Para tu madre."*

He found Seth in the main warehouse, watching the musicians setting up. Ordinarily he would have had an entire army posted around the area, but he knew that Linc wouldn't let Folsom anywhere near this place. Still, he didn't want his partner to get too relaxed.

It was advice he had given himself after his mother had shooed him off in search of Enrique. In the main house with *El Jefe,* one of the workers had told him with a curious look.

"Have to say when you Oregonians set out to party, you do it right," Seth said when Rafe joined him.

Rafe hadn't been an Oregonian for years, but he let that slide. "There's something I have to do, so if you don't see me around for a while, don't sweat it."

"Want me to stay close to the Doc?"

"No, let her have a few hours of freedom." One of the guitarists began tuning. The familiar sound had his gut tightening. He'd loved fiestas. The first time he'd held Danni in his arms was during a fiesta when she'd insisted on teaching him to dance.

He glanced at his watch. It was nearly 1330. He'd arranged to check in with Linc on the hour, using the walkie-talkie locked in the trunk of the Mercedes. "Hang loose, okay? I'll see you later."

Seth nodded. "I'll be here."

Wishing he was anyplace but here, Rafe left the warehouse and started toward the house. The open area between the warehouse and the house was filling up. Makeshift tables had been set up under trees and two teenage girls were laying out condiments. There would be enough food to feed a small country and an ocean of wine. For the kids there would be soda and ice cream and enough junk food to send them all home with tummy aches.

First, however, there would be games for the kids with prizes ranging from shiny new bicycles to a pack of gum. No one left empty-handed. Then came the food and *El Jefe*'s birthday toasts, one given by Eddie on behalf of the family and one delivered by Enrique as the workers' spokesman.

The dancing would start after that. Other things, too, as Rafe recalled. At least one baby was started on Mancini's birthday every year. Sometimes more. And more than one worker ended up snoring drunk, left to sleep it off wherever he'd passed out.

"*Hola,* Rafi," one of the older workers called down from the ladder where he'd been hanging streamers. "Damn near fell off this here ladder when I heard you'd come back packing a gun and wearing a badge."

So the word had spread, he thought while searching for a name to go with the face that had gotten older and more seamed than the one he remembered. "How's it going, Señor Martinez? Still catching the big ones?"

The old man grinned, showing off a gold tooth. "Can't complain," he said with a laugh before returning to his task. Nothing changed, Rafe thought as he skirted the course laid out for the sack race before angling across the driveway toward the house.

He was debating whether to use the front or back door when

someone to the rear called his name. Though he'd prepared himself mentally and emotionally to come face-to-face with the man who'd raised him, his body shot into defensive mode.

Working to level his emotions, he turned and waited for Enrique to catch up with him. The face that had reflected a mixture of Spanish and Indian genes seemed leaner now, and the thick coarse hair that had been as black as night was mostly gray now, but the deep-set eyes that had always reflected a fierce inner pride were unchanged.

Instead of his work clothes, he wore dark trousers and a sparkling white shirt that was crisp with starch. Surprise ran through him when he saw that his father was hatless. It struck him that he couldn't remember a time when his father had been without his straw hat when he was outdoors.

"*¿Cómo estás,* Rafael?" he asked when they stood only a few feet apart for the first time in twenty years.

Because he'd been taught to show respect to his elders, he nodded politely. *"Bien, Señor. Y usted?"*

"The same." Enrique glanced toward the picnic area, his expression stern. "You have made your mother very happy today. She thinks I haven't heard her crying in the night."

Rafe took a careful breath. It hurt more than the years of silence, this tense distance between them. He missed the easy teasing between them, the flashes of wry humor that sometimes crept up on him later, the special closeness between the oldest son and his father.

"I'm sorry, Padre, I never meant to hurt either of you." Locked away for more than half his lifetime, the words came out rough, but at least he'd kept his promise to his mother.

Enrique acknowledged his apology with a slow nod. Silence settled again. Though no one was impolite enough to stare, Rafe felt the surreptitious glances that came their way as the Mancini extended family prepared for the event of the year.

As though feeling those furtive looks as well, Enrique frowned, deepening lines and furrows burned into his leathery skin by countless hours under the blazing sun.

"This thing with Daniela, it's good she has you with her,"

he asked, gesturing toward the house. "She tells me you have been her salvation. And Lyssa's."

Rafe felt a sudden pressure in his chest as surprise jolted through him. He could hear her now, singing his praises to anyone who would listen. Doing her best to mend his fences for him. He wanted to be grateful. He was grateful, damn it. But it still galled him that he'd ended up in this mess.

"I don't know about salvation, but protecting her is my job."

Enrique focused his attention on his badge, and Rafe could have sworn the man's eyes filled with pride. "You work for the government, she said."

"Yes, the Secret Service. It's a branch of the Treasury Department."

Enrique looked both annoyed and amused. "You think your father is so ignorant he doesn't know that?" he chided in a surprisingly gentle tone.

Rafe felt the burn start at his throat and crawl up his neck to his cheeks. When he'd been a kid, he'd sometimes been embarrassed by Enrique's lack of education. After a while, though, he'd noticed how everyone deferred to his opinion, even Mancini himself. Underneath the untutored speech and unsophisticated ways was a brilliant mind. After he'd figured that out, he'd started to pay closer attention to the things his father told him.

"I meant no disrespect," he said honestly. "Not everyone knows where Secret Service fits in."

Enrique measured him with those dark eyes before sighing. "Once, when I was younger even than Lyssa, my father and I went into Puebla to sell a calf. We came to a bridge over the river which was the only way into town from the south. It was an old bridge, only wide enough for a single cart. *¿Comprende?*"

He lifted his eyebrows inquiringly, and Rafe nodded, both puzzled and intrigued.

"On this day we came upon an angry crowd gathered at the mouth of the bridge. In the center were two carts, one leaving, the other arriving. It seemed those carts had been there for hours, neither driver wanting to be the one to back down. No amount of angry protests from others who needed to use that bridge would move them. It was a matter of honor, each declared. A man who is in the right never backs down.''

Rafe drew a careful breath. ''What happened?''

Enrique chuckled. ''The wife of the man returning home arrived with her hungry babies—and a shotgun. She would shoot the burros of each man in turn, she said, unless both men backed off the bridge. Instantly, the two men began shouting protests. In the end, united against a common foe, they negotiated their own compromise. They even ended up in the cantina, making rude remarks about women while getting blind drunk.''

Rafe felt something let loose inside. Habit had him rubbing his hand over his chest before he realized what he was doing. ''I'm tired of standing on the bridge, Padre,'' he said gruffly.

His father's eyes were suddenly damp. ''Me too, my son. Me too.''

Rafe never knew who made the first move, but suddenly they were hugging each other. It had taken him a long time to get there, but finally, thanks to Danni, he'd come home.

After retrieving the walkie-talkie from the trunk, Rafe went into the bathroom off the tasting room and locked the door. The communications equipment Linc had brought with him was so sophisticated that a voice that was barely audible in the field came through clearly on the other end. The men in the field wore ear pieces with tiny microphones attached. The one Rafe carried was designed to look like a cell phone.

Linc replied to his call, informing him tersely that the men were all in place. ''He showed up around noon, driving a white Bronco with Washington plates. Parked in the pull-off and offloaded a lawn chair and a cooler before driving on down the road. Twenty minutes later he showed up on foot. Since then he's been kicked back in the culvert.''

Rafe felt his gut tighten. ''We'll be leaving here at 1600,'' he said, checking his watch. ''Expect us at your location by 1607.''

After signing off, he tucked the walkie-talkie into his back pocket, then flushed the toilet and washed his hands in case anyone was waiting outside. After drying his hands, he unlocked the door and walked through the silent and empty main room toward the exit. As he pushed open the door he saw Eduardo Mancini bearing down on him, a look of fierce determination on his face.

A confrontation had been inevitable from the moment he made the decision to walk Mancini land again. No matter what the man said he didn't intend to lose his temper. But only because he knew it would upset Danni.

Mancini stopped a few feet away, looking even more eager than Rafe to have this meeting over. He didn't extend his hand. Rafe hadn't figured he would and tucked both of his in his back pockets. "Happy Birthday, Patron," he said coldly.

Mancini frowned. "So, you've finally come back."

"Looks that way."

Mancini took a cigar from his pocket, then frowned irritably before jabbing it into the pocket again. "Are you married?" he demanded, pinning Rafe with a pugnacious stare.

"Why would that possibly matter to you?"

"Don't get smart with me, Rafael. I paddled your bottom more than once. I can do it again if I have to."

"I doubt it," Rafe said mildly.

"She still wants you," he said, spitting out the words as though they tasted foul.

"If she does, that's between the two of us."

Mancini narrowed his gaze. The years had added a patrician sharpness to his features and deepened the look of melancholy around his eyes. Rafe's father had told him once that he'd never gotten over the death of Danni's mother. Though he didn't want to feel anything but contempt for the man who'd driven him away, he knew what it felt like to have a part of your heart ripped out.

"For what it's worth, if you're fortunate enough to win my Danni's hand, you have my blessing."

It struck Rafe that Mancini looked exactly like a man feeling the cold barrel of a gun pressed against his spine. Suspicion was as much a part of Rafe as breathing. It sharpened now to a razor's edge. "You sure you don't have me mixed up with someone else, Patron? Someone *worthy*."

"I know who you are. I also know what you are."

Rafe's mouth took on a cynical line. "A mongrel bastard, I believe were the exact words Eddie used."

Anger churned in Mancini's brown eyes. "His words, not mine," he clipped out.

"Words you put in his mouth," Rafe shot back before he regained control of the bitter anger he hadn't quite mastered.

"You're wrong, son." Mancini suddenly looked every day of his sixty-plus years. "What Eddie said and did was wrong. Dead wrong. If I could give you back the years he took from you I would, and gladly. But that's impossible. All I can do now is offer you and your parents my deepest apology."

Before Rafe got his jaw unhinged, Eduardo turned on his heel and started to walk away. Two steps later, he turned back to pin Rafe with another of those formidable looks. "One more thing you need to know, Rafael. You were born on this land. It's your home as much as it is mine. If I had wanted you to leave I would have told you that to your face. Until I do, you are always welcome here."

The sun was kissing the tops of the trees as Danni worked her way through the crowd, catching up on gossip, laughing at a joke she'd heard a dozen times before, admiring a new baby, effusing over an engagement ring, congratulating the groom-to-be.

The sounds and the smells, the laughter and music, the smiles on faces she'd known all of her life—it was all so wonderfully familiar. It soothed her somehow, knowing that there would always be a place for her here.

By the time she made her way to the buffet table she was ravenous. After months of surviving on little more than tea and toast, she was thrilled to discover the queasiness seemed to have disappeared.

A good-looking young man with soulful eyes and long, glossy hair who'd been filling a plate with sweets greeted her shyly before ambling off to join the pretty teenager waiting for him near the pool.

After deliberating carefully, Danni dipped a plump shrimp into the spicy cocktail sauce and popped it into her mouth with a little hum of pleasure.

"Obviously Baby likes shrimp," Rafe commented as he joined her.

She smiled, pleased to see that the stony look around his eyes was gone. "Baby likes just about everything today. I feel exactly like a squirrel storing up nuts for the winter."

Rafe lifted a hand to smooth her collar, his fingers brushing the sensitive skin of her throat. A little thrill ran through her. It was the first time he'd touched her all day. "We need to leave soon, Princess."

Her brow puckered. "Oh Rafe, no! It's way too early. I promised Aunt Gina I'd help her serve the cake. And Lyssa's having such a good time. Seth even talked her into being his partner for the sack race."

"Yeah? How'd they do?"

"They won! I'm surprised he hasn't told you. He's certainly told everyone else who would stand still long enough."

He grinned, but she noticed he seemed distracted. "I imagine he'll get around to it."

"I looked for you before it started, but I must have missed you in the crowd."

"Hmm?" He was searching the crowd, obviously looking for someone. She felt a moment's fear, then realized it wasn't a threat he was watching for.

"I wanted to watch the race with you," she said pointedly. So far this afternoon she'd spent a grand total of ten minutes with him, nine of which had just ticked by. It was not the way she had envisioned this day when she realized he was coming with her.

She poked a finger into his hard belly. "Rafe, I said I wanted to watch the race with you."

He flicked her an impatient glance. "I appreciate the effort."

He was humoring her, she realized, beginning to fume. "I got to award the prizes. I gave Seth the pack of baseball cards.

Lyssa got a copy of the *Kama Sutra.* I figured it was time she learned how to please a man.''

"Great.''

She was wondering if she would break her toes if she kicked him in the shins when his gaze whipped back to her face. "*What* did you say?"

"Obviously nothing that interests you," she snapped before stalking off. He caught her before she'd gone more than a few steps.

He grabbed her but instead of stopping her, he simply changed direction, pulling her along with him toward the path leading down to the pond. As they passed, eyes snapped their way, some startled, some amused. His brother Carlos gave him a thumbs-up. Rafe flashed him a grin that dripped testosterone.

Danni felt her temper start to sizzle. "Rafe, stop this!" she ordered. "Everyone's watching."

"Good for them."

She considered digging in her heels, then realized that would be about as effective as a mouse trying to stop a charging bull. "This is silly," she shouted.

He didn't stop until they were screened from view by the berry vines. Winded, she took a moment to catch her breath, only to find herself spun around to face him. Before she could blast him, his hands came up to frame her face. His eyes were very green as they bored into hers.

"Did you or did you not slug your brother in the face?" he demanded, his voice rough.

Since she knew it was futile to struggle, she pressed her hands against his chest and felt the pounding of his heart beneath her palms.

"Why would you ask that?" she probed cautiously as he dropped his hands to her shoulders.

"No reason—just the fact that his nose is twice its normal size. *Which* I happened to notice when he apologized to me for acting like an ass."

"What did he say?"

His eyes crinkled, but his voice was drenched in pure masculine impatience. "He advised me never to make you mad."

Danni felt laughter bubble in her throat. "Ah."

He glowered. "Well?"

"I might have overreacted just a little," she hedged.

His jaw tightened. He was furious, she realized with a large measure of surprise. "Damn it, Danni, you could have hurt yourself!"

"But I didn't." She risked a tiny smile. "That stupid vest might have gotten a little blood spattered on it, though. I never knew a broken nose could bleed so…profusely."

His scowl was truly lethal. A lesser woman would be shaking in her sandals. "Did you talk to my father, too?" he demanded, his voice silky now.

"Not intentionally. He and Papa overheard me talking to Eddie. For a minute or two I was afraid your dad was going to tear poor Eddie apart. By the time the three of us were finished with him, he was pretty shaken."

He closed his eyes, then dropped his forehead to hers. "What am I going to do with you?" he muttered.

"Love me?" The words slipped out as easily as a sigh. Now they hung there between them like the memory of the last time they stood here together.

His chest rose and fell in a ragged sigh. Tension coiled and hissed around them, and he seemed to be having trouble with his breathing. "God help me, I never stopped."

Because the words seemed torn from him against his will, it took a moment for her seething brain to translate the words. And then joy burst inside her. "Really?" she said in a little voice.

He lifted his head and looked down at her. Lines of tension framed his eyes and bracketed his mouth. "Yes, really."

She heard the irritation in his voice and bristled. "You don't sound very happy about it."

The mouth she loved to feel on hers tightened into a hard line. "I'm not."

Now it was hurt that pulsed through her. "Thanks for sharing that, Cardoza," she declared, wrapping herself in pride.

He ground his teeth. "Ah hell, honey, don't look at me like that."

"Like what?" she asked stiffly.

"Like you don't know whether to knee me in the groin or cry."

"Actually I'm just trying to work out the sequence."

His mouth curled up. "Would you consider an alternative?"

"I doubt it."

He sighed. "The crying I can probably handle, but the other might be a problem, considering I'm hoping you'll consent to have my baby at some future time. Or babies. The number is up to you."

"B-babies?" It was dream, she decided. Or a hallucination brought on by a food overdose.

Rafe saw the shock come into her eyes and cursed himself for handling this all wrong. Probably because for the first time in his life he hadn't taken the time to think things through thoroughly before committing himself. "Babies aren't a requirement," he backpedaled. "We can talk about that later."

Suddenly she had a death grip on his shirt with those tough little fists. "Now," she demanded with a fierce little scowl. "We'll talk now."

He glanced at his watch and hissed out another curse. "I admit my timing is lousy, but it's important that you know how much I...care about you."

"Love. You said you loved me."

Suddenly he felt as though a huge boulder had suddenly fallen on his chest cavity. "I do. More than you can ever imagine. I'm even crazy about Lyssa, although she's probably going to be a hard sell."

"Just what are you...selling?"

Hell. "Uh, well, marriage, I guess. Once your legal status is sorted out, of course."

Those dark elegant brows drew together, and her mouth took on a stubborn line. "Is this by any chance a proposal?"

Hadn't he just flat out said that? Puzzled, he ran over the conversation in his head before he caught on. "You want a big production, right? Flowers and a ring, things women need to make them feel like they've been courted." He slipped his arms around her and felt her shiver. "Give me a little time to figure out how to work it, okay? In the meantime, take this on account."

Afraid to give her time to think, he brought his mouth down on hers and kissed her as though his entire future depended on it. She jolted, then let out a little moan. The hands that had been pushing at his chest relaxed, and then she was kissing him back. Kissing him until his head spun and his knees went weak. It was all he could do to keep from stripping her bare and taking her on the grass with an entire community only a shout away.

When his control loosened, he forced himself to draw back. Her face was flushed, her expression dazed. "Wow," she murmured, letting her eyes drift open.

He dragged air into his lungs, needing oxygen to clear his head. "Time to go, honey."

Still a little dazed, she gave him a puzzled look. "Why are you in such a hurry?"

Damn, he hated to lie to her. "I have my reasons."

"But—"

He silenced her with a quick kiss. "Danni, do you trust me?"

"Yes, of course. But—"

"If I told you I would never do anything to put either you or Lyssa at grave risk, would you believe me?"

She searched his face. "Is it important to you that I believe you?"

"Just about the most important thing I can think of at the moment."

Lifting a hand, she touched the scar where the fish hook had ripped his flesh. "In that case, yes, I believe you."

Chapter 17

From their position fifty feet away, Linc heard Folsom's phone ring. He flexed his shoulders to loosen the muscles, then eased his weapon from the holster. "Heads up," he whispered into the microphone. "ETA, six minutes."

Every man was braced and ready, eyes focused on the target crouched below sight level fifty feet away, his weapon in his hand. A successful result depended on training, split second timing—enough luck to have sweat trickling down Linc's back.

"As soon as he commits, A-team moves. B-team, if he refuses to surrender, make sure you have a clear shot, then take him down. But for God's sake—and the sake of that brave little girl and Rafe—make sure you don't miss."

By prearrangement, Lyssa sat on the right in the back seat with Rafe next to her. Seth drove. To Rafe's relief Danni accepted that as routine. It was his job, what he was about to do, he reminded himself. It was necessary. It was his only option.

He'd minimized the risk, planned for every possible contingency. He and Seth and the team backing him up were part of the Special Ops unit that would be sent in to rescue the president should he ever be kidnapped. Linc would have the responsibility of planning such an operation. In fact, the unit had a multitude of plans already in place—and practiced until they were second nature.

Still, it all hinged on one little girl. It scared him to think what life would be like for Danni—and everyone else involved—if something went wrong. Imagining that had pretty much ruined his sleep and wrecked his stomach.

Maybe it had been sleep deprivation that had had him getting all sentimental down by the pond. Whatever it was, he needed to block it out. Later, he would deal with mending his fences.

Next to him, Lyssa adjusted the ponytail she'd pulled into one of those scrunchy things. She looked more excited than nervous. He was the one with a burning knot in his belly.

While he'd had been tripping over his own tongue, Seth had been taking her though the plan again, step-by-step. Once he was satisfied, he had her call Folsom to say they were leaving in ten minutes.

"How'd you get blood on your vest, Mom?" Lys asked as Seth drove through the gate.

"It's a long story," Danni said, turning to mesh her gaze with Rafe's. He managed to smile back, but his mind was already focusing on the next few minutes. As soon as she turned around again, Rafe took Lyssa's hand and kissed it. She flashed him a smile, then took a deep breath and focused her attention on the road.

He caught Seth's gaze in the mirror and nodded.

Soon. It would be soon.

Jake's muscles were coiled and ready. Excitement churned in his belly and danced through his head and he checked the Beretta one more time. The extra clips were in his pocket, but he doubted he would need them. Among his other talents, Jake Folsom was a crack shot.

Once again, his plan was flawless. His Beretta was loaded with explosive, high velocity death. His escape route north to Vancouver had been laid out in meticulous detail. Soon. Very

soon Jacob Peter Folsom would exist only in the minds of the
dumb-ass cops he'd beaten and the brainless twits he'd conned.

Only one man stood between him and the new life he had
planned. One stupid, plodding government hack, paid peanuts
to put his life on the line out of some pathetically corny belief
in justice.

Jake laughed softly before tipping the liter bottle of water to
his mouth. What justice there was in this country was simply
another commodity like rare gems and fast cars and beautiful
women, available only to those with money.

After capping the bottle he tucked it back into the cooler.
He'd already policed the area to make sure he hadn't left any
clues behind. After he made sure all the occupants of the silver
Mercedes were dead, he would carry the cooler and the lawn
chair to the Mercedes and drive back to the spot where he'd
left his Bronco. By this time tomorrow Michael Carlyle would
be in Canada taking delivery of his own Mercedes, his only
worry what to order for dinner.

Oh yes, life was going to be so sweet.

Soon, now. Very soon.

Through the hole he'd cut in the blackberry thicket he could
see the silver Mercedes Lyssa had described coming toward
him. Only seconds separated Cardoza from the agonizing death
he deserved.

Jake could hardly wait.

"Ow," Lyssa said suddenly, clutching her stomach.

Danni's head swiveled around, alarm stamped on her features. "What's wrong, sweetie?" she asked anxiously.

"I don't feel so good," Lys gasped out, then for good measure, let out a keening groan. The kid was a natural, Rafe
thought with real admiration. Her face had actually turned pale,
he noted, before shifting his gaze to the road. "I think I ate
too many enchiladas."

The culvert was ahead. Bushes blocked the view, but Rafe
knew Folsom was there, waiting. He braced, ready to reach for
the door handle. He was going out after Lyssa on the passenger
side.

"Are you going to be sick to your stomach?" Danni asked, touching her daughter's head where it was bent over her knees.

"It just hurts," Lyssa wailed.

Seth slowed slightly, matching his pace to Lyssa's performance. Countless times during the last week they'd practiced on a country road outside of Portland.

"Stop the car, I'm going to be sick!" Lyssa cried, right on the target. Rafe released her seat belt and his.

"Hang on, kid," Seth muttered for Danni's benefit, braking hard. The Mercedes swerved into the pull-off and shuddered to a stop a good ten feet from the incline. Rafe eased his weapon from the holster.

"I'll help you, sweetie," Danni said, fumbling with her seat belt.

It happened fast then. Rafe threw open the door, and Lyssa scrambled out, her hand over her mouth. At the same time Seth grabbed Danni and pulled her down below the level of the window, covering her with his body in classic duck-and-cover procedure.

Lyssa ran to the edge of the pull-off just as Folsom came charging up, his weapon drawn. Instead of going down and rolling as she'd done perfectly each time Seth had taken her through it, she saw the gun in Folsom's hand and froze, directly in Rafe's line of fire. He veered left to get a clear shot. With a feral cry, Folsom fired. Pain exploded in Rafe's left thigh. He was already falling when another shot slammed into his shoulder. He heard other shots, heard Lyssa scream.

No! his mind shouted just as his head cracked against something hard and then everything went black.

Rafe surfaced slowly, the memory of pain still vivid in his mind. He felt a sense of urgency, an unnamed fear. Something was wrong, something important, but his thoughts kept scattering, bits and pieces.

Danni. Lyssa. The baby.

Noise. Terror.

Gunshots. Had there been shots? He felt his heart rate speed.

He struggled to wrap his mind around those pieces. To pull them all into some kind of sense.

"Rafe, can you hear me?"

Linc? What was he doing in Portland? He felt a hand on his arm. Someone else was holding his hand. He heard odd little beeps, familiar, yet he couldn't quite place them.

"Hey, Rafe, open your eyes, partner." Another voice, a different accent. Gresham. "There's a whole bunch of people hanging out in the corridor yonder who haven't been to bed in almost twenty-four hours while you've been snoring away."

Snoring? What the hell?

Somehow he managed to pry open his eyes. Little by little the blurry images sharpened until Linc's homely face swam into view. He fought to clear the sticky gray cobwebs from his mind. "What happened?" he managed to rasp out.

"We took him down, Rafe." Linc's voice was sharp with grim satisfaction. "That murdering bastard, Folsom. He's downstairs on a slab."

"He used a Beretta like the shooter who killed Alice. It's a good bet the bullets the docs dug out of you will match the ones that killed her," Seth added grimly.

Folsom? Had they sprung the trap without him?

Rafe fought to remember. And then suddenly, panic shot through him. He struggled to sit up, only to have hands hold him down.

"Lyssa?" he croaked.

"She's fine," Seth assured him, pride in his voice. "Damned if she didn't try some of her kick-boxing tricks on the bastard. Distracted him just enough for our guys to get in a shot."

Tears flooded his eyes. Damn but he was proud of her. "Danni?"

"She's fine, too." Something in Seth's voice had his heart jolting.

"She's...ticked off?" he guessed aloud.

Linc chuckled. "Let's say she's not very happy with any of us at this moment."

"She'll get over it," Seth offered. "Both she and Lyssa insisted on riding in the ambulance with you, and they pretty

much camped out in the waiting room until the doc told us you
were gonna make it.''

"Where...now?''

"Her father took her back to the vineyard.'' His partner
needed a shave and his eyes were bloodshot. He looked exhausted. Linc didn't look much better.

"The entire Cardoza family is outside, including a whole
passel of little ones asking about their Tio Rafe,'' Linc said,
his smile strained in his tired face. "Nice people. We've kept
each other company. They'll want to see you if you feel up to
it.''

Rafe managed to nod.

"I'll just go get them,'' Linc said. "Glad to have you back,
old son.'' He pressed Rafe's hand before disappearing.

"Me, too, partner,'' Seth said, rising.

"Seth?''

"Yeah?''

"Tell Danni I want to see her. To explain.''

Seth dropped his gaze. "I'm not sure that's such a good idea
right now, Rafe. She's pretty steamed.''

"Tell her...no, *ask* her, anyway.''

"For you, partner, anything.'' His grin was lopsided, but
Rafe was pretty sure he saw tears in the kid's eyes.

Although it was nearly 6:00 p.m., the sun was still high in
the sky. Sunday was a day of rest, and the vineyard was quiet.
The tables had been put away for another year and the party
debris piled in the Dumpster.

After her father had brought them home from the hospital
around five o'clock that morning, she and Lyssa had gone to
bed in Danni's old room. Lyssa had awakened after a few hours
and had gotten out of bed, which had jerked Danni out of a
restless sleep. Still high on adrenaline, Lyssa was unable to
settle. Since it had turned out to be another perfect day, Danni
had suggested a swim. While Lyssa worked off excess energy,
Danni sat at a poolside umbrella table, trying to work a cross-
word puzzle to distract herself.

Seth had found them alone at the pool and presented his case.

"What is there to explain?" Danni asked, staring at the tired looking man seated across from her. He was still wearing the same jeans and shirt, sadly wrinkled now, and his jaw was rough with whiskers. At the moment he looked more Wild West than Ivy League.

"Rafe could have gotten my daughter killed. Nothing else is relevant." She narrowed her gaze accusingly. "*You* could have gotten her killed."

He shifted uneasily. "The way Rafe set it up the chances of that were very slim, Danni."

"*Slim* is still a risk, which is more than I would have permitted, had I been asked. But I wasn't, was I?"

Something flickered in his blue eyes, but to his credit he kept them steady on hers. "No, you weren't asked."

"Rafe's orders, right?"

A trapped look came into his eyes, before he nodded. "Look, I know you're upset, but—"

"Upset? Oh no, Seth, I'm so far past upset what I'm feeling isn't even on the chart."

"Hey Seth, watch this!" Lyssa called from the edge of the diving board.

He turned in his chair to call back, "I'm all eyes, toots!"

Danni's stomach contracted as Lys stood poised for an instant, then performed a ragged jackknife, the same dive she'd been learning before the accident. She came up wiping water from her eyes and grinning. "How was that?" she asked eagerly.

"Looked terrific to me!" Seth called back.

"Your best today," Danni told her. "Why don't you take a break now, sweetie. Remember what your therapist said. Exercise followed by rest to let the muscles recover."

She looked ready to protest when Seth added, "There's something in the Mercedes for you. On the front seat with your name on it."

"Killer!" she shouted before hoisting herself over the lip of the pool. Seth stood to toss her a towel. "What is it?" she asked, her voice muffled as she dried her face.

"Go and see," he told her. "Mostly it's from Rafe. I'm just the delivery boy."

"I love presents!" Grinning, she wrapped the towel around her still dripping body.

"Wear your flip-flops," Danni ordered. "The grass has burrs."

Impatiently, she slipped her feet into her thongs. "Be right back," she shouted as she raced through the open gate in the fence around the pool area.

"What did you bring her?" Danni asked tightly.

Seth sat again and stretched his legs. "Four tickets to the Acid Aliens concert in Seattle next month. Front row center."

Gratitude mixed with resentment. "I won't forbid you to be there because I know Lyssa would resent me for it, but if Rafe shows up, too, we will leave."

Danni knew real misery when she saw it. His was acute. "Danni, please don't do this. Give him five minutes. Let him give you his side of this."

Danni felt the baby kick and wanted to weep. How could he have put this child at risk as well? So many things could have gone wrong. She'd experienced all of them in the nightmare hours she'd spent since gunshots had exploded around her yesterday.

Closure, Danni. Remember? No lingering feelings to tie the two of you together. Her heart contracted at the memory of the kind of closure she'd once envisioned.

"All right, five minutes, not a second longer. Make sure you tell him that. Not a second longer."

Rafe sensed her an instant before he opened his eyes. Hungry for the sight of her, he let his gaze skim every inch of her, from the glossy hair caught back with a yellow ribbon to the pink polished toes peeking out of her sandals.

She wore an oversize pale yellow T-shirt with the Mancini label on the front, the same kind that was sold in the gift shop, and the white slacks she'd worn to the fiesta. Her face was pale, but composed.

His need to touch her bordered on desperate. To feel her melt against him and tell him she understood. To fill his senses with the clean scent of her hair instead of the medicinal stink of the hospital.

She didn't smile as he greeted her, but she'd brought flowers from the garden. A good sign, he told himself—and almost believed it.

"These are from Papa and Aunt Gina," she said tightly, her eyes cool and remote as she set them on the bed stand. "Don't worry about returning the vase. We have plenty."

His hopes hit the floor. She was beyond angry. "Thank them for me, okay?"

"Of course." She glanced around at the monitoring equipment, then at the leg they'd put in traction after repairing the broken femur in surgery. "How are you?"

"Damn tired of getting shot." He tried to make it a joke. She didn't laugh.

"Will you walk again?"

His jaw tightened. "Yes."

She nodded, her expression remote. "Good. I'm glad."

He shifted on the pillow, trying to get a read on the best way to plead his case, but she was giving him nothing to work with. She had pulled everything inside, where he couldn't reach her. His face was suddenly icy, and yet, inside, he felt clammy with fear. "Sweetheart—"

"Don't call me that!" she exclaimed, her eyes suddenly hot. "Don't ever call me that again! If you do, I'll walk out."

Anger he could handle. It was the icy indifference that terrified him. "Will you walk out if I tell you I love you?"

The heat in her eyes faded as quickly as it came. It was hurt that simmered there now, the kind that came from deep inside. But when she spoke again, her voice was eerily calm. "That lovely scene we played out by the pond, it makes perfect sense now. Why you were so eager for me to *trust* you. You knew exactly what was going to happen in just a few minutes and you were covering your butt."

It stung. Stung more than the pain in his leg which was screaming. Stung like hell because she might be right. At least partially.

"I meant every word I said," he said quietly, his voice hoarse. "Maybe the timing was wrong, but it just…happened that way."

"But this obscene plan you concocted to use my daughter, that didn't just happen, did it? That was deliberate. In fact, according to Lyssa, you had her practicing for days."

He hated explaining himself. It seemed like begging. For her, though, he'd try. "In my gut I knew he'd get to you. It was the only way to make sure he didn't."

"Ah, so that makes it right? You would sacrifice Lyssa to save me."

"Damn it, Princess, it wasn't like that at all! I had Lyssa covered. I knew he'd go for me first."

She seemed to pale even more. "But what if he hadn't?"

"But he did, damn it! And now he's dead. He can't get to you. Or the baby." Deliberately, he let his gaze rest on her tummy. A man fighting for his life sometimes fought dirty. "Not now, or not years from now. Or have you forgotten the threats he made?"

She took a breath, then seemed to grow even more remote. He felt her slipping away from him, and fingers of panic clawed his spine.

"I knew you were strong-willed, Rafe. I knew you could be stubborn and determined. I didn't realize how ruthless you could be when you wanted something. In fact, it occurs to me that in many ways you and Folsom are exactly alike."

He felt that to the bone. It was beyond hurtful. "Damn it, I'm not anything like him!"

Her gaze stayed steady on his, but the hands resting on the bed railing tightened. "No? Let's see, shall we? Jonathan deliberately set out to deceive and betray me. So did you. Jonathan seduced me for his own aims. So did you. I thought I was in love with Jonathan, but as you so wisely said, I was really in love with the man I thought he was. With you—"

"Enough! You're wrong. Dead wrong." The pain in his leg

had edged past screaming to excruciating. He blocked it out. "I didn't deceive you. In fact, I told you things I've never told anyone else. As for seducing you, yes, I wanted you. I've always wanted you, but you were willing. More than willing."

The faint tinge of pink coloring her cheeks encouraged him to cover her hand with his. With a cry, she snatched it back, damn near unmanning him. He took a deep breath and tried once more. "Danni, I meant it when I said I love you. I've always loved you. Maybe I did make mistakes, but if I did, it was because I needed to keep you and Lys safe. It's part of who I am, what I am. If you can't see that, if you can't accept that, then there's no hope for us."

For an instant doubt seemed to shimmer in her eyes before they filled with tears. "There's never been any hope for us, Rafe. On some level I'll always regret that."

He'd lost her. His mind screamed a protest. He couldn't lose her, not when they were so close to having it all. "For God's sake, Danni—"

"Please don't ever contact Lys or me again. You're welcome at the vineyard because it's your home as well as mine, but I'd appreciate it if you wouldn't plan your visit for a time when Lys and I are there. Holidays we can work out somehow."

"Danni, don't do this. Please."

Her smile was bittersweet. "Sorry, your five minutes are up." She turned and fled.

He never knew how the vase got into his hand. He had no memory of throwing it. Only when it hit the wall and shattered did he realize what he'd done.

It didn't help one damn bit.

Danni woke up to find Lyssa huddled into a ball on her side of the bed, trying desperately to stifle her sobs. Danni hastily turned on the lamp, then turned back to comfort her daughter.

"Oh, honey, don't," she said, rubbing Lyssa's back. "I know you were scared, but it's all over."

"It was my f-fault Rafe got hurt," she stuttered out between sobs. "I knew what I was supposed to do, but I messed up. If I hadn't he wouldn't have almost died."

Lyssa's words took her aback. It sounded as though her daughter hadn't been worried at all about her own safety. "No, honey, it's not your fault. It's Rafe's for putting you in that position."

Lyssa turned to look at her. "I *wanted* to help, Mom. I liked it that he and Seth trusted me to help. I *hated* Jonathan for what he did to us!"

Danni took a careful breath. "I thought it was Rafe you hated."

Lyssa swiped a hand over her wet cheeks. She had changed, somehow, since Rafe had come into their lives. "I did at first, but even when I said nasty things to him, he never got mad. And he made you laugh, you know? Like Daddy did. Sometimes he made me laugh, too. I kept thinking he was being nice to me on account of wanting to impress you, only even when you weren't there, he was nice. And he talked to me like I was a grown-up and not a kid." Her smile trembled. "He said he respected me on account of how I was so hurt in the accident and had to go through therapy and all. He said he knew how awful it was seeing Daddy in the wreck. He said I was the strongest person he knew next to you."

"I'm glad you like Rafe, sweetie. And he's right. You are strong and brave and so very dear to me. I keep wondering what I did to deserve such a great kid." With a hand that trembled, she stroked the soft hair that had been peach fuzz when her little girl had been born. Sometimes she woke up in a panic, thinking about how close she'd come to losing her, too.

"This whole thing with Jonathan, I'm so sorry I made such a mess of things, sweetie."

Lyssa sniffed. "Rafe said it wasn't your fault, about Jonathan. He said Jonathan had cheated lots of other women, too. He said it was what he did best."

"He was certainly good at it, all right. But now, thanks to you, he won't ever hurt another woman."

Lyssa's eyes glowed with pride. "And Rafe and Seth and Mr. Slocum and the other guys."

"Yes, thanks to them."

Lyssa wiped her cheeks with the sheet. "Can I see him, Mom? Rafe, I mean. To tell him I'm sorry I messed up?"

Rafe was doing his best to force down some really foul white stuff that was supposed to be good for him when Lyssa walked in. His heart raced as he looked behind her for Danni, but she was alone.

She was wearing shorts for the first time and a shirt identical to the one Danni had worn. She had a scrape on her arm, but otherwise, she looked unhurt. Her eyes, though, were red-rimmed, and she was skittish.

"Hey, champ," he said, managing a grin. "How's it going?"

"Okay." Her gaze darted from the arm they'd stuck in a sling to ease the strain on his shoulder to the contraption holding his leg. "Does that hurt?"

"Only my pride," he admitted with a grimace. "I have to tinkle in a jar."

She laughed. "These are from Rosaria," she said, thrusting a square plastic container at him. "Chocolate chip with pecans. She said they're your favorite."

"She's right. Thanks." He took the container and put it on the movable tray next to the pathetic excuse for breakfast. "Uh, where's your mom?"

"Back at the vineyard. Grandpa Mancini brought me. He's waiting downstairs."

"Does your mom know you're here?"

"Uh-huh. I told her I wanted to come, and she said it was okay, just this once."

He felt as though his heart had been sliced in two jagged pieces. Despite all of his care, he'd fallen for this little one almost as hard as he'd fallen for her mama. He'd come so close to everything he'd ever wanted. A wife, a family. But life wasn't horseshoes.

Later, he would figure out how he was going to get through the next hour, the next day. The next month. Right now, Lyssa was looking at him with troubled eyes.

"So, Ms. Fabrizio, you did it! I'm proud of you."

Her gaze dipped. "I messed up."

"Heck no, you didn't. You did it exactly right."

"But—"

"Lyssa, no one knows how he or she will react when faced with a loaded gun pointed their way. What you did was exactly what I did first time. Darn near peed my pants, too, I was so nervous."

She blinked. "Really?"

He grinned. "Really." He held out his free hand and when she put her hand in his, tugged her closer. "According to Linc, you pretty much saved my life."

Her eyes glowed, and her cheeks turned pink. "Really?" she asked again.

"You bet. That means I owe you, snooks. Anything you want from me, it's yours."

A cagey look came into her eyes, and her lips curved. He felt sorry for the guy that finally won her heart. His life was going to be anything but tranquil. "Anything?" she echoed.

"Well, I won't break the law for you, but anything else, yeah."

Her smile became a grin. "Will you marry my mom and be my dad?"

Pain exploded inside him, followed by a soul deep bitterness. Now what, slick? The truth? A diplomatic lie? Hell if he knew. He rubbed his thumb over the back of her hand, feeling the fragile bones and rubbery veins. Her hand was so small, so delicate, so easily broken. Like her heart.

"Lys, I'd like nothing better than to be your dad. And I'm more honored than you'll ever know that you would want me, but it's not up to me. It's up to your mom, and she turned me down."

Dismay crossed her face, and her fingers tightened around his. "But she couldn't have! She loves you. I know she does. I can tell by the way her eyes smile when she looks at you!"

A hole opened in his gut. "It's complicated, Lyssa. You'll just have to take my word that we both tried to make this work. The fact that it didn't doesn't have anything to do with you. I need you to believe that, okay?"

A frown worried the pale little mouth that was achingly like her mother's. "Can't you try again, Rafe? I know she's upset, but she gets that way sometimes. After a while she gets over it."

"I don't think she's going to get over this, Lys. I—God, don't cry, honey. Please don't."

With a little cry, she flung herself at him. Pain shot up through his shoulder, but he ignored it as her tears wet his neck. He curled his arm around her, and let himself pretend she was his. Just for a few minutes.

"Rafe?" she whispered, her breath moist on his shoulder.

"Right here, honey."

"I love you."

His breath dammed in his throat. God was lobbing mortars his way this time. "I love you, too, my brave little warrior," he whispered, rubbing her back. "I'll never forget that you trusted me."

"Oh Rafe..." Her voice choked, and then suddenly, she tore herself out of his arms and ran out of the room, leaving him alone.

Big tough government agents didn't cry, he reminded himself—before turning his head into the pillow.

Chapter 18

"This can't go on," Margie said as she sank down next to Linc on the sofa. Because Rafe's townhouse had stairs, they'd talked him into staying with them until the cast came off his leg. "He won't talk to me, and I can get anyone to open up. Just keeps saying he's fine."

"Maybe he is," Linc muttered before taking a swallow of scotch.

"Oh sure. Fine as in thin as a rail, hollow-eyed, brooding. Seth said he darn near took his head off yesterday for even mentioning the concert next week."

Linc hunched forward, his glass cradled in both hands. "I've already tried damn near everything I can think of." He sighed. "He's talking about resigning."

"You can't let that happen, Lincoln. His job has always been the most important thing in Rafe's life."

"Not always." He drained his glass before setting it on the coffee table. Turning to the woman who was his whole life, he held out his hand. "I want to make love to you before I leave for Portland."

Her smile was a precious gift. "I love you, you old softie."

He pretended outrage. "Hey, I'm not old."

She laughed as she curled her fingers around his. "I dare you to prove it."

Linc smiled. There was nothing he liked better than a dare.

"All in all the shelter's not bad," Cindy Habiz said as Danni walked with her to the door of the waiting room.

"It'll be better once you settle in," Danni said as she opened the door. Shock filtered through her when she caught sight of Lincoln Slocum sitting in the corner, reading a magazine.

"See you next week," she told Cindy who waved from the door before leaving.

Rafe's boss rose, a surprisingly kindly smile creasing his weathered cheeks. "Hello, Dr. Fabrizio. I hope you don't mind my coming by without an appointment."

A sudden fear sent chills running through her. "Why did you?" she asked curtly, afraid of the answer.

"The simple answer is to talk. The more complex answer takes longer." He glanced toward the door. "I was hoping you'd allow me to buy you dinner."

"How do you know I don't have another appointment?"

"Do you?"

She thought about lying. "No. Cindy's the last."

"Good. I made a reservation at Allegro's. I understand it's your favorite place."

"How do you know that?"

He smiled again. "You'd be surprised what I know about you, Daniela."

"I know that you thought your First Communion dress was ugly and deliberately spilled punch on it so that your aunt would let you wear the one you'd bought with your allowance. I know that you had a crush on your ski instructor and ended up breaking your arm trying to impress him." Linc took a sip of a really fine Mancini Cabernet Sauvignon. "I know you cry at commercials and carry spiders outside rather than kill them. I know—"

"Stop," Danni said, her thoughts in turmoil. "What's your point?"

"Obvious, I think. I'm trying to show you how much a part of Rafe you are. How much a part of him you've always been."

"You're saying he told you all those things?"

He lifted a graying eyebrow. "Of course. How else would I know?"

She let her skepticism show. "Please don't treat me like an idiot, Agent Slocum."

"After Rafe was shot the first time, infection set in and he was delirious for a time. Margie and I took turns sitting with him. Part of the time his mind was back in Oregon, with you. *That's* how I know."

He sat back. The bar was packed with the regular Friday afternoon crowd, but the dining room was still half empty. It was Michela's evening to cook, and vintage rock pulsed from the speakers.

Too upset to eat, Danni pushed her plate away, then took a sip of water. It soothed the dry membranes of her throat, but did nothing for the nerves pulsing just below the skin. "All right, you've made your point. Rafe has obviously talked to you about me. So what?"

"So the man is besotted with you. My wife, who I admit has a tendency to speak in hyperbole, says he's lovesick all the way to the bone. Me, I just see a man who's about to blow his life apart because of what you did to him."

What Rafe did or didn't do was none of her business. It would be a mistake to even talk about it. God knows, she's made enough of those. "Why do you mean, what *I* did to *him?*" she demanded when all of his words sunk in.

"He's thinking about turning in his badge. For years his job has been what he is. Who he is. I can't imagine how he'd survive without it."

There was a knot in her stomach and a hard lump wedged in her throat. "What does this have to do with me?"

For the first time real anger surfaced in his deep blue eyes. "Don't play the naïve game with me, Daniela. We both know you cut the man off at the knees. I thought he'd pull out of it, but he hasn't.'' He leaned forward to make sure she got the point. ''To tell you the truth, I think what you did was pure chicken…manure.''

Danni's breath hissed out, and heat rushed to her face. ''I beg your pardon?'' she said coldly.

''You live in a sheltered world, Daniela. For the most part people in your world follow the rules, care about each other. I'm glad that you have that luxury. One of the reasons you do is because people like Rafe and Gresham stand between you and sociopaths like Jacob Folsom.''

''I know that,'' she said impatiently. ''It's the *way* Rafe did it that was wrong.''

''Bull! It was the only way he could make sure the man didn't blow you away. Make no mistake about it, Folsom would have gotten to you. If not before the trial, then after he got out of prison. The way the system works now, that wouldn't have been all that far down the road. Two, three years, probably.''

Danni hadn't considered that. It was the trial she'd been focused on, but not what might happen afterward. ''But why should he care then? He would be out, free.''

''A normal person would think that. Folsom wasn't normal. He had no sense of conscience, no thought for anyone who stood between him and what he wanted. In his mind you had done him wrong, and he wouldn't rest until you paid. He would have come at you then. Without warning, when you least expected him. Maybe you would have opened the door like Alice MacGregor did and had your face blown off the way she did. Or maybe your daughter would have opened that door. It wouldn't have mattered.''

Danni felt horror race through her. ''I admit I…hadn't considered that.''

''But Rafe had, and he couldn't stand the thought of you being hurt. So he figured out a way to keep you safe.'' His face turned frighteningly hard. ''Yes, there was a very slight risk Lyssa could have been hurt. About the same risk we all take crossing a street. But Rafe didn't make the decision alone.

He ran it by Gresham and then by me. We all agreed it was the only way.''

He took his napkin from his lap and put it on the table before rising. "I love the guy like a brother. Of all the men I know in law enforcement he's the one I would chose to take my back in a tough spot. The fact that he chose you above all women to love is the only reason I won't let myself despise you for what you've done." He took out a money clip, peeled off a hundred dollar bill and dropped it on the table before walking out.

Propped up with one crutch, Rafe was shaving in the Slocums' guest bathroom when someone tapped on the door. Before he had a chance to find out who it was, Margie walked in, a portable phone in her hand.

"Hey, there's a half-naked man in here," he grumbled, rinsing his razor under the hot tap.

She grinned. "And such a fine physique he has, too, but alas, I'm still hooked on the old guy," she said before waving the phone in his face. "Call for you."

He frowned. "Who is it?"

"Lyssa Fabrizio."

The cab dropped Rafe off in front of the Tacoma Dome where the concert was being held. The cast on his leg had been replaced by a plastic-and-metal splint that was lighter but still gave him fits. Worse, he still needed crutches which made getting around a pain.

According to Seth who'd flown to Portland two days ago in order to attend Lyssa's kick-boxing meet last night, the three of them would wait for him in front of the main ticket window. The next few hours would be rough, but he'd prepared himself. Lyssa was the one who had invited him to the concert. It was Lyssa he'd come to see. He needed to remember that.

The area in front of the Dome was organized chaos, with cops and security maintaining a visible presence. The crowd streaming in was mostly composed of teenagers and young adults in a party mood, although, as he made his way carefully through the rush of bodies, he was surprised to see a number of adults his age or older salted in with the kids.

Sweat was trickling down his back by the time he spied the ticket window. "Rafe!" He turned to see Lyssa running toward him, her hair flying. She looked taller, or maybe it was the skinny jeans and tight top she wore. A lump formed in his throat as he braced himself on his good leg. "Hey, champ," he said as she folded herself into his arms.

"Oh, Rafe, it's so good to see you!"

"You, too, honey."

She drew back but kept her arms around his waist. "You got skinny."

He'd dropped a few pounds, yeah, but he wasn't about to tell her that he'd been pining away for her mom. And her. "Us government types call that lean and mean."

She giggled. "Mom's gotten humongous. Kind of like a blimp, you know? And real sensitive, 'specially about her bummy. She thinks she looks like an elephant from the back. Only don't tell her I said, okay?"

"Too late, young lady. I already heard."

Rafe had himself well in check. Still, the sound of Danni's voice wrecked his insides, sending his heart racing and his gut into a spasm. As Lyssa's arms fell away, he turned in the direction of her voice and watched her walking the last few feet that would bring her to him.

Humongous had never looked so good, he realized, his gaze skimming her big belly. But it was her face he needed to see. The dark, liquid eyes that could snap with anger or warm with a smile. Or turn sleepy with passion. The little nose with those seven freckles. The lips that felt so right beneath his.

It had been a month since he'd seen her. A month of trying not to remember the feeling of contentment she'd given him that single night they'd slept together. Of fighting the need to see her one more time. Of trying not to worry about her and the delivery that was coming up in less than a month.

A month of living with guilt wedged like a jagged bone in his craw.

A month of pure hell.

He frowned thinking about the way he'd screwed up his second chance, and the corners of her mouth that had started to turn up froze. Behind her Seth shot him a disgusted look.

"Have any trouble getting here, partner?" he asked as he joined them.

"Darn near drove security crazy with this cast, but I flashed my badge and pleaded line-of-duty injury. Impressed the heck out of the ladies. The guys just looked bored."

Seth grinned. "I scoped out the section where we're sitting. It's got ramps instead of stairs so you should manage okay."

"Did you bring the earplugs, too?" he asked, earning him a wounded look from Lys. "Just kidding, honey. I can't wait to hear those guitars tearing my eardrums apart."

She laughed. "That's what Mom says, but she likes that classical stuff." She grinned at her mother. "And Barry Manilow."

Danni glanced at her watch. "Honey, why don't you and Seth go on in? I need to talk to Rafe a minute."

Lyssa and Seth exchanged looks before he held out his hand. "C'mon, toots, we'll let the old folks take their time."

"I want to get a tour T-shirt before they're all picked over," Lyssa said as she took his hand. "See you guys, later, okay?"

"We won't be long," Danni said with a smile.

Rafe fought a sinking feeling as he watched them wend their way through the crowd which had thinned noticeably while they'd been talking. A half dozen times before he'd gotten on the plane at noon Washington time, he'd taken out his phone to cancel. Danni thought he was ruthless. Hell, a ruthless man only thought of himself, right? Why should he care if Lyssa was disappointed?

He cared, damn it. He cared too much. So far he hadn't figured out how to stop. But he would, because this way was killing him.

Reluctantly, he shifted his attention to Danni who wasn't quite glaring at him, but she looked far from happy. He leaned on his crutches and braced himself for another blast. He couldn't fathom what he'd done wrong this time, but he figured to find out soon enough.

"Seth has become the brother Lys always wanted," she said, her expression softening. "She's trying to fix him up with her algebra teacher."

Now that was a curve he hadn't expected. Her game, he decided, so he'd play it her way. "Is this teacher a blonde?" he asked, watching her eyes for clues to where she was going with this.

"Blondish," she said after reflection. "More like strawberry."

Still puzzled, he played along. "Long legs?"

Her lashes flickered. "All the way to her neck."

"Two out of two, that should do it."

It was worse than she'd anticipated. Danni thought with a sinking heart. He was polite. He even smiled. But his eyes reminded her of the deepest part of the river where they'd fished, reflecting her own image back to her, but revealing nothing beneath the depths. Only when he'd first seen Lyssa had he seemed like the man who had opened his heart to her by the pond. When his gaze had shifted toward her, however, that man had gone away, to be replaced by an impassive stranger. It hurt, she realized, taking a breath. It hurt terribly.

"I, uh, appreciate you letting Papa know you'd be spending time with your folks for the next few days." She hadn't meant to sound stiff. Nerves always made her retreat into a studied politeness.

He didn't understand, she realized as his mouth hooked up at one corner, giving his face a sardonic look she'd never seen before. "Just following the rules, Doctor."

There was a pressure growing in her chest, making it difficult to breathe. She arched her back slightly, trying to free space for her lungs to work. It only made it worse. "I suppose you know Seth has managed to locate bank accounts Folsom opened under various aliases in Canada and Mexico."

He nodded. "You'll have to share with the other victims, but at least you'll get something."

"Enough to pay off most of my credit card debt." The front

of the Tacoma Dome was mostly empty now. The concert was about to start. As she glanced around an industrious middle-aged scalper wearing a Mariners' ball cap held up two tickets, his expression hopeful. She shook her head, drawing Rafe's gaze to the man who looked away as soon as Rafe made eye contact. She knew the feeling. Those green eyes could be lethal. They could also blaze with passion or crinkle with wry humor. But it was the tender look that had shimmered there when he'd asked her to marry him that she saw every night in her dreams.

"So, uh, how are you doing?" she blurted out, her well-practiced, logical plan scrambling.

His gaze narrowed. "Depends on what you're really asking, Daniela." His beautiful mouth hardened. "If you mean, do I still feel as though you stripped out my heart and slammed it in the dirt, the answer is yes, but I'm getting over it."

She heard the bitterness and the pain. It stabbed deep, like a blade aimed at her heart. "I, uh, wanted to apologize for saying you were like Folsom. I...overreacted."

"Did you?"

She noticed he had begun to look terribly tired. Or was he merely impatient to escape? It was difficult to tell. "I'm sorry, Rafe," she said quietly as a police cruiser drove past slowly. "I seem to be so...incompetent lately. I don't seem to be able to handle even the simplest things."

Something lashed out at her from those eyes, as quick as a slap. "Which simple thing are we talking about?"

Patching up a broken heart, for one thing.

"Do you mind if we finish this sitting down?" she asked, gesturing toward a raised concrete planter filled with flowering perennials in the center of the sea of cement. Without waiting for an answer she turned and walked toward the man-made island to sit on the wide concrete lip designed as a bench. A large jay perched on one of the rhododendron bushes scolded irately before finally taking noisy flight.

Behind her he cursed under his breath, but he followed. In the three weeks since he'd been out of the hospital, he'd become fairly proficient using the crutches and managed to sit without too much trouble. After putting aside his crutches, he crossed his arms over his chest and waited.

"If you're going to close me out, there's not much sense in my saying anything," she said with a pointed look at the brawny arms straining the ribbing of his maroon polo shirt. Losing weight had added a sparse austerity to his features and added more definition to his impressive musculature.

Sighing, he uncrossed his arms, bracing his hands on the seat instead. "Obviously, you're not real eager to hear the Acid Whatevers," he said, watching her.

"Are you?"

"God, no!" There was a brief glimmer of humor in his eyes before he wiped it away. "Suppose you tell me why I'm here."

She toyed with the strap of her purse, realized what she was doing and folded her hands atop her stomach. His gaze flickered over her tummy, and then her breasts, and she felt her nipples reacting. Heat bloomed inside her, part desire, part fear. "You asked me a question the day Folsom was shot. I didn't give you an answer. I'd like to give you my answer now." She took a deep breath and tried to block out even the smallest possibility of rejection. "I'd be proud to marry you, Rafe. If you still want me." Her heart was racing so fast she couldn't count the beats if her life depended on it, and her mouth felt dry. The pressure in her chest was agonizing.

"That must have been some speech Linc handed you," he drawled, his gaze fixed on the parking lot where row after row of vehicles waited patiently for the freeway snarl to begin again.

"Did he tell you we talked?"

He shook his head. "Not a word."

"Then how did you know."

His mouth softened slightly. "Deductive reasoning. Margie has the world's most romantic soul. She's also worried about me. Linc suddenly left on urgent business without telling me where. I'm sure she sent Linc to talk to you, and even though I imagine he considered it worse than any duty he's ever pulled, he did it because he's crazy about his wife."

She sighed. The baby stirred, punching out with both a foot

and a fist as the little one shifted from one side to the other, trying to get comfortable in her rapidly decreasing space. The smothering feeling was all too real. Somehow she managed to take in a deep breath.

"I can't recall the entire conversation verbatim," she said. "Two things do stand out, however. One was the part where he told me he considered my behavior chicken do-do."

That got to him, crinkling his eyes in that half mischievous, half amused way she loved. "Knowing Linc, I figure you sanitized that some."

"Actually, his language was pretty much G-rated, although the look in his eyes would have been censored for violent content."

His mouth curved wryly. "What shows is only a fraction of what's inside."

"Is that the same with all you government types?" she wondered aloud.

His smile hardened away. "Pretty much, yeah."

A roar went up from the crowd inside, followed by the muffled sound of music pounding through state-of-the art speakers. She glanced toward the huge rounded structure before returning her gaze to his forbidding profile. "The other part was where he told me he couldn't quite despise me because you…cared about me." She took a breath. "Or used to, anyway."

He shrugged the shoulder that hadn't taken a bullet. The one bearing the scars of her nails. He was giving nothing away. She felt the baby kick and rubbed the spot. His gaze flickered to her hand then jerked away.

"Cut to the chase, Danni. What exactly do you want from me?"

"Exactly what you offered me by the pond, Rafe. Love, a father for my daughters, marriage, more babies. A boy, I think next time. With green eyes and his father's dimples."

Rafe stared straight ahead as the image she'd painted hung in the air. It was as though she'd seen into his soul and taken a snapshot of his deepest longing. He felt as though all his internal walls were cracking, threatening to release emotions so powerful he'd kept them hidden deep.

Something twisted inside him when he realized he'd tried so hard to kill off his feelings for her he might just have succeeded. "Why me?"

"Because I love you."

"Why?" he asked again, feeling as though he'd just swallowed nails.

She took a breath. "These are not necessarily in order of importance," she said before taking another, deeper breath. It should have pleased him that she seemed as nervous as he had that day of the fiesta. Now he wasn't sure how he felt. Impatient mostly, he realized as she squared slender shoulders. "Reasons why I love Rafael Cardoza," she recounted as though saying a piece in school. "Because I only have to look at his body and mine goes all soft and hot inside." She ran her hand over the thigh that wasn't in a cast and he felt his muscle contract involuntarily. She grinned. He frowned.

"I have this deep desire to laugh with you again in the shower and argue about silly things over cookies and milk on a rainy Saturday and plan important things in front of a fire while our children are asleep," she said, her voice suddenly soft and intense. "I want to know that I can go home after a day that's left me feeling limp and discouraged and feel those strong arms close around me, shutting out the world long enough for my courage to return. I want to be there for you when you're discouraged or sad or furious because you can't quite make yourself perfect enough not to make mistakes. I want to take our children to the vineyard so your family and mine can make a fuss over them."

She took the hand he hadn't realized had curled into a fist and pressed it to her belly. "I want this to be the hand holding mine when this little girl is born. I want it to be your face she sees next to mine when she opens her eyes for the first time. And I want to give her your name as well as mine."

He felt the baby moving, a soft little nudge against his palm as though a downy little head were nuzzling against him. The cracks in his inner walls opened wider. "I'm still the same man you rejected," he said, staring into her eyes.

"I was scared," she admitted. "And hurt because you shut me out."

"You know why I did that."

"Yes, but it took me a while to push aside the emotion I'd piled up. Linc helped." Her mouth curved. "Actually, he did more exploding than pushing, but the result was the same. I went home that night and realized how empty the house was without you."

He cleared his throat. It still felt scoured. "I'm...flattered, and you'll never know how much I want to accept all you're offering."

Fear dilated her pupils until her eyes were deep black pools. "Oh God, why do I think there's a but coming?" she muttered.

He curled his fingers tighter around hers. "A month ago, I would already be hustling you to the nearest jeweler, but..."

Sadness crept over her face, tearing at him. "But it's too late? Is that what you're telling me?"

"Maybe. Probably," he admitted reluctantly. "For years I've tried to make myself stop loving you. God help me, I don't know how I feel now, and you deserve more than that from a man."

Danni studied that dear face with the lines of suffering and experience gouged deep, studied the eyes filled with wariness and another emotion that looked like regret. Studied the mouth that paradoxically seemed intensely...vulnerable.

"You're scared," she blurted out as the truth dawned. "That's it, isn't it?"

He glowered at her. "Government types are never scared," he muttered.

Excitement burst inside her. "Oh yes you are. It was easy loving me when it was just in the abstract, but now all of a sudden it might turn out to be real and you're having second thoughts." She felt strong, suddenly. Powerful. For the first time in months—years—she felt whole. She allowed her lips to smile. "I've learned something these past weeks, Rafe. Do you want to know what that is?"

His face tightened. "Do I have a choice?" he asked tautly.

She laughed. "I've learned that material possessions aren't

essential to happiness. I loved my house and my beautiful Lexus and my antiques, but when I heard those gunshots exploding, all I could think about was that I might be losing the two people I cared about most in the world. And for what? Because some jackass ripped me off and I wanted him to pay.'' She took a breath and kept her gaze steady on his. His hand had tightened around hers and his breathing wasn't as steady as it should be. All good signs, she told herself.

"In that moment I didn't care about my stuff or justice or some greater good. All I cared about was you. I realize now that you felt the same way. Maybe you're more, um…'' She paused, groping for another word for ruthless. His mouth moved.

"Ruthless?'' he suggested with a hint of a smile.

"Single-minded,'' she compromised before lifting his hand to her lips. She felt him tense as she kissed his hand. "If you need to walk away to protect yourself from all that scary stuff like commitment and the day-to-day hassles of living with a teenager and a baby, I understand. But be warned, I'm tenacious when I want something and I want you.''

His brows drew together. "You do?''

"Oh yes, amazingly *mucho*. Once this baby is born, I intend to pursue you shamelessly. If I have to move to Washington, I will.''

His frown took on bewildered edges. "You'd do that?''

"In a heartbeat.'' She took a chance. "I'm not afraid of loving you, Rafe. And I know you love me. I can feel it. All I'm asking is that you give us a chance.''

A tormented look came into his eyes. "What if I don't love you, Danni?''

"Impossible.'' She touched his face and felt his tremble. "Feel what I can do just by touching you. Imagine what an impact I could have if I rubbed my fat little body all over yours.''

The smile started in his eyes. "That's probably not a good idea at the moment,'' he muttered hoarsely, glancing around.

A knot of cops and security types were hanging out near one of the light standards. One or two cast a speculative look their

way. Rafe recognized the expressions. A few more minutes and
one of them would amble by to see what was going on. He
shifted his gaze to the face he'd never forgotten. Her beautiful
face.

How many chances did a man get to grab a handful of star-
dust? he wondered. To hold his dream in his arms. Maybe he
wasn't the brightest guy, but he knew when Fate had handed
him one more shot at happiness.

"If you take me on, it'll have to be forever, Danni," he
warned, his voice growing rougher. "I don't believe in divorce."

"Neither do I."

"I'll be your husband and a father to your babies, all of
them. I'll love them without holding anything back, the way I
love you. The way I need to be loved, despite my many flaws,
several of which you have already—and repeatedly—pointed
out."

He lifted an eyebrow and she nodded, her eyes sparkling. "I
do love you," she murmured. "Despite those, um, regrettable
lapses in perfection."

He felt those walls crumbling one after the other, leaving
him wide open to her. It didn't just scare him—it flat out terrified him. But he figured he'd get used to it. "I'll never keep
anything from you again—unless it has to do with my job. I'll
be there for you when you need me. I'll protect you and the
kids and you'll never have to wonder if I'm faithful to you."
He stopped, frowned. Tried to think if there was anything else.

"Can I kiss you now?" she asked, her smile soft.

"Not yet, there are conditions." That wiped away the smile,
he saw.

"What conditions?" she asked warily.

"From this moment on that baby doing handstands in that
humongous tummy of yours is mine, no one else's. When she's
old enough, we'll give her bare bones about the man who provided the sperm, but in every way that counts she's mine." He
narrowed his gaze. "Agreed?"

Her smile was the sun and the stars and a light in the dark.
"Agreed."

"We get married before she's born so she doesn't have to live with any kind of stain."

A look he couldn't quite read came into her eyes. "Agreed, but the Mommy Brigade would be crushed if we didn't have the wedding in Portland."

"A week, no more."

"Agreed."

He felt the tension drain away. "Then it's settled. You'll marry me?"

"Happily! Eagerly."

His throat felt thick. "You can kiss me now," he prodded.

"I thought you'd never ask." She tugged on his hair, pulling him down for a long, smoldering kiss. With a growl, he pulled her onto his lap, wrapped his arms around both her and his daughter and rested his cheek against hers.

The cop that had been approaching smiled. "Everything okay here, folks?"

Danni's grin blazed. "Perfect, officer. This big hunk has finally decided to make an honest woman of me."

The cop grinned. "Congratulations. Being as I have six myself, I think I ought to advise you to do it real quick like. Just in case."

Rafe nodded. "As soon as our daughter's finished ruining her eardrums, we're fixing on doing just that."

Danni waited until the cop was out of earshot before turning her face up to Rafe's. "It's taken us so long, but finally, I think we've found what we've always known we wanted." She lifted her free hand to his face and touched her forefinger to the scar at the corner of his mouth. "I adore you, my dearest Rafe. My own gift from God."

* * * * *

Feel like a star with Silhouette.

We will fly you and a guest to New York City for an exciting weekend stay at a glamorous 5-star hotel. Experience a refreshing day at one of New York's trendiest spas and have your photo taken by a professional. Plus, receive $1,000 U.S. spending money!

Flowers...long walks...dinner for two... how does Silhouette Books make romance come alive for you?

Send us a script, with 500 words or less, along with visuals (only drawings, magazine cutouts or photographs or combination thereof). Show us how Silhouette Makes Your Love Come Alive. Be creative and have fun. No purchase necessary. All entries must be clearly marked with your name, address and telephone number. All entries will become property of Silhouette and are not returnable. **Contest closes September 28, 2001.**

Please send your entry to: **Silhouette Makes You a Star!**

In U.S.A.	In Canada
P.O. Box 9069	P.O. Box 637
Buffalo, NY, 14269-9069	Fort Erie, ON, L2A 5X3

Look for contest details on the next page, by visiting www.eHarlequin.com or request a copy by sending a self-addressed envelope to the applicable address above. Contest open to Canadian and U.S. residents who are 18 or over. Void where prohibited.

Our lucky winner's photo will appear in a Silhouette ad. Join the fun!

HARLEQUIN "SILHOUETTE MAKES YOU A STAR!" CONTEST 1308
OFFICIAL RULES
NO PURCHASE NECESSARY TO ENTER

1. To enter, follow directions published in the offer to which you are responding. Contest begins June 1, 2001, and ends on September 28, 2001. Entries must be postmarked by September 28, 2001, and received by October 5, 2001. Enter by hand-printing (or typing) on an 8 ½" x 11" piece of paper your name, address (including zip code), contest number/name and attaching a script containing <u>500 words or less, along with drawings, photographs or magazine cutouts, or combinations thereof</u> (i.e., collage) <u>on no larger than 9" x 12"</u> piece of paper, describing how the <u>Silhouette books make romance come alive for you.</u> Mail via first-class mail to: Harlequin "Silhouette Makes You a Star!" Contest 1308, (in the U.S.) P.O. Box 9069, Buffalo, NY 14269-9069, (in Canada) P.O. Box 637, Fort Erie, Ontario, Canada L2A 5X3. Limit one entry per person, household or organization.

2. Contests will be judged by a panel of members of the Harlequin editorial, marketing and public relations staff. Fifty percent of criteria will be judged against script and fifty percent will be judged against drawing, photographs and/or magazine cutouts. Judging criteria will be based on the following:

   - Sincerity—25%
   - Originality and Creativity—50%
   - Emotionally Compelling—25%

   In the event of a tie, duplicate prizes will be awarded. Decisions of the judges are final.

3. All entries become the property of Torstar Corp. and may be used for future promotional purposes. Entries will not be returned. No responsibility is assumed for lost, late, illegible, incomplete, inaccurate, nondelivered or misdirected mail.

4. Contest open only to residents of the U.S. <u>(except Puerto Rico)</u> and Canada who are 18 years of age or older, and is void wherever prohibited by law; all applicable laws and regulations apply. Any litigation within the Province of Quebec respecting the conduct or organization of a publicity contest may be submitted to the Régie des alcools, des courses et des jeux for a ruling. Any litigation respecting the awarding of a prize may be submitted to the Régie des alcools, des courses et des jeux only for the purpose of helping the parties reach a settlement. Employees and immediate family members of Torstar Corp. and D. L. Blair, Inc., their affiliates, subsidiaries and all other agencies, entities and persons connected with the use, marketing or conduct of this contest are not eligible to enter. Taxes on prizes are the sole responsibility of the winner. Acceptance of any prize offered constitutes permission to use winner's name, photograph or other likeness for the purposes of advertising, trade and promotion on behalf of Torstar Corp., its affiliates and subsidiaries without further compensation to the winner, unless prohibited by law.

5. Winner will be determined no later than November 30, 2001, and will be notified by mail. Winner will be required to sign and return an Affidavit of Eligibility/Release of Liability/Publicity Release form within 15 days after winner notification. Noncompliance within that time period may result in disqualification and an alternative winner may be selected. All travelers must execute a Release of Liability prior to ticketing and must possess required travel documents (e.g., passport, photo ID) where applicable. Trip must be booked by December 31, 2001, and completed within one year of notification. No substitution of prize permitted by winner. Torstar Corp. and D. L. Blair, Inc., their parents, affiliates and subsidiaries are not responsible for errors in printing of contest, entries and/or game pieces. In the event of printing or other errors that may result in unintended prize values or duplication of prizes, all affected game pieces or entries shall be null and void. **Purchase or acceptance of a product offer does not improve your chances of winning.**

6. Prizes: (1) Grand Prize—A 2-night/3-day trip for two (2) to New York City, including round-trip coach air transportation nearest winner's home and hotel accommodations (double occupancy) at The Plaza Hotel, a glamorous afternoon makeover at <u>a trendy New York spa</u>, $1,000 in U.S. spending money and an opportunity to <u>have a professional photo taken and appear in a Silhouette advertisement</u> (approximate retail value: $7,000). (10) Ten Runner-Up Prizes of gift packages (retail value $50 ea.). Prizes consist of only those items listed as part of the prize. Limit one prize per person. Prize is valued in U.S. currency.

7. For the name of the winner (available after December 31, 2001) send a self-addressed, stamped envelope to: Harlequin "Silhouette Makes You a Star!" Contest 1197 Winners, P.O. Box 4200 Blair, NE 68009-4200 or you may access the www.eHarlequin.com Web site through February 28, 2002.

Contest sponsored by Torstar Corp., P.O Box 9042, Buffalo, NY 14269-9042.

SRMYAS2

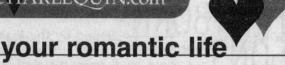